Devotion
and
Corrosion

Michael Warren Lucas

Tilted
Windmill
Press

Copyright Information

Devotion and Corrosion

Michael Warren Lucas

Contents

Acknowledgements

How do you thank people for helping you endure over a decade of writing? Some folks due my gratitude have moved on from my social circle, moved on from writing, or flat-out moved on from life. But let's take a stab at it. If I've missed your name, it means only that the electrified pudding filling my skull is feeble.

So, ahem: dear Laura Bickle, Blaze Ward, Glen T. Brock, ZZ Claybourne, Brigid Collins, Ron Collins, Rob Cornell, Leah R Cutter, T. Thorn Coyle, Colin Harvey, CJ Jones, Richard Jones, Alex Kourvo, Matthew Kroll, Mark Leslie Lefebvre, Kate MacLeod, Juliet Nordeen, Josh Peterson, Sharon Reamer, Amanda Robinson, Robert Rowntree, Kristine Kathryn Rusch, Dean Wesley Smith, Lucy A. Snyder, and Clarence Young: y'all rock. So do many other people, whose names have rusted away in my corroded memory.

I also must thank my Patronizers, the lovely folks who send me money every month for no legitimate reason. I keep reminding them that going to patronizeMWL.com and signing up is a terrible deal, but they don't listen. Kate Ebneter, Stefan Johnson, Jeff Marraccini, Eirik Øverby, and Phil Vuchetich supported both the electronic and print versions of this book. John Hixson, Craig Maloney, Florian Obser, Maximilian Kühne, Ray Percival, sungo, and Peter Wemm supported the ebook.

My biggest thanks go to Liz, who charitably shoved flat food under my office door during more than one writing binge.

Foreword Motion

ZZ Claybourne

"I have love in me the likes of which you can scarcely imagine and rage the likes of which you would not believe. If I cannot satisfy the one, I will indulge the other."

From the Kenneth Branaugh movie adaptation of Mary Shelley's Frankenstein

The insidious thing about love is we define it to suit us. There are people who think they're so logical that no variety of something so basic as love sways them. A simple whisper or well-placed compliment flips their world. Artists will bring all their craft and time to bear on a project, then, for love of craft, never release it for fear it's not good enough.

Would most of us do anything for love? In the same way there's the erroneous envisioning of hope as some soft cloud of dreams, love is too often cast as a diaphanous thing ladling orgasms and picnics upon the world. Love is a Depression-era photo of a mother who'd snap the neck of God to make sure her children survive. Fortunately, humans come into the world slippery, hard to grasp, and weird, and generally stay that way. We're all children or parents.

Invoking Shelley's creature requires an understanding of the human condition. Invoking Ozzie Osborne requires honestly declaring how love eventually makes hypocrites of we angels. We may think we wouldn't do that for love, but then find ourselves doing it twice. Granted, maybe not the way we think "that" would play out. Maybe we wouldn't put Bambi on train tracks for love, but we can see ourselves laying a haymaker on a doe if it got too close to a baby. We can see ourselves testifying against our addicted twin if it meant they'd be remanded to medical care. Sacrifice is love. Self-preservation is love. Construction is love. Destruction is love. Truth is love. Lies are love. We'll burn a hole through the Earth for love of profit. We'll plant a million trees for love of forests. Devotion. Corrosion.

Shakespeare and balladeers never told us love was the stark Coin Flip of motivations.

When I was a teenager, my suicidal brother went missing during the worst of a Michigan winter. He was a few years older than me. I'd never really liked him, could've hated him. He was mean, selfish, and had a putdown for anything anybody held up as an accomplishment. I didn't know anything about depression then, but I knew his mind. I knew the note he'd left wasn't for show. So I wrapped my feet in bags, slid them into my threadbare boots, and walked alleys hoping to find him. Not alive. Just hoping to find him. I got home nearly frostbitten. Never found him.

I loved my brother.

Love drills nails into our lobes if we hand it the right power tools.

As an adult, love had me comforting the guy whom the woman I loved cheated on me with, the revelation coming when I knocked on her apartment door and he answered wearing my bathrobe. Weeks later, at 3AM, she called me. Except it was him from her landline. Wondering why she didn't really love him.

That was an hour conversation.

I'd do it again.

There are so few times in life when we're not touched by a bit of this glorious insanity. Smart people might postulate glorious insanity as the only thing sticking humanity together; I'm willing to give them that. We might not have had Toni Morrison, Prince, Alice Coltrane, or Johnny Cash otherwise. Wondrous love for a billion lights in the sky drives us to be creative. Creativity drives us to be compassionate. This is why my only mantra is *Despite everything, create.* Love *demands* we build, that we bring healing into lives that forever reach for succor like a confused infant in the eye of a storm.

A line I wrote a long time ago: 'We're all the ones who know so little, and I'm the one you least need fear.' Folks reading this foreword know fear is the mind killer. Even when there's every reason to fear, love factors into everything. My latest books are love letters to perseverance, community, and every mysterious grace that keeps life interesting. *The Brothers Jetstream: Leviathan* is love for adventure. *Afro Puffs Are the Antennae of the Universe?* Love's in every word of the title.

Sometimes love forces us to create in order to destroy. Devotion and corrosion.

Devotion and Corrosion, the collection: Each story is Hieronymus Bosch writing a love letter to Charlie Brown's little red-haired girl now grown and so weary she aches. Can you grasp that? Can you grasp an Elmore Leonard Hallmark romance? Or H.P. Lovecraft exorcising his demons as a kid out of love for himself before they calcify his adult heart? Does familial love—like rat familial love—get its due in your life? Rat familial love amasses in the thousands, and always with ready teeth. What Lucas has done is present the xenomorph from ALIEN going in for a French kiss: burning things to the bone so that the unspoken underpinnings show through. It'd be one thing if our species remained simply insane, but there's that "glorious" part. That glorious devotion. Love, per Chuck Tingle, is real. Love is also a product of the imagination. We feel what we believe.

The 11 surprising, inventively immersive stories in *Devotion & Corrosion* know you know that fact. They share a fierce belief at their core, a belief that love can make things—if not right—better. Love will find a way to dig through us to the other, safer side. During times of insane politicians, alternative facts, and people considering putting ultraviolet lights up their butts, that belief might be the only type of love that moves us through our days. Because any time lying, pride in ignorance, or putrescent bigotry feel like love to some? We can do better than that.

We are better than that.

We know love. Somehow, we do.

Otherwise all is corrosion.

Winner Breaks All

Tyler Rowan knew how to win.

No, scratch that. He had no idea how to win.

But he knew *how* to know how to win, if that makes sense.

Tyler was famous for caring about his people. He somehow knew the names of each of the four hundred men and women who worked at Detroit Nanobiotics (NYSE stock ticker DNBX, currently valued at $781.44/share but predicted to grow forever by any analyst who had eyes). He'd started the firm in his parents' basement, building it into a research powerhouse, until he finally flat-out bought a whole wing of the razed-and-rebuilt Packard Biotechnical Research Park just north of Downtown, right by the big tree farm where the Gratiot Tram Line met the Conant. The scientists and HR types lived right there in the high rises of Indian Village or the mini-estates of Poletown, while the janitors and shipping crews commuted in from the slums of Grosse Pointe, which really aren't *that* slummy.

People had tried to buy Tyler out before. He refused. He needed the company, for reasons he'd never tell anyone. I knew, of course. How could I not?

But when lab receptionist Harry Muldoon had wrecked his back in a car accident and the surgeon declared that current nanobots couldn't fix it, Tyler had called a friend over at Cadillac Medical Equipment's R&D wing and borrowed a prototype chair that detected nerve signals and adjusted itself to minimize

Muldoon's agony. The guy found himself more comfortable at work than home in bed.

I've always known Tyler was a soft touch.

If Harry hadn't been able to work, Tyler would have sent a company concierge out to his home. DNBX employed three concierges for precisely such situations. But because Harry felt so much better at work, he was able to take care of his kids and wife on his own time.

A receptionist costs a little more than a concierge, so at least the soppy bastard came out ahead.

The only thing Tyler loved almost as much as his people was his company. The office areas were painted sky blue and yellow and rose, and those weren't prints on the walls, they were actual paintings. Not the most expensive art, he kept the Eschers and Michelangelos and Teskes at home, but still. The industrial carpet was chosen for easy cleaning, yes, but it was the most plush and luxurious industrial carpet money could buy. The air handlers had the best filters—Detroit wasn't nearly as smoky as it had been back in the Oil Age, but still, he didn't want his people breathing in all that crap. Besides, unfiltered air was bad for the décor.

And the lab space? Making money requires spending money.

Smart nanobiotic researchers who feel happy, believe their work matters, and have the best equipment can make a whole bucket of money.

So the lab had all the tools. Not the toys—Tyler had a doctorate in nanobiotics and a real numbers-and-contracts MBA, not one of those bogus Internet ones.

Even the sysadmins had the best ergonomic keyboards on the market, and those buggers didn't care so long as they had something better than manual typewriters.

So: Tyler's employees loved him like he loved them.

And he loved the company almost as much.

The company couldn't love him, of course.

But humans are frail. Fallible.

A corporation can be eternal.

If he played the corporate game right, sometime in the thirty-first century his portrait would be hanging in the lobby of the worldwide powerhouse DNBX's global headquarters. Wait for the forty-first and it might be the galactic headquarters.

That's the final goal of nanobiotics, of course. Immortality.

Tyler Rowan only had to live long enough to live forever. What more thrilling game could there be?

And Tyler loved to win. He loved winning a whole bunch.

Tyler wasn't willing to hurt people to win the game, though.

I didn't mind hurting people, if it meant winning.

But as long as Tyler kept that damned psychopathy suppressor in our skull, filtering me away from the world, I'd never get the chance.

2

It began in Tyler's office. The office befit a rich man. There was the low lemon stink of furniture polish, and every surface was smooth as glass. I approved of the cherry-wood desk with enough space for a rousing game of Capture the Flag and enough monitors to make the game interesting. His leather chair was only a little bigger and a little plusher than those he gave his employees. I'd checked the catalog for something more bad-ass, but he'd already chosen the biggest and plushest chair on the market. When I urged him to buy the employees chairs just a notch or two down, though, he'd flat-out ignored me.

The employees made Tyler rich. He thought they deserved to be *comfortable.*

I could urge him towards rewards that don't hurt anyone. The tiny glass-fronted liquor cabinet was my idea. Most days I couldn't get him to take a drink at work, but sometimes at the end of a grueling twelve-hour engineering meeting or after he'd been juggling bank numbers until the company could hold together another year, I could get him to sip a couple fingers of Laproaig. What's the point of working so hard when you don't reap the rewards?

The guy wouldn't even hire a call girl. Tyler had this weird idea that you had to *know* a woman, that you had to give a shit what she felt, like she was something more than a bunch of warm slick holes.

I could have compromised on knowing a woman if it got me laid, but no.

Forty-one years old and stupid wealthy. We ought to be swimming in it, and it's been fifteen years.

And I knew the guy was just as desperate as I was.

We were both psycho horny, but he was lonely too. He wanted a family, but couldn't imagine fathering children who'd inherit his "defect." Desperate, aching loneliness.

So: I win.

And I was going to win the long game, too, one whisper at a time.

Tyler had an antique credenza from the 1920s, also cherry, with all kinds of intricate little doors in the front to stash office supplies that hadn't been relevant for a century. He kept printed stock reports in there and plastic models, for impressing empty-headed board members and gullible reporters.

I wanted to think that the wicker basket of seasonal fresh fruit on the credenza was my idea, but realistically it was probably ours. Part of staying healthy enough to live forever. The Quebequois peach crop had finished, sadly—those were our favorite—but we had some nice Oregon oranges, which were pretty tasty.

No matter who'd come up with it: Expensive. As. Hell.

Did I mention the soundproofing? He'd wanted good sound-proofing. I'd suggested the phrase *good enough to hide a chainsaw massacre*. He'd thought it was just a clever way to explain it to the contractor, but that's what we had.

At least he'd had the walls hand-polished. You had to be damned rich to have real human beings polish your walls.

But I didn't like the *way* he'd done it.

Tyler's brother Forrest didn't have Tyler's business drive or, frankly, his intellect, so he worked with the old geezers who'd served in the Second Civil War. I wouldn't have called it a "war," more of a "feisty disagreement with a whole bunch of guns." No nukes no war, that's my rule, but whatever.

Tyler thought that supporting aged vets was good and noble work, well worth Forrest's time.

Without the Second Civil War, Tyler wouldn't have had the damn suppressor since birth and I'd be out in the real world.

Anyway, Tyler hired those damn vets to polish the wood. He got them a little wheeled garden cart to sit on and an extension pole so they didn't have to get up on a ladder. The ceiling's not that high, he should just let the geezers stretch up to hit the top of the wall or fire them and get someone who can do the job.

I got a satisfied thrill every time some peasant came in and saw the gentle swirls of hand-rubbed wax. But every time I noticed those same swirls, I got pretty ticked off.

Not too ticked off. I don't control the adrenals.

At that moment, though, the adrenals were running just fine as Tyler paced back and forth in front of the desk, his feet sinking half an inch into the lush carpet.

"What do you mean, we can't get Tyrnex solvent?" Tyler's deep, rich voice had this annoying softness. I knew he could be more firm, but he doesn't *like* to be. "They're right across the complex from us!"

Research chief Jason Mill's voice came from the speaker hidden in the white acoustic tiles overhead. "I mean that the Novalon Biologistics is unwilling to sell us any solvent, at any price." He sounded calm and collected, even in this disaster, and make no mistake, it was a disaster.

The patent on Tyrnex ran out a dozen years ago, but Novalon had a couple hundred defensive patents around it. You could brew your own Tyrnex, so long as you had a completely unique method to deliver it that didn't involve any of the chemicals that didn't interact with it. Oh, and you needed to not use any of the standard Tyrnex instruments for measuring it, because the interfaces were all patented too.

And a whole bunch of DNBX projects relied on Tyrnex. Projects that had been running for a long time. Projects that had critical delivery dates.

Without Tyrnex, the gears of Detroit Nanobiotics would grind to a halt.

Tyler clamped a head to his forehead to try to contain the pounding headache. His shoulders ached from shuffling through lab reports all morning and cash flow reports all afternoon, and his tongue tasted like coffee's corpse, and now he had to deal with (*fucking incompetence)* supply problems.

"Other labs," Tyler said. "Have you talked to Jake over at LXI?"

"Of course," Mill said calmly. "He's the one who told me what was going on."

Tyler took a deep breath, trying to smother his body's completely natural reflex to beat someone over the head with a rock. "Going on. Tell me."

Mill's voice should have picked up an inflection, but he sounded just as unruffled. "Novalon contacted the legal departments all of their customers late last week, specifically reminding them that the licensing terms on Tyrnex do not permit them to resell or redistribute the solvent and that violations of the license would result in loss of their own access to Tyrnex."

Tyler felt a chill. "So this is deliberate."

Tyler hated what he called *corporate bullshit*. The rough-and-tumble brawl of business. He'd built a nanobiotics research firm so he could invent medical miracles and license them to manufacturers specifically because he didn't want to "compete" in the marketplace. Once his people invented something and nailed the patents down, they'd won. Next project. He only fought properly when he had to.

I lived for those times Tyler busted a fiscal knuckle on someone else's stock price. Smacking someone down felt *good*.

Mill said nothing.

Tyler's spirits firmed up. "Right. Leave it with me."

"Yes sir." Mill disconnected.

I rejoiced. We were going to have a fight!

3

Tyler followed the same ritual every time he needed to have a business throw-down. He started by walking over to the wall and pressing the hidden panel to open his private closet. "Ivanka. Is Minnie White still CEO of Novalon?"

Thirty years ago I'd suggested he name his digital assistant Ivanka, after the pop star. Every time Tyler spoke her name, it reminded me what I'd like to do to her. With her. Whatever.

"Affirmative," she replied in that delicious sultry voice.

Tyler pulled his shirt off and threw it in the hamper.

The closet was barely big enough to stand in, but it had the basics. A variety of clothes, from neatly folded polo shirts in blue and green to a sharp-pressed custom-tailored suit in dark blue. A dozen ties so powerful that they almost fought for dominance. At the back, a little glass shelf held a tube of odorless deodorant and a spray bottle of cologne that had a fancy French name but I thought of as Leather and Sage and You Want Me Now.

"Ivanka. Give me the precis on Minnie White and Novalon."

Tyler paused to select his weapons. The polo shirt would be too casual, the suit way too formal. He needed to approach as an equal.

"Minnie White." Ivanka's voice lit something primal. "Doctorate in nanobiotics from University of California, 2079. Inventor of the White Splenic Accelerator and the White Ovarian Stabilizer. Founder and director of the White Consortium. Purchased majority of Novalon shares in 2091 June and voted herself corporate President. Added Novalon to the White Consortium 2092."

Tyler's hand wavered over the bleach-white button-down cotton shirts, the sort that men had favored for centuries. His manicured fingers paused over the one ironed to a razor's edge—*no, you'll look like a supplicant.*

"Forty-eight years old," Ivanka continued.

Thankfully he listened, picking a dressy but softer shirt with a loose collar and fashionably tiny bright red buttons. It felt really nice sliding across our back and chest.

"Unmarried, no children, no romantic partners on record."

Everyone had romantic partners. Everyone but Tyler, that is. He could hire a snoop, get the real story.

"Large scale Novalon projects begun during her tenure include kidney supplantation based on the Harvard Emmer-Twix paper of 2097 and lung efficiency enhancement based on the Saskatchewan Labs Dipole paper of 2096."

We'd read those papers. They had possibilities, but he was way too nice of a guy to see them. Fortunately, the same law that castrated me meant that nobody else would see those possibilities either.

"Identified confidential projects include test beds in neural network integration and sleep acceleration. Research source unknown."

Everybody did neural integration and sleep acceleration. Whoever cracked those first would make another fortune. I hadn't encouraged Tyler to follow those, though. I had better things to urge him towards.

While Ivanka's sultry voice had distracted me, Tyler had grabbed a somber blue silk tie with a double-helix crosshatch. I shouted for him to skip the tie, or at least to pick the red one instead. What was he trying to do, play sober banker instead of business tycoon?

I knew damn well what he was trying to do. Get along. Not cause trouble.

We already had trouble.

Someone had made it for us.

And I itched for a good fight.

He looked at his hair. Not graying yet, thankfully. This was a comb job, not the big plush wide-tooth brush. I really liked that brush. It had a wonderfully curved handle and widely spaced, soft teeth. It felt like a scalp massage. But right then it was three strokes with the comb, then he adjusted the tie into a loose double Windsor. Not too tight, good. He couldn't look like he'd dressed up for this call. And this would be a video call.

"Ivanka," Tyler said. "Verify Minnie White's pets. Does she still have the rats? Mickey and Donald?"

How the hell had Tyler remembered those vermin? Last year White had appeared at Detroit's Gold Anniversary Armistice Ball with a tiny little black-and-white neorat on each shoulder. They'd clutched her shoulders with their tiny paws until she stopped, then scuttled around and offered to shake mitts with anyone who came near. Silly bitch couldn't shut up about how smart they were.

"Confirmed. Two Smith and Wesson neorats, registered to Novalon, named Donald and Mickey."

Don't get me wrong. I was glad he remembered them.

They'd be useful. Just like Tyler.

I wouldn't want to get rid of him completely.

Put me in the cockpit and I'd listen to him far more than he ever listened to me. With his social skills, he'd be a powerful tool.

He checked his image in the full-length mirror mounted behind the door. Teeth clean. Collar straightish, but not too rigid. His fingers adjusted the smooth silk tie, loosening it a little further.

Perfect attire for seven-thirty PM. He looked like he'd just stepped away from an important after-hours discussion to handle this routine annoyance.

The red tie would have been better. But he'd do.

"Ivanka." Tyler casually leaned his butt against the front of his desk, looking out into the empty space. "Request a call to Minnie White of Novalon. Priority..."

Two, I urged. Two.

"One."

Dumbass.

"If she requests video, accept."

Not surprisingly, the holographic image flickered into midair almost before he finished making the request. Tyler's office had excellent hologear and it looked like White's was just as good.

Tyler's eyes insisted Minnie White was sitting right in Tyler's office, in a great big overstuffed black leather recliner, facing him.

Her raised feet showed off the pink fuzzy slippers. No, bunny slippers—the ears flopped down around her ankles. She wore breezy cotton pajama pants, dark blue with little rocket ships printed on them, and an oversized white T-shirt bearing the Doctor Who 130th Anniversary logo. The shirt did nothing to hide the bit of a paunch she was working on. Her frizzy white hair shot back from her head like she'd been licking one-ten volts. And if she was going to take video calls and make the rest of us look at her, couldn't she try some makeup or something?

Really nice tits though.

Tyler won't look, so it's my job to notice those things.

One hand cradled a great big daquiri cup, complete with half a fruit stand on a stick and half full of red slush.

The appearance was a message.

Tyler had dressed for competence.

Minnie had dressed for *I do not give a shit.*

4

"Miss White." Tyler offered her a smile barely large enough to be polite. "Thank you for taking my call so quickly. How are Mickey and Donald?"

White nodded her head a fraction of an inch and raised the daquiri for a slow sip.

I wanted to slap her. She hadn't made us wait on hold, so she would make us wait for her to answer. We rated just below a sip of daquiri. "I've been expecting your call. Took you long enough."

"Then we skip the pleasantries." I told Tyler exactly how to firm his voice, and he listened. "What's going on, Minnie?"

White reached to set her daquiri down. It disappeared beyond the edge of the hologram, taking her hand with it. The hand reappeared a second later. "I'm ready to resume Tyrnex shipments immediately. The manufacturing plant is right on the other side of the Packard complex, and I have a courier standing by twenty-five-eight to deliver a case as soon as another additional twelve and a half percent of Detroit Nanobiotics go on the market."

Son of a bitch.

I let Tyler do the math. Simple math, he could handle it.

Tyler's brother Forrest owned five percent of DNBX.

Tyler himself owned fifty seven percent.

Losing twelve and a half percent meant losing control of the company.

And with Millie White being the one asking, we both knew damn well what would happen.

"No," Tyler said automatically.

Millie raised her hands in a shrug. Those really were nice tits. "I'm prepared to offer you an even two thousand dollars a share."

Tyler's hands were clenched around the edge of the desk. Normally I'd approve, but this wasn't the time. "I'll take this to the Federal Trade Court."

"If you like. I believe they have a four month queue." She reached out to recreate the daquiri. "I suspect you can continue operations for another five weeks without Tyrnex. Maybe you can stretch your funding to carry you through three dead months."

"The trade court will hit you with a penalty larger than Nanobiotics is worth." Oh, he's so gloriously angry. The way his heart thrums makes me feel truly alive. But he's still clenching the desk, his fingernails digging into the antique cherry. He's not only displaying his hand, he's going to scratch the finish.

"They will."

Dammit, Tyler, let me handle this.

But he doesn't even hear me.

White said, "But by then, what's left of Detroit Nanobiotics will be part of the White Consortium. I'll happily pay the fine."

Tyler stood up. "Listen, White. What is it you really want. Licensing? We can arrange something—"

"Don't take this personally, Tyler." White gave this big smile, bright white teeth in a kind of doughy face. The sort of lovely smile that I'd just love to fill with a fist, then something else. "It's only business. You've rebuffed more subtle acquisition attempts. And our business technology strategy says I absolutely must own your entire portfolio. You'll do well."

"Not interested." Tyler's brain scrambled through options, trying to assemble alternatives to Tyrnex. He even considered bootleg options, which lit my cold little soul, but there was no time for any of that. His hand rose to make the cutoff sign.

White raised a hand. "Hold on for a moment. Let me say the last bit. No matter what, I'll employ all of your current staff for not less than one year. You sell out now, completely, and walk away? I'll pay the full two thousand for each and every one of your shares. But you stay on, you run the new White Nanobiotics Detroit office, and inside ten years you'll be rich enough to start your own company without any stockholders at all."

Tyler's anger ran tsunami-high.

And I saw my chance.

I'd waited forty-one years for this moment. Ever since the psychopathy suppressor got shoved into our head. Ever since I learned to walk. Ever since I wanted to bash stupid Forrest in the head with a plastic building block for stealing my graham cracker when I wasn't looking and discovered I couldn't.

I shouted as loud as I could inside our skull.

She's going to destroy everything you love.

Everything you've built will be gone.

The people you love? Their lives? Ruin, ruin, ruin.

This is the end.

Tyler raised his hand to make a swiping motion across his throat, ending the call.

But I was pretty sure he heard me.

5

Ninety percent of the rules are written for ten percent of the people.

The function of rules is to be exploited.

The more rules you have, the more they can be broken.

I'm not talking about rule breakers. Everyone spits on the sidewalk or throws an apple core into the recycle bin now and then. I'm talking about the people who look at the rules and say, *If I do this and that, I'll get an advantage.* You want a strong social safety net for the permanently disabled? Someone will figure out how to get money they don't deserve. You want money for old folks and the poor? What lines define *old* and *poor*, and how can they be subverted?

Most people who aren't desperate figure out these loopholes and say: that would hurt people. It would be wrong.

Legal penalties are enough to deter most of the others.

We psychopaths? We don't care.

All that matters is the winning.

Rules got evaded. Regulators and legislators wrote more rules. More rules mean more exploitation of rules. People got boxed in tighter and tighter, while we psychopaths had a grand old time beating the system.

We enjoy beating the system.

The never-ending legal spiral led to the Second Civil War, universal testing for psychiatric disorders, and mandatory treatment at birth.

Strictly speaking, Tyler's psychopathy suppressor doesn't suppress much. It bolstered our brain's flabby empathy centers. It filtered the most primal of urges, like violence and sex, keeping them from hitting his decision centers.

Filters. Not eliminates.

I'm wired way, way too deep to eliminate.

So I'm sieved out of his mind.

Like every psychopath, Tyler loved winning.

He just loved people a little bit more.

Teenage Tyler had snuck into the library more than once to read about psychopathy. The librarian would have helped him find age-appropriate books, but she might have guessed why he wanted them.

Nobody really talked about these disorders—it's no more interesting than the story of how you were born with extra webbing between your toes and the doctor had to snip it away. A whole bunch of the insipid holos Tyler liked, the ones that didn't involve explosions and fistfights, had whole plots built around how to tell the New Love that you had a schizophrenia or homophobia or racism implant.

None of them mentioned psychopaths, though.

"Hey Sally? Without my implant? I'd kill you to win this hand of penny poker."

Not romantic material.

Tyler was absolutely terrible at friendly poker games.

But getting furious because someone was trying to strong-arm you out of the company you built from nothing? Trying to take the research you cut your teeth on, the patents you had your own plans for, the dreams you'd nurtured ever since you were a pimply-nosed teenager and found out that ten percent of the population shared a tiny degree of your secret shame?

Getting really, really angry at a time like that... was *normal*.

6

Tyler stalked through the building.

I provided the running commentary.

The sky-blue walls? You had them painted that color to calm and soothe all your people, the people you love. They'll be painted Minnie White white in a month.

Your feet feel pretty good on that carpet, don't they? Jerry down in Shipping, he's told you so often how he loves it. White loves tile, harsh clacking tile that tells everyone that other people are coming up behind them.

Tyler swept through the empty offices of Accounting, trying to burn off nervous energy, trying to think. I kept offering him my honest, sincere opinion.

Phrased in a way he could understand, of course.

The air sure smells great here, doesn't it? She won't use that expensive air filtering. They'll get all the Industrial Age dust floating around out there.

Love is a brutally edged blade without a handle. Touch it and you'll get cut. The only way you can hold it is if you let it slice you to the bone.

People love you because you hire enough to handle the crush season. Nobody works late unless they really want to. The White Consortium is huge. You think she *knows the name of everyone who works there?*

Tyler trotted up the echoing stairwell to the lower lab level.

If Tyler got us through this, we needed to decorate the stairwell. Hang some ridiculously expensive art between each floor. Nobody'd see it, but word would get around.

I hoped his swirling emotions, all that fear and anger and desperation, would conceal my excitement. I'm not sure my excitement is any different than his fury, but it's not like I had many chances to compare.

And the suppressor was already increasing its hold. My thoughts were getting fuzzier and harder to hold on to. I was pushing its limits. Without that damned thing, I would have already had White's beating heart in my bloody hands. With it, he might have just folded.

He couldn't fold. He couldn't surrender.

I'd waited too long.

Tyler slammed the door to the research level open, shoving the push bar so hard its metallic clang echoed down the stairwell. The reception area up there was as lush as his office was smooth, displaying his winnings in a whole different way. The walls had thick rich carpeting in shades of blue with a very fine pattern of double helixes and nanobiotics woven through it. Beside the bronze-faced elevator, an indoor huckleberry bush thrived in its pot, its eternal crop scenting the air. The carpet swallowed his stomping steps.

I had one last chance, a beautifully dirty move.

The lab's expansive reception desk, after-hours vacant except for a dark flat screen and a phone handset.

That blue automatic chair behind the desk? Designed for intractable spinal injuries? You got it for Harry Muldoon when he hurt his back. White would have paid his disability and sent him home, all tidy and legal and even right, but you gave Harry his dignity. You let him keep going with work that let him value himself. You went above right. You did good. You think Minnie White is going to love your people that way?

The suppressor damn near lit on fire. My thoughts crumbled to ash, leaving me only with sensation and emotion.

Tyler's frenzied pulse. The breath scorching through his throat.

Even if Tyler failed, even if I failed, I would treasure this memory for a long, long time.

Tyler used his code to get through the security door and sweep into the lab complex's sterile white hall beyond. Numbered windowless doors a dozen paces apart marked separate research labs. The air here was drier than the office, conditioned and filtered beyond sanity and reason, except nanobiotics give a lot of really good reasons.

Oh, please. Please please please.

Tyler wasn't thinking. He was *acting*. Tyler was stripped back to his primal self, his pre-verbal glory, his brain running on animal instinct propelled with a whole great big dose of purely human fuck-you. He hadn't made a conscious decision.

But I thrilled when he turned left at the intersection.

Only three doors that way.

We swept past the neonatal cancer lab.

Through the suppressor, I felt a possessive glower. That project promised to make a fortune. I'd be damned if I'd lose it to White.

Two doors left.

Tyler shot straight past the nanobioneurolingustic programming lab without slowing.

Yes.

Was he going to? Was he really going to do it?

87191?

Tyler didn't even flinch as he punched his personal code into the biggest lab in DNBX, the one dedicated to psychopathy.

Tyler didn't know how to win.

But he knew how to know how to win.

7

Psychopathy is treatable, but not curable. It's wired right into the core of the brain. Tyler dreamed of curing it. Not just curing it, but getting into his genes and ripping it out.

Impossible? Yep. Exactly like heavier-than-air flight and regrowing a chopped-off dick.

And Tyler was highly motivated.

If he scrubbed my taint from his sperm, he could be honest with a woman.

After all, nanobiotics might fail. Even if Tyler lived to be a hundred, he might not develop the tech to live forever. And if he died, who would inherit all this? Who would benefit from his work?

He'd dedicated the biggest lab in the building to the top-secret psychopathy research.

One out of ten human beings had some degree of psychopathy, after all. And treatment was mandatory, not just in the States but across most of the Earth. His closest friends hadn't needed much convincing.

I'd wondered if some of them had guessed his deep dark secret.

Tyler had wondered, but dismissed it. They were his friends. He trusted them, mostly.

The lab could do a whole bunch of research in simulation and a bunch more on animals. Pigs have a surprisingly high rate of psychopathy—not as high as cats, sure, but labs that trepan cats attract protestors. People care about bacon, not pigs.

Eventually, though, a lab needed to test on human beings.

And that meant turning off the suppressor.

No suppressor came with an off switch, but any technology could fail. The same radio mesh that provided our phones and data and monitored vital statistics like biomedics and credit, the circuits every home and office building used to maintain our civilization, watched for failed suppressors. You couldn't walk down the least used road in the most pissant village in the Western Hemisphere without a sensor picking a busted suppressor and summoning every cop in the county. It's not that they wanted to beat you senseless, but if your psychopathic suppressor had failed… you were a psychopath. You might bite a face off or rape the nearest orifice or something as they got you to the hospital.

No, I'm not being sarcastic.

One moment of freedom in my whole life?

They'd be idiots to send anything less than every damn cop.

It'd still be a total blast.

DNBX had an on-site suppressor lab. They strapped a volunteer into a comfortable gurney in a highly padded and very well secured chamber. When the volunteer was all nice and cozy, two techs on the outside entered access codes and held down buttons twelve feet apart. So long as both buttons were pressed, the suppressor was off and the volunteer gets to be all maniacal or xenophobic or whatever.

Tyler wouldn't even try the damn thing.

What a wuss.

Once in a while, a test went a little bit awry and set off the alarm. At DNBX Tyler had gotten those false alerts down to less than once a year, but the cops were still pretty ticked off when they showed up for nothing. Tyler apologized, paid for the call, and made sure the research team fixed whatever had set off the alarm.

Alarms were the price of doing business. DNBX had some of their brightest minds working on psychopathy. Digging deeper into rewiring the brain, discovering how these neural pathways worked. Not all of their research was successful.

Some of the projects failed in extremely educational ways.

Educational failures are the best.

The very best? Educational failures that demonstrate horrific possibilities.

Almost smothered by the suppressor, I still managed to pray to my nonexistent god. *87191. 87191.*

Tyler marched past the rows of towering monoliths of aluminum-cased assemblers the size of commercial refrigerators and long ceramic counters covered with microscopes and hand lasers and micrometers and pipettes and all the other tools of nanobiotics research. The glass-cased dark spindles and spires of the 3D printers usually drew Tyler but no, he paid them not a lick of attention as he marched to the fabricator console.

The back of his mouth tasted like ancient copper pennies and he'd sweated through the shirt.

Even crushed beneath the suppressor I felt more alive than ever.

87191, I beseeched the indifferent cosmos.

Tyler flipped a wall switch, and the oversized wall screen lit up. Another switch made the nearest assembler hum to life.

His hand print unlocked access to the entire DNBX intellectual property repository.

Humans do terrible things in anger and fear.

But the worst things, the most deliciously awful things, are done from love.

Tyler typed in 87191.

Fifteen seconds later, the assembler spat out red and green gelcaps, each the size of a fresh blueberry.

He pocketed the green gelcap, and my world went black.

Tyler had closed his eyes.

His heart had never beat so hard, so fast.

Then the horseradish-sharp but so spiritually sweet taste of freedom gushed between my teeth.

8

You couldn't shut down a suppressor without triggering alarms and summoning law enforcement.

Experiment 87191 had been intended to reroute some medulla functions around part of the aggression center. If it had worked, it would have permitted removing a few—a very few—of the neurons responsible for psychopathy.

Instead, it added a key pathway around the suppressor.

The suppressor continued functioning.

With those pathways in place, though, my nature just flowed around it.

Tyler's hands were clenched on the edge of the work counter, his fingers digging into the underside. The horseradish taste made him want to gag. I'd never liked horseradish, but suddenly it became my very favorite flavor in the world.

If I ever needed to bite someone's nose off, I'd smear horseradish on it first.

He was afraid. The fear rattled through his body, blending with that all-consuming love and anger and fury and impotence. He had his eyes clenched tight, and–was he crying?

He was.

Pansy.

The suppressor was still squashing me flat, or I would have congratulated him.

Tyler's face grew hot. Sudden sweat slicked his skin, the thick nasty sort you get when you've been exercising long and hard enough to get dehydrated.

Hot bile splashed in the back of my throat. Was he going to throw up? Gross.

87191 had performed in the lab more than once, but that was a long way from proper field testing. No wonder he was scared. This might fry our brain.

For me, though, a chance to play a hand was a win.

A shudder rippled his body, then quieted.

I open my eyes.

My eyes.

My. Goddamn. Fucking. Eyes.

I'd seen the lab many times. Now, with most of the overhead light panels out and the equipment in gauzy shadows, I see details I'd never noticed before. The unimpeachable white tile down the aisles are a little worn and have stopped taking wax. The tiny dots in the off-white hexagonal sound-dampening ceiling tiles form a pattern that makes gentle arcs and waves across the whole ceiling. Lab bench twelve, something dark and scorching had happened to the closest leg, and nobody had mentioned it.

My staff thinks they can hide things from me?

I snarl, then choke it back.

No.

Think long term.

This is a long game.

My first impulse is to snatch the green pill from my pocket and fling it into the disposal, but that's short-term thinking. If I'm caught, if things go horribly wrong—

No, don't think about that. That won't help.

Prepare for it.

I can feel Tyler in here with me. He's just short of panic. We're melded together now, this tangled mass of feelings and passions. That nasty empathy is still there, a bogus imposed passion that's even worse than rape because it's being done to *me*, but that's a

36

very long-term plan and I don't have the opportunity to do anything about it right now.

We don't think in words. Our brains form words, but the words bubble up out of our passions. I know this better than anyone.

Right now, Tyler's passions threaten the whole thing.

I tell my legs to straighten.

They obey.

It is glorious.

Hot freedom sizzles in my blood, my brain.

Enjoy the freedom. Tamp down the fear.

I horrify Tyler. We horrify us.

Deal with that.

My gut says that walking should be hard, because I've never been in charge of it before, but my stride is even more confident than usual. Tyler has pride, but he doesn't have swagger. I straighten the collar and run a hand through my hair as I—

There. That assembler. It's the size of a fridge, and the front is a sheet of mirrored aluminum. There's a few lights, but they won't interfere with what I have to say.

I study my hazy steel-shaded reflection.

My face is a sweaty mess, and my eyes look like my brain is trying to pop them out of their sockets. It kind of is. Sticky sweat, too thick to run, gives my skin this gleam and glues my expensive shirt to my body. No matter, I'll throw it in the basket and one of the pee-ons, whatever her name is, can handle it.

But my face has the biggest you're-gonna-eat-my-shit grin I've ever worn.

Maybe I can think words at Tyler. But right now, I need to run on instinct. I need to do my thing without making him any more alarmed than he already is. I'm going to fuck the guy over so damn hard, but he can't know it yet.

Right now, he needs to believe that everything will be okay.

I turn the smile down.

It's really, really hard.

Especially when I want to giggle.

I rest my palms on the cool mirrored metal of the assembler and stare into my reflection's face. It's familiar. We shaved that damn mug every day for years, but right now there's a whole new spirit inside the skin.

"Listen up, Tyler," I say. "I'm going to solve your problem. And I'm going to help keep your people all safe and happy, just like you like."

The fear surges. What the hell is wrong with him?

"Why?" I let the smile come back. "Because right now, the game is DNBX. Those people are part of the game. Yeah, I'd squeeze them down for a few extra bucks. But I'd do it for me— not because some cunt with a Snow White fetish makes me do it. Those people are the prize, and I intend to fucking win."

Tyler's fear pops like a child's balloon.

He knows that feeling, just not at my intensity.

His green eyes always looked kind of soft and muddy. My eyes are sharp as emerald lasers. I stare into them. "But there's a price."

This has to be believable.

Maddeningly reasonable, even.

"Dude, we have *got* to get laid. I want it. I know you want it. Lucy, the accounting head? When she inflates those tits at you, it's not a threat display from a goddamn nature documentary. You could fuck her on top of the board table during the annual meeting and all she'd scream is *harder*. Or Doctor Subramanian? The one doing Pancreatic Enzyme Supplantation, not the one in Cardiac Optimization. He'd blow you just for the joy of practicing his craft. You want to salve your feeble little conscience? There's professionals who really, truly enjoy their work. Sign up for a goddamn delivery service, tip them well, they'll think you're a truly decent human being. Throw in some flowers and a really nice dinner if you want to. I enjoy the Brazilian steakhouse, yeah, I know it's ecologically damaging but who gives a fuck."

I lean a little closer to the metal, making my eyes look bigger. "Twice a month. That's not too much to ask, is it? Twenty-five times a year. Yeah, if a flight takes you out of town I'll cut you a little slack, but make it up. You're a young, decent looking guy who can afford to—" no, that'll revolt him, don't make him think I'm that scary "—to hire someone to shake your dick for you after you piss, so get someone to squeeze the damn thing."

My feelings are a weird stew of worry and anger and frustration, but… is that a little splinter of rejection in there?

"I don't have any leverage here," I say to the passenger behind my eyes. "But here's the deal. I'm going to solve our problem. I'm going to take real good care of the people you love, the people who love you. Because I don't lose. Once you're back, you're going to take care of me. Otherwise, the next time you need me?" I put my face inches from the assembler. My hot breath puffs back up against my cheeks and nose, but I can see only my eyes. "Otherwise, the next time you need me, or if something goes wrong? I won't be so… accommodating."

Tyler is this tight knot of emotions filling my throat.

But I recognize the grudging capitulation that loosens it.

It feels utterly luscious.

I have my backup plan.

If the worst happens, at least we'll get some action.

I lean back. "Then that's settled." No, wait—let's fix that thing too. "Oh, and by the way? Janet was fifteen years ago. Use your imagination. Get some new mental footage for your one-handed shower sessions. I suggest an extensive research program. *Extensive*."

I tug at the shirt's shoulders, straightening it. "Now let's kick some White ass."

9

There's a joy in ordering lab flunkies around, telling post-docs to create a new liver regenerator or diverticular polyp polisher.

But working with the nanobiotics is its own joy. I'm building tiny machines to rearrange life, designing cells, arranging polymer compounds. It's not the first time I've worked alone in the lab, but I haven't for, what, three years now?

I need to play God more often.

I'd worried that if I ever got out, I'd move straight to the pillaging. A lifetime is a long time to spend repressing yourself. I'm able to hold my composure better than I thought, though. Having a worthy goal helps.

Minnie White wants to break me? She's gonna get a really nasty surprise.

And it's not like I'm a whole new person. I'm still mostly Tyler. I'm just all of Tyler, for the first time in my life. If someone gets in my face right now, yeah, I might punch them. But it's late and my, *my* company is damn near empty.

Two hours in the lab, brewing up a nice batch of unlubricated fuck-you.

A remote-control drone from Daycare. Why the hell did Tyler help support those little parasites? Don't I pay them too much already?

I change my shirt. A green polo this time, because it's late and there's no way I'd be wearing anything even vaguely formal.

A ninety-minute late-night walk around the Packard Biotechnical Research Park, to "stretch my legs." With my new awareness the night is razor sharp. Even with Detroit's light pollution, the sky looks full of stars stabbing holes in the firmament. Every breath of fresh-mown grass and the fresh air of the tree farm fills my chest with purely sensual pleasure.

Around on the east side of the complex, almost as far away from DNBX as I could get, I rest for a moment, leaning my back up against an elm. The cool bark soothes the back of my head and between my shoulder blades.

When I walk away, I leave the hand-sized child's drone and its special cargo behind. I have to trust that it scuttles away behind me, on its mission to climb up the drainpipe by the Novalon manufacturing plant.

I'd thought a whole bunch about Tyrnex solvent over the years. How it was one of my empire's choke points. I'd considered its weaknesses.

At eight fourteen and thirty-one seconds AM, a previously unforeseen combination of airborne late twentieth century industrial particles combined with an undetected manufacturing defect in a solvent container will make a tiny corner of the Tyrnex shipping facility go up in a puff of gas. A puff of horribly toxic gas. Probably kill a couple Novalon employees and lung-burn a couple dozen more.

They should have gone to work for me.

The whole industry would lock down Tyrnex use while the investigation went on.

Yeah, DNBX would grind to a halt. My stock would take a hit.

But the White Consortium's stock would plunge right into the composter.

I win.

I circle back towards my wing of the industrial park, filled with pleasant daydreams as I walk through the night.

Shine up the records first. Make DNBX's supply and manufacturing records unimpeachable.

Wait for staff to start to arrive. The DNBX kitchen staff arrives around five AM. I'll stagger down from the lab looking for a cup of coffee. Tell them I'd spent the night working on a new idea, but it'd been a wash. Grab a shower.

No—wait on the shower. Time things so I'll be *in* the shower when Novalon has its 8:14:31 AM debacle. Running out to shout *what's happening* wearing nothing but a towel, with shampoo in my hair, would give me a shot of credibility. And witnesses.

Plus, the showers are near Accounting. Maybe I'll give Lucy of the Inflatable Tits a good eyeful of my pecs and abs. Hell, when the second set blows the towel might slip. That would totally happen if I didn't know it was coming. I'll grab it quick, and look all embarrassed and run away. Lucy and I have our usual Friday meeting coming up day after tomorrow. Watching her try to talk to me about 'figures' while she's got that picture in her head would be fun.

It might even lead to something more, right there in her office.

The green pill feels like a lump of red-hot iron in my pocket. I want to fling it into the night, or stuff it into the lab waste bin and break it down into its component atoms.

But if I have to see a doctor, I'll need the pill. My brain is lit up in its full psychopathic glory. The most cursory diagnostic scan will summon an armed response unit.

But I'll be spending a lot more time in the lab. There must be a way to fool the diagnostics. I can probably create a new implant that broadcasts a fake signal into medical sensors.

Meanwhile, I'll go home and call a delivery service. Get me a double order, a brunette and a redhead.

This will be the greatest day of my life so far.

And tomorrow promised to be even better.

I give the night receptionist a carefully restrained nod, choking my grin until I'm safely in the stairwell and can run back up to the lab level. A bit of tedious paperwork and I'll be totally in the clear.

Then I open the secured door to the psychopathy laboratory to find Minnie White.

With a bomb.

10

White's in a lab technician's scrubs and jacket, both in bright DNBX yellow. She has her wildly frizzy white hair pulled back in a matching yellow velvet ribbon and wears a gauzy hairnet over the whole thing.

White is a pretty good looking piece. Seriously. Those wide lips need good hard kisses and then some.

But in one hand she's got this nasty black box about the shape of a cantaloupe. A heavy cable made of many smaller wires braided together hangs off one side. It's a carbon-oxygen molecular nanoassembler module, used specifically to attach those types of atoms together.

She's standing right by one of the big nanoassemblers, next to the junior tech's lab bench just to the left of the door. The assembler's aluminum front hangs open, making it look even more like a refrigerator.

The module in White's hand doesn't have a spray-paint stencil label that says BOMB, but come on. It's round. It has wires for a fuse. And she's installing it inside my equipment, when she has no right whatsoever to be here.

White freezes, shock sprayed across her face.

I don't.

Her presence here changes everything. I don't know what game she's playing, but my new game is Gleeful Blackmail and I'm going all in.

I keep my steps regular, non-threatening, as if I'm just going on with my day and hadn't quite realized who she is. Half a second later she gives this little jump, but it's too late and I'm close enough to give her a shove and she stumbles backwards, right into the assembler's innards, letting me reach out a hand and grab the big metal door and slam it right into her once, twice, three times, drowning out her scream with all its lovely surprise and pain and this nice note of rage too, giving me a pleasure like perfect milk chocolate melting on my tongue but my tongue is clenched tight behind my jaw and my heart is beating and I am so goddamn alive for the very first time in my whole life and it's pure unadulterated joy.

White slumps to the white tile.

Jewels of blood spatter the dark leather of my dress shoes.

I swing the door open wider, trying to get a really good crack in before I slap her awake and explain the new facts of life to her.

Her head sags beautifully.

The yellow velvet hair ribbon slips off that shock of hair, hitting the red-dotted tile with a thud far too heavy for cloth.

An automated voice proclaims from a speaker in the ceiling. "Failed sociopathic suppressor in the Psychopathy Lab."

I stop to stare at the yellow hair ribbon.

It rolls a couple inches like metal, then tips into a wobbling spin before stopping on the ground.

"Lab is in lockdown," the alarm declares. "Armed response is on their way."

The game isn't blackmail now. There isn't one psychopath in here. There's two, and we're both sitting bare-ass naked with our brains burning with glorious madness and she's fucking unconscious, blood running from her swelling purple nose and these luscious gashes on her face and arms where I'd slammed her into the machine innards.

I grab a tablet loaded with access software off the nearest test rig bench, then snatch the "velvet" hair band. It's cool and hard, maybe some kind of ceramic. The hair band doesn't respond to wireless signals, but there's a tiny access port on the inside edge, so I grab a lead and plug in.

I've never seen these menus before, but I recognize all the language in the labels.

It's a psychopathy suppressor inhibitor.

It shuts down the suppressor, but provides a masking signal.

I use the tablet to check her suppressor. Without the influence of the hairband, it's resetting itself back to normal.

Dammit.

The cops will be here in five minutes, and they're going to find one psychopath.

I let out a torrent of desperate obscenities.

Then I study my image in the assembler's mirrored aluminum surface. I look deranged.

I haven't said anything about my plans out loud. He won't be sure. Not really sure.

Of course I'd think about doing Lucy. He would too, if he dared.

But he thinks the best of everyone.

Even me.

"Listen," I say to the feeble little bastard behind my face. "I've kept my word. You'll be happier without the bomb anyway, won't you? And you're getting control back."

I dig the fucking green pill out of my pocket.

"If you can't come up with a peaceful loving way to save DNBX with knowing that Minnie White is a goddamn psychopath, that she came here with a bomb, then you don't deserve to be running DNBX."

No, one last thing.

I dash all the way across the lab to the bench I'd been working on. I'd left a mess of tools and parts, but there—the drone remote.

A tap shows the drone hasn't delivered its cargo yet.

I stop the program and tell it to hold.

Tyler will have to get it tomorrow.

I raise the pill—no, dammit, one more thing.

I dash back to White. Seize her suppressor-suppressor.

Stuff it into an interoffice envelope. Scrawl HOLD FOR TYLER ROWAN - PERSONAL AND CONFIDENTIAL on the front, and rip the protective sticker off the glue strip.

Then stuff it down the mail chute.

The mail crew knows my scrawl. They love Tyler. It isn't the first time Tyler has mailed something to himself. They won't let jack shit happen to that envelope before it gets back to me.

Him.

Shit goddamn fuck.

I bite the pill.

||

It was noon before White and Tyler ditched the cops.

They were working late, trying to develop a new product to detect sociopathy as part of a possible partnership. She slipped and fell inside the assembler. Her face bounced off the nasty gears and rods inside, then the door ricocheted back and knocked her again.

Tyler had run over to rescue her and tripped right on top of her, making everything worse.

Sorry, Officer. We're CEOs, not big strong responders like you.

The signal? A rogue from the test equipment. Just like last year, remember?

They remembered all too well.

Tyler promised to pay the fine.

They vanished back into the city.

Did they believe us? We had money. We didn't have any kind of sociopathy. So I didn't really care. Tyler cared, but he was tired enough to wave them away with a smile.

Tyler felt like he'd been beaten everywhere with rubber mallets. Not that he'd ever been properly beaten, so how would he know? But fatigue burned in his eyes and made all his joints ache.

Me?

I was the back seat driver again. Ah, fuck.

But I could already tell that Tyler intended to keep his side of our "unholy" covenant, so: yay, fuck!

He also intended to never let me out again.

But he still intended to live long enough to live forever.

And "never again" isn't a long time, compared to forever.

I could wait.

Meanwhile, he'd invited Minnie White into his office. He'd left strict instructions that they were not to be disturbed.

And closed the door, with its excellent soundproofing.

The room smelled of hot coffee and a whole heap of sandwiches. Roast beef and cheddar on rye, with really nice sharp mustard, all on a tray perched right on the antique credenza. The paneled walls still had their hand-polished gleam, and the carpet still swallowed footsteps.

With the door closed, the only sound was White's partially smothered breathing.

She slouched in one of the guest chairs, defeated and crumpled. The DNBX medical officer had put a regenerator patch across her busted, swollen nose and applied salve to the scratches on her face and arms. Nothing but time would handle the impressive black eye, and her shock of hair was a tangled mess. Tyler had offered her a clean lab uniform to replace the one with her blood on it, but it didn't quite fit.

That nice body, looking all disheveled and beaten?

I was good.

Tyler poured coffee into an incredibly expensive, delicate china cup. He'd ordered the West Texan beans, lightly roasted. Probably the best coffee on the planet these days.

Then handed her the cup.

Good. We had the power. Treating her like a guest would remind her of that.

Tyler laid a sandwich half on matching china and placed it on

48

the credenza. "I do believe roast beef and cheddar is your favorite?"

"You would know that," she said.

"It's been a long night." Tyler took his time collecting his own coffee and sandwich before settling in his chair. And a sandwich would really hit the spot after all this running around. "So, let's try this again. How are Mickey and Donald?"

Nice and civilized. Excellent.

Minnie rolled her eyes. "Please. You're a psychopath, same as me."

Tyler leaned back.

No, you idiot, don't show surprise!

He raised a coffee to cover. "Why do you say that?"

She shook her head. "You moved too quick. You struck too quick. You didn't even hesitate."

Damn, that coffee felt like life in a cup. "You were in my company's most private lab. And I bet when I take that assembler module apart, I'll find a bomb."

"I was stunned," she said. "I couldn't, couldn't find my body, but my ears? They worked just fine. I heard you talking to yourself. Talking about your bargain. That's why you have every single psychopathy-related patent sewed up. You're trying to do something about yourself, aren't you? For yourself. So, where were you?"

As she spoke, this lovely streak of indignant rage at her presumption bubbled up inside Tyler. By the time she finished, I was really looking forward to him totally crushing her. He had her in the palm of his hand, and only had to close it to make any supply problems with the White Consortium disappear forever.

When he said "Sabotaging your Tyrnex factory," the words

draining away all the anger with them, I'm not sure if he or I was more floored.

"A bomb of your own," she said.

Tyler sipped his coffee. "Not exactly. With just the right proportions of coal ash, asbestos, and Freon, you can make Tyrnex vaporize."

White frowned. "Lethal?"

Tyler set the cup down. How is he so relaxed? "Less lethal than a bomb in a crowded lab, but yeah."

"My stock price would have tanked." White sipped her own coffee. "I have to admit it, that's pretty nice."

The coffee? Or my bomb?

"So seriously." Tyler picked up his sandwich. Mustard dampened his fingers. Damn, but I *was* hungry. "What is it you want? What is this really about?"

White set her cup back on the saucer and leaned forward. "You know perfectly well what it's about. Nobody talks about what we are. This," and her face twisted beautifully, "this suppressor, it makes society safe from us. But it doesn't make us safe from society. You know how hard it is to form a real connection with someone when you can't tell them the truth about yourself?"

That sandwich tasted really good, beef and cheddar and expensive ground mustard all mingled together. I encouraged Tyler to chew slowly. "Yeah," he said. "I do. And we're close to real immortality."

Her eyes burned. Now that she'd started talking, it was like a reservoir of bitter words had ruptured and was exploding out of her. "Is it going to be like this forever? Or am I going to take action? Psychopathy isn't my area of expertise, but expertise you can buy. Nurture. Either I do something, or it's forever."

Tyler swallowed. "You're overlooking the other choice."

I could see his thoughts rising, and wasn't sure I liked them.

White frowned. She didn't look like she'd like them either.

"We do this together. You're no slouch. You built that anti-suppressor hair band, didn't you?" At her nod Tyler continued, "And you've got the economic empire. We could do between us."

"I built the suppressor." White had recovered her poise. Even holding a coffee cup, she looked good. "What have you done?"

No, don't just spill—

"Me?" Tyler gave his most charming smile. "I've got two pills. One bypasses the suppressor. The other shuts down the bypass."

Her eyebrows went up. "Nice."

"But that's not it," he said. "That's not really the important bit."

White set the cup down and settled her hands in her lap.

Tyler stood up and walked to the closet

I didn't like turning my back on White, but I didn't get a vote anymore.

A second later we returned to stand almost close enough to White to touch her. In one hand, he offered her his luxurious wide-toothed brush, handle out.

"The real thing is," he said, "I am sick of not being able to tell anyone the truth. I'm sick of being alone. I'm sick of nobody knowing. I'm sick of being so ashamed of what I am that I don't dare tell anyone. We damn near killed each other last night, and you know what? Talking to you now is a relief. I have a nanobiotic chip in my head that keeps me from being one of the worst people in the world. So do you." His voice dripped ruptured frustration, and I felt his face heating, but the brush didn't move. "If you and I can't find something in common, some way to get along together, some way to help each other and maybe even take care of each other, just a little, then we might as well quit trying. Because we are never going to find another person so willing to go all the way for what they want."

Damn.

Tyler isn't bad.

White studied Tyler's face for a beat, then one end of her battered mouth crooked up in a smile. "Mister Rowan. I do believe I like your style."

With long, delicate fingers, she reached for the brush. One of her fingers drifted across the edge of his palm, just a little but deliberately, as she folded her fingers around the handle.

Tyler smiled. "Then let's have some lunch and discuss it."

She raised the brush to tug it through her blown-away hair, an interested spark in her blue eyes.

I just might get my paws on those tits after all.

And something tells me that locked behind those brilliant eyes and that ravishable mouth, there's a person that I'd really, really be interested in getting to know.

Final Gift

|

When November's wind clawed at the plank walls of the old wooden barn where Mha lived, when it set the flames in the rusty coal stove of the grooms' quarters to flickering, when the hard-used joints between her ancient orcish bones swelled enough to make every motion torment, when her crumbling guts refused to release the giant turd-brick wedged inside, Mha couldn't help asking in the secret pit of her heart: why hadn't her children eaten her?

She already knew the answer, even on this bitterest of days.

Mha had borne two sons for her Uraz-n'Tass. One son died in the Great War; the other, crushed beneath a falling crane at the Port of Detroit. Other clans had claimed her three daughters.

They had done right by their children.

Even if it left them alone.

Even if a son had survived and kept the clan alive, she would still draw breath. This horrid America of 1927 left the old to rot alive.

And she and Uraz had rotted. Mha couldn't remember ever seeing an orc as old as them. Her beautiful bald purple-green scalp had sprouted long strands of hair, like a human's or a dwarf's but far coarser. Her steel knife couldn't hold enough of an edge to shave away the shameful strands no matter how carefully she worked the whetstone, so she used a piece of old tack she'd found in the barn to tie the strands into a lump in the back of her skull. During the Spanish-American War, her hands had been dexterous enough to work Lord Gatling's famous machine gun, but now her knuckles were the size of walnuts. She'd broken a tusk off short gnawing on a marrow-bone, and the roots of the rest of her teeth felt only tenuous. Her nose had grown weak, but not weak enough she didn't know she stank of something that wasn't quite mildew or decay or bad meat, a stench that could only be called old orc.

At least the barn had plenty of space to do the butchering, even with the giant heap of coal and the age-warped timbers wasting away and the open-top carriage that hadn't been used since before Mha's birth. Scattered barrels held scraps of wood and bits of iron and other detritus someone hadn't bothered to properly discard. Dusty shelves offered mysterious half-full bottles and tools so corroded they imploded at a touch. The six stalls hadn't seen beasts for ten years at least, but the stinks of hide and manure and horse-sweat had sunk into the dirt floor like wasted blood. Not that Mha would waste any of Uraz's blood.

The barn was for lost and useless things.

Like an orcess with no clan and no labor.

Like Uraz, Mha was naked. She didn't want to get his blood or grease on her clothes. The grooms' quarters had the tiny stove, but out here in the main barn, November's chill whistled between gaps in the plank walls, turning her breath to white plumes and raising bear pimples on her sagging skin.

Mha knotted the heavy hemp line around Uraz's ankles. She needed two tries to toss the line over the central beam, a mere fifteen feet up. Rusty saw blades in her spine and an even more agonizing brick in her throat, she hauled the line hand-over-hand to hoist her warrior's naked body so that his dangling hands hung inches above the floor. A double loop and quadruple half-hitch around one of the beams supporting the hayloft held him there.

Had the wind picked up? Did November approve of her efforts?

No, she couldn't think that. Orcish gods never gave. They only took. They commanded, never succored. She only thought she'd lost everything. If she dared protest to November or the Sun or Moon or even the sleeping soil, they would find something else to claim.

Watching Uraz's empty shell swing from his ankles, arms dangling almost to the hard-packed wooden floor, Mha fought for her own breath. It wasn't enough that her bent back cramped her lungs and the brick in her throat nearly choked her, the sight threatened to squeeze gasping tears from her. She knew every inch of his skin. That long twisted scar on the back of Uraz's ribs, where he'd had taken a sword blade meant for the human Lieutenant Harrison. The thick knot of scar where an overstrained rope had snapped, burning through his skin clear to the muscle. A lump where the first orc to try to claim their daughter Kiva had gouged a talon's width of meat away. And so many smaller scars, where she'd marked him each time they joyfully ravished each other. Though those lusts had died twenty years past, her memory held each scar as firmly as his flesh did.

Her warrior's body mapped their lives together.

Uraz had left her this final gift. She had not dishonored him by sobbing when she woke to find him cold. She had not cried when she'd undressed him, gently tracing each of his scars for one last time. She would not soil his memory by even hinting at ingratitude. Even if she was alone for the first time in forty years, even if the rocky lump in her throat swelled enough to wholly choke her, she would not cry.

An orc lived for their clan and their work. She had neither, but Mha would show the gods that taking everything but her breath would not break her. Like the warrior she had been.

When Uraz stopped swinging, she set the broad tin pan beneath him. As she'd hoped, it was exactly wide enough.

Now the worst part.

The first worst part.

Mha didn't dare hesitate. November would think her reluctant. She would not tolerate that.

So many orcs in America, not that she and Uraz had seen any in the last few summers, kept their talons indecently trimmed. How could an orc be an orc without talons? She set her thumb to the side of Uraz's neck. "Thank you for your final gift," she whispered. Not that Uraz would hear, but November would know that she honored her warrior.

She needed to be gentle. She didn't want to set Uraz swinging and disrespect his blood by splashing it across the dirt. She wanted to savor every bite of blood sausage.

Mha flicked her thumb against Uraz's still carotid.

Her talon hit hide—and cracked.

The pain in her thumb was minor, but the shock of breaking a talon on Uraz's hide wholly halted her breath. She stared at the cracked talon, heart thudding in her ears.

She'd cracked talons before, of course.

But age had taken even the power to truly claim her warrior.

Maybe her breath would never start again. Perhaps November would decide she had finally earned death.

But in another heartbeat, her treacherous ruin of a body demanded air.

She had to use the feeble knife to cut Uraz's throat. It wasn't sharp enough to cut him properly, but at least it wouldn't snap. She cradled the back of his head with one hand as she sawed, trying to keep the swaying to a minimum.

An awful minute later, thick red blood pinged into the tin pan.

Mha's vision blurred. How dare she? The barn seemed even colder than before—had November witnessed her shameful tear? She refused to raise a hand to wipe her eyes. If the tear had been seen, she had condemned herself. If it had not, she would not draw November's eye.

The barn's chill would slow his blood. He would be there for hours.

She couldn't put it off any longer.

If she could preserve Uraz's meat and tan his hide properly, so that his remains could succor her for as long as she lived, she could choose a proper final sacrifice for him. If she couldn't, if his whole body had to be consumed in a single feast or be wasted, she would have to sacrifice it all.

You couldn't smoke meat over a coal fire, so she'd have to salt-cure him. A lot of salt. The little box in the groom's quarters didn't come close.

If she found salt, she would tan Uraz's hide with his brains. If she couldn't make the necessary sacrifice, she'd surrender his hide with the rest of him.

If she found salt before she needed to eat or drink, her warrior could still shelter her against the world.

And in the pit of her heart, Mha so desperately wanted something of Uraz to stay.

That meant calling upon that most un-orcish of human customs.

A favor.

2

Stepping out of the dim barn into the clear morning, Mha blinked and raised an arm against the painful light. The winter-weakened Sun had dragged itself a quarter of the way across the sky, but November stole so much of its warmth the frost still gleamed across the vast grassy lawn. Drifts of dead leaves from the surrounding forest raised a stink of decay from their sheltered steaming innards, almost smearing the crisp cold air. November's wind slipped through gaps in the old horse blanket she'd stitched into the coat and cut straight through her canvas dress. She'd debated over the skulls of her three failed suitors, but decided to leave them on their shelf. Humans wouldn't understand the significance.

Her warrior hung in the barn behind her, turgid blood draining into a bucket before he froze, and the Sun shone as though the world hadn't ended. Maybe this year would be different. Maybe December Sun-Eater would fully devour the Sun. Plunge the world into a darkness as complete as that inside her.

December would not grant that fiercely held hope.

If she was to have anything at all, she must find salt.

Her only hope was the big white farmhouse at the far side of the meadow.

Frozen dirt crunched beneath her boots. The Army had issued her these misshapen boots when they'd claimed her labor for the Spanish-American War. Thirty years on, she'd worn the third set of soles so thin that only the cardboard liners kept the dirt out. If she could keep some of Uraz, she could make new boots. Proper, truly orcish boots.

Every other step sparked a flare of pain in her left hip. Each month, each week, that hip ached more. A slow-growing pain, demanding a hair's thickness more from her every day. Perhaps she needed to finally surrender to the humiliation of a staff? Using a staff while Uraz lived would have been an admission that she was too feeble to be worthy of him, but now...

She brushed the thought away. She would deal with Uraz's gift honorably. Making that last sacrifice, she would stand on her own feet. She could bear the pain one more day.

Nothing compared to the pain of relying on a favor.

Uraz and Mha had saved Lieutenant Harrison's life in the war. They had only done their duty as soldiers of the US Orc Army, but Harrison claimed a human sort of blood debt. Not a proper blood debt, where Harrison would serve the n'Tass clan all his days, but a human favor as feeble as a man's thighbone. The young human had fumbled trying to explain favors to a young Mha and Uraz, finally settling on *when you can't take, I will give.*

Senseless, senseless words behind a senseless human idea.

But favor had sheltered Mha and Uraz in Lieutenant Harrison's barn for these last three summers, even after the Lieutenant's death last summer. It had granted them the freedom of the woods, a heap of coal every month, oats and beans and bacon and a handful of salt or sugar or lard left at their door every week.

A feast of humiliation every day, for orcs who did nothing to earn it.

And now, Mha needed to invoke favor again.

A ten-pound bag of salt was nothing to a man. Perhaps Mha could do some service to earn it without the demeaning favor.

The humans here didn't work the soil, or care for cows or horses, but surely they had some labor that would merit a bag of salt? Even age-twisted, she could carry a load that would cripple all but the biggest men.

Her finger caressed the knife-trimmed edge of the talon she'd broken against her warrior's neck, and wondered if that was still true.

A horseless carriage growled down the road beyond the line of trees at the front of the property. One of the new Model Ts, or Model As, or Model Another Stupid Meaningless Human Word. What was a T? Or an A? You couldn't point at a tree or a human or dirt or the Sun or even a despicable elf and say This is a T. More than one human had told her they were marks on paper, but that had to be a human prank. Why would you give marks on paper a name? You could make countless marks, of any sort you wanted, before using the paper to scrape your ass clean.

Perhaps the walk would shift the brick blocking Mha's guts.

It wasn't as painful as the brick in her throat, though.

Mha trudged past the human outhouse to the farmhouse's back door. The farmhouse was built so sturdily that it might have been intended for short orcs. The doorframe was timber, painted a shining white, and the door was solid planks of oak fit tightly together, sanded to be inseparable to human eyes, and stained a dark brown.

Mha had grown accustomed to the barn. The ceiling of the grooms' quarters was so low, her awful hair brushed the plaster. The barn doors were comfortably tall. In the time since Uraz had brought them here, Mha had not once approached a building truly meant for humans.

The sight of this door added another layer of self-revulsion to her heart.

She had been strong. She had been tall. Her heart remembered being the sort of orcess that picked up a young recalcitrant cow under each arm before tossing them up onto the scale.

A normal human door should come up to her chin.

Her head could clear the farmhouse door without so much as a nod.

Heart shuddering anew, Mha's breath trembled in her lungs. Had age stolen so much from her? Was she so stooped? Her traitorous eyes threatened to erupt with tears again, so she squeezed them shut until they obeyed her.

If she'd worn her skulls, any orc that saw her would challenge her boast.

Humans wanted you to knock on their doors to request admission, then built doors that would fall off the hinges at the lightest touch. She rapped the back of her knuckles against the door, light as she could. The dim thud, inaudible even ten feet away, sent another shudder through her.

She was weak. Old and weak and useless.

Maybe once she'd cared for Uraz's gifts, the gods would let her die.

She knocked again, a little harder.

A muffled cry beyond the door answered. The humans knew she was present.

Mha made herself relax. She needed to be calm. Humans worried when an orc showed so much as a tusk, or breathed too deeply, or farted. Her sharp ears picked up the sound of slippered feet crossing a wooden floor, along with a peculiar double thump. Moments later, the door rattled and swung open.

The gaunt human wore a faded white house dress—she, the human had to be a she, only women wore dresses, even though her skin hung so loose she might be sexless. She was even more bent than Mha, relying on a cane in each hand to keep her upright, head twisted almost cruelly forward so that she could see ahead. Wire-framed glasses with heavy lenses loomed on her beak-like nose, transforming her rheumy eyes into giant bloodshot orbs. She stank of grease and spearmint.

"Yes?" The woman started. "Oh, it's you!" She leaned on one cane to peer around Mha's flank. "It's usually your husband."

"Woman," Mha said formally. "I must invoke favor."

Before Mha could explain, the woman said, "But of course!" She retreated a step, working her canes and legs in combination like a nightmare spider-horse. "Come in, come in! Wipe your feet, come in!"

What sort of human invited an orc into their home? Even in Mha's decrepitude, too bent to breathe well, one sneeze would shatter the old woman's spine. Human homes were full of breakable things spaced too closely together.

But Mha and Uraz were completely, un-orcishly dependent upon Lieutenant Harrison's favor.

Mha stepped inside and meticulously wiped the soles of her boots against the boar-bristle mat.

"Shut the door, shut the door," the woman said. "These old bones freeze too easy."

This had to be a kitchen. It had a coal stove, and a counter, and even one of the fancy iceboxes just like an Army mess hall. It didn't look anything like a mess hall, with smooth-plastered walls painted a pale blue and a pristine white ceiling. The smells of a dozen different dried spices and baking bread filled Mha's sinuses. A china cabinet displayed delicate white porcelain plates and tiny cups, all bearing identical intricate blue sketches that Mha's old eyes couldn't quite make out. An antique wooden claw-foot table dominated the room, surrounded by masterfully carved ladder-back chairs that any of Mha's children would have broken with a hard look. The floor was so brightly polished that Mha could see the shape of her reflection, if not her features.

Mha had never smelled any place so weirdly clean.

The woman waved to a sturdy-looking bench. "Sit, sit. At our age, our bones need all the rest they can get. I was just putting water on for tea, it's no problem to add a little more."

Did favor require tea? Uraz drank tea each time he begged for food? What were favor's rules?

"Could you grab one of those big brown mugs off the top of the china cabinet before you sit?" the woman said, pouring water into a kettle. "I'm afraid it's a mite too heavy for these old bones."

The woman wanted her to go near the most breakable items in the kitchen? Was this a test? Did aged humans test orcs the way the Army had? And why would she keep a mug she couldn't reach and couldn't use? Keeping her steps as light as her treacherous hip permitted, Mha held her breath and plucked a mug down. It would hold perhaps a quart, and had a nearly orcish heft.

The woman set the kettle on the stove and tottered towards the table. "Sit, sit, my dear."

Mha sat. The bench was almost high enough to be comfortable.

"While that heats—oh, dear." The woman blinked. "I fear we've never been introduced, have we? And you, of course, are Mantis."

Humans! They couldn't speak an Orcish name properly if you stuffed them with apples and fennel and slow-roasted them over a hickory fire. "Mha-n'Tass." Maybe a little garlic. Garlic went well with man.

Ignoring her correction, the way humans always did, the woman turned a chair to face Mha and settled down. "My name is Rose, but everyone calls me Thorn. You must do so as well."

She had a name, but others refused to use it? Perhaps "Mantis" was as close a feeble human throat could get to her name, but "Thorn" sounded nothing like "Rose." How did humans stomach such disrespect?

Still, the woman had demanded a labor of using a wrong name. Mha would swallow the insult, so long as she didn't have the gall to ruin Uraz's name. Mha sucked her cold-chapped lips to moisten them. "Thorn."

"Just so!" the woman said. "What brings you out here, and not your fine orc husband?"

The knot in Mha's throat swelled until it threatened to burst. She didn't dare shout past it. Such words demanded to be shouted, but shouting would scare Thorn and might make her summon the police. "My warrior is dead."

The woman leaned back. "Oh, you poor thing! I am so sorry. How can I help you? Do you need help with arrangements? Should I send word to someone?"

Mha's heart pounded. This tiny birdlike woman, intruding on Uraz's final gift? Her hands twitched with the instinct to leap across the room and swipe her talons across the old lady's throat. The urge lacked heat, though. Mha's old blood didn't boil the way it once had. And could her talons pierce even human hide any longer?

"No," Mha said. "I need salt."

Thorn raised a hand to her mouth. "Orcs bury their dead with salt? I had no idea! Bristol would never talk of his time serving with orcs, you know. Except for the part where you and your husband saved his life." She leaned closer and reached out a hand, almost as if she wanted to touch Mha. Which was silly. Humans didn't touch orcs if they could avoid it. "You gave me another twenty-nine years with the man I love. You don't have to worry. The barn is yours as long as you live. It's in my will."

What did Thorn's willpower have to do with the barn? Mha was sixty years old, and still understood nothing of humans. "It was duty."

"Now don't discount yourself!" Thorn lightly slapped both her knees. "Your man shoved Bristol out of the way and took a bayonet meant for him. The fall popped his knee, so you carried him away to safety before he got trampled. I know the whole story, see?" One side of her mouth cricked upwards. "By the time he healed up, the war was over. You were sent by God to keep my man safe, and I won't forget it. Whatever you need that I can give you, is yours."

Mha needed worthwhile labor. She needed a hip that didn't pain and hands without giant swollen knuckles and a back so bent that she could walk through a human door. She needed the hair to fall away, restoring her beautiful green-purple scalp.

Thorn's offer meant nothing.

And sent by God? Human gods did not even notice orcs.

On the coal stove, the warming kettle hissed and spat.

"I can work," Mha said. "For salt."

"Oh don't be silly!" Thorn said. "How much do you want?"

Silly? Mha's pulse throbbed in her vision. How was offering labor for salt silly? No, she couldn't let human strangeness distract her. The best way to deal with humans was to ignore the senseless things, swallow the insults, and say what you needed. "Ten pounds. I can move firewood. Or rocks."

"Nonsense." Thorn waved her hand. "In the pantry. Let's take a look."

Would she refuse labor? Did humans count favor so strongly? Mha set the mug on the bench and followed.

In the Army, a pantry was a food warehouse. Thorn's pantry was the same, on a smaller scale. Big enough for Mha and Thorn to stand side by side, with wooden shelves lining the walls and tiny cans and boxes and jars lining the shelves. Sacks of flour and sugar and rice filled the floor space beneath the shelves. Mha had never imagined one person having so much food, so many different kinds of food. She recognized the beans and the red goop of tomatoes. But what were the jars of yellow orbs suspended in dark liquid standing in precise rows, ready for inspection whenever the Lieutenant returned? Were those peaches? Humans could have peaches all year long? Mha's mouth watered at the thought.

"My nephew, the ungrateful wretch, comes by every weekend to make sure I have everything I need and to do a few chores," Thorn said. "He brings me more than I can possibly eat. He says it's because he's afraid I'll get snowed in, but I'm sure it's just because he doesn't want to drive all the way out to Clinton Township when the weather's bad." Her head turned as she studied the bags and boxes. "He thinks I should move down to Detroit near him, like I would ever leave the home Bristol made for us. My son thinks I should move out to New York City with him, where he's got his fancy bank job. He's a vice-president, you know. He had the phone put in and everything." Her cane thrust out. "There. That little cask. That's the salt, left over from last year's canning. Here, let me out and you can pick it up."

The cask was big enough for twenty pounds of salt. How full was it? Mha's hope thrummed. She tried to dampen it before November noticed and was compelled to thwart it. She made herself watch Thorn's two-cane shamble back to her seat, refusing to surrender to dangerous hope.

"Go on, then," Thorn said. "Pick it up. I'll make the tea."

Mha lifted the keg's loose lid.

It was nearly full.

If Thorn permitted her the whole cask, Mha could accept every scrap of Uraz's final gift. Not just the meat, but the organs and bowels as well.

Mha commanded her heart to slow. "I could move coal for this."

"Oh, you go on," Thorn said. "Take it, take it. You more than earned a few pounds of salt."

Earned? How had Mha earned this?

No, she couldn't get angry. She'd already lost her pride by living too long.

The cask felt far heavier than twenty pounds.

Thorn said, "I have a jar in the cupboard I use for cooking. When Pete shows up this weekend, I'll send him tooty-sweetie for another box."

Escaping the pantry had its own challenge. If she turned around, her backside would probably bump the canned peaches, or maybe the bag of flour. Or the sugar—how did humans stomach that awful stuff? Mha backed up, each unnatural step triggering an unfamiliar ache in her rotting hip, glancing left and right before each motion to be sure she wouldn't accidentally knock down a wall.

Not that she could wreck a human's house. Not anymore. Not like when she was young and worthwhile.

She emerged to find Thorn had set a china cup and the mug on the table, and was pouring hot water into a teapot barely bigger than the mug. "Set that by the door and have a sit. I still have some cookies left from yesterday's baking. And prunes, but you don't want them. Nobody wants them, but I get stopped up something fierce and nothing clears you like a prune. It happens to old ladies like us."

Thorn thought she was like Mha? An orc was nothing like a human!

But...

They were both old.

Both lived alone.

They'd borne their children. Those children had gone away.

Like Mha, nobody remained to eat Thorn.

"Sit a spell," Thorn said.

Mha shoved her disquieting thoughts away. Even if she wanted to eat with a human, she could neither eat nor drink until she made Uraz's final sacrifice. "Uraz-n'Tass needs me."

Thorn's entire face drooped. Was she disappointed? "Of course, of course. It's selfish of me." She set the kettle back on the stove. "Listen. It's just us ladies now. We can't be all formal. If you get lonesome, you just come up and knock on that door. We'll have tea and chat, and you can tell me what you need my nephew to bring for you. I'm sure you get tired of oats and lard, don't you?"

Get lonesome? Mha's entire life would be lonesome. Uraz had nuzzled her neck before sleeping last night. That would be the last true contact she would have in all her days, and she would treasure that memory in the pit of her heart as long as she lived.

And when she died, she'd rot until she was found.

Chatting with a human would shorten her days when her heart burst from frustration.

And what sort of human would welcome Mha to her fragile dainty kitchen?

3

November had stripped away the forest's greenery, leaving an impassible tangle of vines and low-hanging branches on all sides. Every time the breeze surged, it carried scents of burning leaves and distant coal and November's constant decay. Leaves crunched beneath her bare feet as she trudged down the path, a knot of bloody gristle in each hand. The knot in her throat had not eased, but thirst had added its burn.

Make sacrifice, then she could drink. Eat a scoop of leftover porridge. Spend half an hour in the outshed Uraz had built behind the barn, heaving at the brick in her guts. Begin cutting and salting and tanning.

And undress.

An orc's final sacrifice must be made naked. Anything she wore, anything she carried, the gods would strip from her like the scudding clouds stripped the Sun's warmth from her skin. Mha kept her thoughts as empty as she could. Her greatest treasure were memories of Uraz. She would not offer any more of those than she must.

A few minutes hobbling through the woods brought her to the clearing she and Uraz had chosen. Wide enough for a dozen orcs to brawl, with long brown grass that cracked and crackled at each step, just like her bones. The ankle-deep stream still flowed freely, but its mocking laughter sounded cold.

The Sun was almost at its highest point when she reached the rock. She and Uraz had sat on it yesterday on their daily walk through the woods. They had stopped here more and more often, Uraz saying he would share the Sun's gift of light with his woman. She had thanked him, refusing to shame him by noticing his shallow breath.

Even when Uraz could no longer claim her body, he claimed her heart every day.

Her warrior had fought for her until the end.

She knelt before the rock.

Sobs threatened to come ripping straight up from her and out her face, spilling scornful tears and broken breath. Swallowing them was even harder than cutting Uraz's throat, harder still than choosing what to sacrifice.

Mha opened her hands.

In the left, Uraz's heart.

In the right, his privates.

The blood hadn't finished draining, but they were still pale and shrunken.

The cuts should be smooth, like orcish talons. Not brutally hacked from his flesh by a knife more saw than blade.

Mha took a deep breath. She must say this clearly. She must not be misunderstood.

When she thought she could speak, she raised her face and stared at the Sun. "Sun! Light of day. I thank you for Uraz's life. He fought for me all his days."

Her throat tightened again, her guts clenching around the brick of turd.

The Moon was not visible, but it would hear. The Moon knew everything. "Moon! Keeper of secrets! I thank you for Uraz's nights. He brought me pleasure in every one!" The pleasure had faded, but as she aged she'd found warmth alone a milder pleasure.

Her next breath was brazenly ragged, a disgrace. Her chest refused her commands, so she pushed her air out as hard as she could, hoping that volume could make up for shakiness. "November! My Uraz sought death all his days. I thank you for granting it to him."

She should be surrounded by the clan. Even if orcs born in America would not end their elders, would not take those final gifts, she should at least be surrounded by sons and their wives and their babes. She should be living with her own blood, not left alone in a barn in the wilderness with a strange human woman who would offer her tea.

No. No distractions. Complete the sacrifice.

Mha bowed her head to stare at the rock. The heart that had driven the passion of his spirit, the privates that had driven the passion of his flesh. Two pathetic shriveled offerings, left on cold stone.

More of an offering than she would leave of herself.

She could barely force the words out. "I thank you for my love. My warrior. My Uraz."

There. She'd left his name for the gods. She would never speak it again.

Bitterness overwhelmed her. She had lived her whole life as an orc ought. And she would end her days here, without a warrior? Without useful labor? With no reason, no purpose? The gods took everything from an orc, but couldn't they at least grant her death in return? Why couldn't someone, anyone, just eat her?

The Sun peered around a cloud.

Mha's breath caught.

She'd knelt at her warrior's last sacrifice, and dared to demand?

November had certainly witnessed her. Had the Sun seen as well?

It didn't matter. There was nothing November or the Sun could take from her. If either claimed the barn she called home, December the Sun-Eater would freeze her blood to her bone.

And she would welcome it.

Stifling the groan, she rose to her feet and walked from the clearing without looking back, leaving her warrior's shriveled heart and orchood and name behind. When she returned, if she ever returned, they would all be gone.

The wind gnawed at her bare skin, sucking away what little warmth she still held. She refused to let it speed her step. An orc endured, even when the wind tried to make her skin as cold as her heart.

She'd left her coat and dress by the outshed her warrior had built. Before pulling them on, she dipped water from the rain barrel and washed the heart's blood from her hands and empty breasts. Five orcs had suckled at them. Another had once admired them. Now, as useless as the rest of her and even more annoying, the way they flopped around.

It was done.

And he would still nurture her. A bite of meat, every day. New boots. A leather dress. Bits and drabs of her warrior, to shelter her and warm her and protect her.

Mha was reaching for the barn door when she heard the soft cry.

Between the human outhouse and the farmhouse, a figure in white flailed at the ground.

Grateful for any distraction, Mha stomped towards the farm-house.

Thorn had fallen, arms and legs and canes flying every which way. The woman sucked in breaths bigger than a tiny human should be able to hold. One hand still held a cane. The other cane lay well out of her reach. Eyes watering and blinking, she stared up at Mha. "I seem to have fallen."

Humans, explaining the obvious, would never stop annoying Mha. But she needed to think of something else, anything else, other than her warrior and the gut-wrenching task that would fill the next few days. "Are you hurt?"

Thorn raised her hands and flexed her legs. "I don't think so. My other cane is missing, though. Can you see it?"

Mha knelt to pick it up.

"It's my own fault," Thorn babbled. "It's the prunes, you see. They help when things stop, but when they start again I get in such a rush and the grass was still icy underneath. I can't abide the old chamber pots."

Mha offered her the cane.

Thorn said, "Could you offer a hand?"

Mha had helped wounded human soldiers to their feet before, helping them get upright so they could keep a little self-respect by hobbling off the battlefield. Thorn's tiny hand felt like helping a butterfly aloft.

"Thank you, my dear," Thorn said.

Did the woman think Mha roamed the woods eating grasses?

Getting her canes braced beneath her, Thorn said, "If you'd care to come back in half an hour or so, or any time, we could have that tea. Just knock on the door."

Why did she persist in that offer? Was Thorn so lonesome she would take an orc as company? The only thing Mha could think to do was offer the human parting respect chant and walk away. "Thank you, human."

"Do call me Thorn, I said."

Mha nodded. "Thorn. Thank you, Thorn."

Halfway back to the barn, Mha stopped.

She had knelt at Ur—at her warrior's final sacrifice, heart overflowing with bitterness at not having her clan or labor or her warrior.

November and the Sun had heard her.

And answered.

An old, decaying, worthless orcess wanted labor? Then let her help an equally rotting humaness. She'd thought the gods could take nothing more. They had taken the dare, and followed it by claiming her dignity, her patience, her peace of mind.

Mha ached to bellow reproach at the Sun itself.

But if she did, the gods would find something else to take. She couldn't imagine what remained, but they would find it.

Instead, she trudged back to the barn, fragrant with long-dead horses and the coppery stench of her warrior's still-draining blood. November's chill would help preserve his blood and meat.

She found her boots. Sat on the chunk of tree stump she used as a stool. Tried to ignore the aches in her heart and her throat, and the more concrete pain in her gut. And thought.

She must have a reason. An orc could not pound on a human's door without a reason.

Some time later, the outhouse door slammed on its spring. In another dozen breaths, the farmhouse door shut. Thorn was back in her home.

Mha steadied her breath. Hoisted herself to her feet. Perhaps she should carve a cane from her warrior's thigh bones? That would allow him to support her even more. No, that was for later. For now, she would obey the commands of season and Sun.

Heart pounding and November wind at her back, she trudged across the yard and knocked on the door, as instructed.

When Thorn's delighted face appeared Mha said, "Tell me of these prunes."

Not Getting Away With It

Beth Stone wondered how an eighty-two-year-old woman with enough osteoporosis to rival the Hunchback of Notre Dame had gotten herself into such a ridiculous place that she had no choice but to rob the village museum.

But here she was.

A sliver of midnight moon and the smeared light of the Milky Way offered just enough light for her to discern the Frayville Museum's pebbly white front walk. The black canvas satchel of tools in her left hand dragged at her shoulder, setting up an ache that'd last for days. Her hips felt pretty good tonight so she didn't truly need the wooden cane, but she used it to meticulously probe the path ahead before each step. Getting caught would be embarrassing, but shattering a femur during a robbery offered complete humiliation.

No, not complete.

A forged Matchpawn painting offered pride of place, for every tourist to see? *That* was complete humiliation.

Frayville couldn't afford a real Matchpawn—the whole blessed county didn't have the kind of money to buy even one of her grandfather's paintings, and Beth had willed both of hers to the Red Cross for the good work they did, but still, they could have hung a nice print or a reproduction or even just called it an *homage* to her magnificent ancestor.

But no.

And that foolish boy who ran the museum had proved he wasn't going to listen to her. Wouldn't admit that a woman could know better than he.

Far as Beth knew she was the only living person who had read Grandfather's diaries, filthy things that they were. They made it clear, he never would have painted an otter.

The painting in the museum wasn't merely a forgery—it was flat-out *fake*.

Even twenty years ago she would have jogged up to the museum's front door, confident that her lungs would work as well as the bellows over in the Children's Historical Museum, that her heart would trip-trip-trip along as it always had. Tonight she walked slowly, careful not to run out of air. When had her lungs grown so inflexible? She couldn't feel her pulse in her temples and wrists, the way she used to when she jogged down to the store, but tonight her heart rattled against her ribs in a way it never had before.

When had she gotten so *old*?

Old or not, she still loved Frayville. The breeze carried the heavy scent of feed corn almost desiccated enough to harvest, and just a hint of the healthy waters of Lake Huron only a mile away. People felt comfortable walking the sidewalks of an evening, not like those madhouse big cities. Maybe the City Council had needed to put speed bumps on the road into town to convince the tourists to slow down before State Road 861 turned into Frayville's Main Street, but they'd held the modern world at bay. CBS and NBC out of Flint carried out news of the world, the awful frame-up the liberals were doing on that noble President Nixon and the Russians having their own space station, but that only made Frayville all the more precious.

She could not let a young punk soil her beloved home with lies.

Or her famous—if privately flawed—ancestor with work he would not have done.

The museum's front door dated from the 1800s, a sturdy oak frame surrounding mullioned glass panes. Reflected moonlight showed how the glass had rippled and flowed in a hundred years. The bright girl what lived next door to Beth, the one who taught the sixth grade, what was her name? She'd said glass was really a liquid, just a really thick one. Beth had laughed and said *isn't that the darndest thing* meaning it was wrong cause everyone knew glass was solid, but under that sliver moon dang if the old glass didn't look just like Plummer's Creek frozen mid-ripple.

Breaking it was going to be a shame, but burgling started with getting into the building. She had the masking tape and a hammer in her satchel, just like on Perry Mason and Ironsides, along with a couple other tools from Harold's garage, rest his soul.

Harold would have been a great help here.

Yes, he'd been a man, and like all men he had this need to Get Away With It. Grandfather Matchpawn's diaries had told her all she needed to know about men and their need to Get Away With It. But Harold had been satisfied by Getting Away With an extra beer on bowling night, not like Grandfather's shameful young ladies.

Harold would have spoken to that boy of a curator. Put him in his place right sharp.

If that hadn't worked, Harold would have handled tonight's business.

But Harold had been in his grave this last sixteen years. Beth herself had to save the truth about her grandfather.

The good truth, not the whole truth.

She should be home asleep—or, if not asleep, drifting on nature's cricket symphony. Perhaps counting their chirps to draw her to sleep, rather than counting *on* them to drown the tap of her cane on the dewy concrete walk.

Curator Tapper slept in the flat above the museum. Quiet was essential.

Best she finish this quickly and go home. A nice cup of herbal tea in front of a crackling fire, that was the thing. Sip chamomile and watch deceit in oil paint curl into ash. That'd put her right to sleep, the well-earned sleep of the righteous.

She'd seen the museum door countless times in her life, a dozen in the last week alone. It had a bolt just above her head and a lever handle that would have been the perfect height twenty years ago, before her spine began its corkscrew twist. If she taped up that one pane halfway between them, she should be able to push the lock-button on the handle and pull the bolt. The handle for sure. If she couldn't stretch her arm far enough around to pull the bolt, she'd have to take a second pane.

I have this, she hissed to her fluttering heart. Criminals break and enter all the time, and not even our brave boys in blue can catch them all. And criminals aren't that smart. I can out-think a criminal, especially when you see all their dirty tricks on Matlock.

Beth tugged the wide masking tape from her satchel and tore off a strip. First cover the pane with tape, then tap it with the hammer. The tape would muffle the sound of the glass breaking and would keep splinters from flying all over. That young curator wouldn't have any idea of how to pick up broken glass, not properly, and Beth didn't want any kids getting hurt.

Next to the pane of glass, the dangling strip of tape looked even skinnier. Covering the whole pane was going to take a whole mess of strips.

Maybe this was a bad idea?

No, she wouldn't let a spot of work put her off. Get in. Take the painting off the wall. Go home. Taping the windowpane was the most tedious, time-hungry part, but she'd get it done.

With both hands she pressed the tape into place. Yes, she'd need a good dozen strips cover the whole pane. She let a hand drop to the lever handle while she fumbled for the roll of tape with the other.

The handle sagged under her.

Beth stopped, puzzled.

Not daring to trust her luck, she tugged the handle.

The door swung open. The faint creak barely penetrated the cricket chorus.

It was one thing to not lock your house—out here in the country, nobody locked their doors—but here? The City Council had entrusted Curator Tapper with their historical museum, and that fool couldn't be bothered to lock the door after hours?

He deserved to be robbed.

Once she resolved the matter of the false painting, she'd have to take it up with the City Council. If anonymous ruffians were going to pillage their treasures, the museum needed better locks.

Satchel in one hand and cane in the other, Beth hobbled into the darkness. The door shut behind her with a quiet click, shutting out the night breezes and insects and all Michigan's autumn glory and replacing it with a dusty mustiness that tickled her sinuses.

Beth gave her eyes a moment to adjust to the perfect blackness, but it stubbornly refused to ease. Grimacing, she fumbled in her satchel for the heavy flashlight. It ate those big blocky batteries but Harold had sworn by it and there's no chance she'd go against her husband's word.

The light splashed against the polished wood floor and cast a halo of light up through the museum. The high ceiling loomed, made mysterious by the inverted shadows of all the tables and display cases around Beth. She grimaced and clapped her hand over the flashlight lens, trying to block out some of the light before a passer-by noticed the sudden illumination inside the museum. No, wait—the so-called curator might not have locked the door, but he had drawn the heavy drapes over the tall narrow windows and pulled the shade on the back of the door.

Nobody from outside would see a light.

Not even if she burned that loathsome painting right in the middle of the museum.

Cool your blood, missy. That was short-term thinking. A real Matchpawn would go for millions at auction. Everyone would think that the thief walked in the front door, scooped it up, and took it home. Even if they somehow suspected Beth and convinced a judge to search her home, they wouldn't find anything but perhaps a few ashes from the first fire of autumn.

Well-burned ashes.

Leaving the satchel right inside the door, she kept the flashlight low and hobbled up into the next room.

The Frayville Museum had been the home of Stuart Randall, mayor from 1880 through 1898, back in the days when folks dreamed of living long enough to see their grandparents. Beth knew Randall's story better than her own, how he'd brought in mining equipment and starting pulling the best gypsum known to man out of Michigan's soil, just a couple miles from town. Once he'd made his fortune, Randall had hired master builders and craftsmen to assemble the finest building Frayville had ever seen. As a child Beth had studied the intricately decorated plaster ceilings to pick out the hidden faces. Those same eyes and mouths looked bloated and menacing in the reflected light, all gaping in horror and shock as she quietly snuck between the exhibits.

All she had to do now was not make noise. Don't wake Tapper, snug asleep on the floor overhead.

And there, at the back of the last room, hung the shameful painting.

A Matchpawn.

Thirty inches square, on canvas.

Beth had to admit that the forger had captured Grandfather's technique perfectly. The light reflecting off the glossy wood floor exposed all the tiny brush-strokes and Grandfather's masterful palette of colors.

The painting hung above the abandoned fireplace in what had once been a dining room meant to hold a dozen people while leaving the servants room to gracefully bear their heavily loaded sterling silver serving platters. The placement let the painting loom over the delicate ceramics displayed throughout the room.

Ceramics! As if that was real art. Yes, Lucy Powliss had been a very skilled craftsman, and her little studio had brought good trade to Frayville, but plates and cups and bowls were utilitarian. They weren't real art, even if they could be dandied up.

And how incredible could Powliss be if she could leave all of these *unsold* pieces to her home town?

It was only right that a piece of real art, a Matchpawn no less, should lord over her lowly tradecraft.

If only the museum had chosen a real Matchpawn.

Instead, they had an otter.

Beth had read her grandfather's diaries more than once. The first time had been hard—once Grandmother had passed, he'd spent more pages on his assignations than on his craft, but still, he'd made his loathing of otters clear. They weren't even native to Michigan!

He would never have painted one.

Especially one looking so blasted... *cute.*

Cute was for children. Not serious art.

And Grandfather Matchpawn was nothing if not serious.

Beth hobbled forward, hurrying enough that she had to use her cane. All she had to do was knock the abomination down, drag it three blocks to her little house, and this shameful episode would vanish into Frayville's archives—

"I've been waiting for you, ma'am."

Beth twisted in surprise, the rubberized end of her cane almost popping off the floor.

Gawky Curator Tapper stood in the opposite doorway. He'd jammed his oversized plastic-rimmed glasses onto his face but hadn't taken the time to straighten them or comb his remaining hair. His bathrobe hung misaligned on his shoulders, the sash knotted in a lopsided bow. The light reflecting off the floor gave his features an unnatural cast, his nose casting a shadow up between his eyes and making his mouth a dark pit.

Beth's innards plunged, her heart lurching into higher gear like the big trucks trying to get up one of the steep hills of M-23, even as her brain ground to a halt.

"Not even going to say hello, Missus Stone?"

She'd been silent.

If she panicked, the whole town would know.

She had to convince Tapper, and convince him now.

"You have a duty." Beth hated how her voice had grown thinner and more reedy over the decades. She tried to will gravitas into her tone. "The city entrusted you with our history. You are here to safeguard it, not shill us with lies."

"Missus Stone," Tapper shook his head. "We've been through this. I swear to you, that is a real Matchpawn. By your grandfather. Painted on his 1891 trip to Vancouver."

"It's not in his diaries!" Beth snapped.

"Which you've been most definite about not letting anyone else read."

Beth clamped her teeth. He'd mentioned the otters in the diaries, yes—he'd called them "insipid, much like my companion Charity, but the latter possessed of much greater intimate charms." Aloud Beth said, "And wouldn't you, and every one of those danged professors, just love to dig through his personal thoughts."

"We all would," Tapper said. "He was a great artist."

"This is a fake!" Beth jerked a rheumatic finger up at the offending painting. "You won't even have it sent to a specialist to check it. Foolish boy."

"I'm fifty-three—" Tapper shook his head and pulled off his glasses to rub his eyes.

"If the city council won't make you fix this disrespectful lie, then I have no choice." Her voice still sounded too querulous, as if she had doubt. Curse this mortal shell.

Tapper pushed his glasses back onto his face, taking the extra half-second to align them correctly. "Listen. Missus Stone. It came authenticated."

"It was in the New York Times interview," Beth said. "August twelfth, eighteen ninety-six. 'Nature is God's majesty and grace incarnate, and it is my duty to bring that to the people. Charming is for children, and I do not paint for children.'" She shook her hand at the otter. "And that, sir, is nothing but charming."

Tapper closed his eyes and slowly shook his head. "I can see you're on top of things."

"I might be old, but I'm not daft! Not yet."

"All right, then. All right." Tapper's mouth twisted, but with a sudden charge as quick as flicking a light switch his face erupted into a cocky grin. "You know, I think I'll tell you what's really going on."

"What's going on is that you're an idiot," Beth said.

"That painting's a total fake. Nicely forged, if I do say so myself."

Beth stopped.

Whatever she'd expected, it hadn't been that.

"You know?"

"Of course I know!" Tapper raised his spread hands and let his smile swell. "That's not the best part. The best part is…" He leaned his head a little forward, as if trying to see her more closely without moving his feet. "The best part is, every single item in this museum is a fake."

"Ridiculous! I've been on the heritage committee for almost forty years, since before you were born!"

"I'm fifty-three."

"Whatever!"

"Didn't anyone on the committee ever wonder how you attracted an actual curator to your museum? To work for a pittance and a flat?" Tapper giggled—the man actually *giggled*. "Because piece by piece, I've replaced every exhibit with a forged duplicate and sold the original."

"Oh, don't give me that story," Beth said.

Still grinning, Tapper plucked up one of Powliss' oh-so-haughty ceramic dinner plates to hold it beside his head. "This plate? I can order them from Japan, just like this."

"Stop this foolishness."

Tapper brought his arm down in a single sweeping crash.

The sound of ceramic shattering against the corner of the table echoed through the museum.

Beth's breath froze in her throat.

"I know you're upset," Tapper said. "But please don't break any more ceramics, Missus Stone."

Beth knew that expression. She'd seen it on the face of every young man in town. Boys had a time when they thought nothing really bad could happen to them, that they could run and jump and even leap off Dead Moose Rock into Lake Huron without getting hurt. Life eventually abraded away that certainty, unless a boy broke a leg or a back or a neck and all the others caught a whiff of the Reaper brushing past.

Even in her grandfather's diaries, every encounter he'd written of with a young lady had dripped with certainty.

Her Harold only had a little touch of the look, and only once in a while. A beer didn't rate much of a victory.

But Tapper's grin carried a whole bunch of repressed Getting Away With It.

The sight set fury sizzling down Beth's nerves.

"It's amazing," Tapper said. "There's nothing like a really great con, you know? Once I have the last few bits replaced, I'll just…" He waved a hand. "Fade away."

Pillaging her town's museum? Stripping one of the decent spots in the world? "I can't believe—nobody's so greedy!"

Tapper laughed. "It's not for the money. Not just about the money." His face lost its humor. "It's the joy of craft. Your grandfather painted. Miss Powliss cast ceramics. And I… my craft, my joy, what lights up my soul?" He stepped closer. The inverted illumination made his face not only macabre, but menacing. "Fraud, my dear Miss Stone. And it's so very rare that I get to tell *anyone* about it."

Beth knew what that meant. It was the sort of thing the kidnappers said before "disposing" of their victims, though why the TV shows wouldn't just say "murder" she was sure she never understood.

And he was going to blame her for ceramics that *he'd* busted up.

Fortunately, she was far too angry to be afraid.

"Perhaps that's why I had the painting made," Tapper said. "So I could finally tell someone."

As if Beth could care about why he'd committed such a crime. She shifted her cane and took a step sideways, bringing her right up against a display table. "I have one thing to say you, young man."

"Oh?" The smile returned. "And what is that?"

While Tapper waited for her to speak, she shifted the heavy flashlight to shine right in his face.

Tapper shouted and raised an arm to protect his vision.

Beth dropped the cane, snatched a priceless Powliss ceramic

off the table, and flung it straight at Tapper.

By the time it sailed past his head, the second and third cups were airborne. The second bounced off his stomach, but the third ricocheted off his forehead into his raised arm and back into his shadowed face.

Tapper shouted in surprise, maybe in pain.

Ceramic crashed against the floor.

Beth stepped forward to snatch at a stack of saucers, hurling them two at a time. "How dare you!"

Tapper jerked his hands protectively out in front of his face. "Stop it, you crazy bitch!"

"I'm crazy?" She grabbed a serving bowl but its weight yanked it out of her hand when she tried to lift it, so she snatched at a gracefully curved gravy boat instead. "Crazy is thinking you could steal my town's past!"

The gravy boat hit Tapper square on the chin.

He staggered in surprise. One bare foot came down on an unbroken teacup, which shot out from under and took the whole foot with it, throwing his body back.

The sound of Tapper's head hitting the floor made Beth wince.

She'd only gotten a twelve, maybe fifteen good whacks in with her cane before the police arrived.

❋

Beth was angry enough to chew tin cans and spit nails. They'd put her in the back of the police car, where the criminals went, where it smelled of bleach and puke and damp. *Her* on the sticky ragged vinyl seat, not the charlatan Tapper.

If Tapper was even his real name.

That young officer (whatever his name was) stayed in the car with her, but he wouldn't even take a proper statement. He'd stopped writing everything down hours ago, and he'd just kept nodding and yes, ma'am-ing her like she was a child that wouldn't shut up even though Beth kept saying what that lying liar had told her.

Exhaustion weighed her down. Her every joint hurt. Her back ached from the tip of her tailbone up to the crown of her skull. She'd gotten used to the odd white night, when sleep evaded her, but she'd never before gone burgling. Throwing all that cutlery and wielding her cane had sapped her strength. Only indignation kept her up.

And a "silent alarm?" Who had ever heard of such a thing?

The sun had started to stain the eastern sky pink before Sergeant Fox trudged out of the museum's front entrance. The boy babysitting her perked up. "About time," Beth said. "I've known Sergeant Fox since he was a boy. Maybe *he'll* listen to me."

"I sure hope so, ma'am."

"Don't you get fresh with me, young man."

"I wouldn't dream of it, ma'am."

The police car rocked as Sergeant Fox eased his bulk behind the wheel. "Missus Stone. Have you calmed down?"

"I am the picture of calm, Sergeant Fox." Beth struggled to straighten her spine, despite her exhaustion. "As always."

"Yeah." Stone raised a hand to rub his forehead. "Listen to me, ma'am. Mister Tapper could press charges if he wanted."

"Charges? Whatever for? He's the criminal!"

"Assault."

"I never laid a hand on him!"

"Your cane is a deadly weapon, ma'am."

"That's a highly backwards way to look at things, young man." She could feel the anger driving her words, but felt too tired to pull its reins. Once the anger ran out, she'd collapse. "You need to remember who changed your diapers."

"That's how I persuaded him to not press charges," Fox said.

"I should hope so."

"Instead, we're going to have Doc Smythe check you out."

Beth scowled. "If I wasn't fit, could I have given that cheat what he so plainly deserved?"

"What did you think you were doing?" Fox said.

"I've explained it all to your young man, but he's simply not listening."

"But I had to deal with Mister Tapper while you did that." Fox's face tightened. "You've been here your whole life. I could trust you to behave, not like a newcomer."

Was he really trying to sweet-talk her? "You're no better at sweet-talking than your boy here."

"Ma'am." Fox's teeth clamped together. "What. Were you. Doing. Here. Tonight?"

"Getting rid of that forgery. He even admitted it was a fake."

Fox glanced at the younger officer. Once the kid nodded Fox said, "Did you throw all those cups and saucers at the curator, then hit him with your cane?"

"He threatened to do away with me." Even as she spoke, she realized how pathetic she sounded.

Fox heaved out a breath. "Here's what's going to happen. I'm going to take you home. Doc Smythe will be by this morning to do his exam. We'll decide from there."

Beth found the strength to clamp her own mouth shut.

What could she say?

She could say how Tapper had confessed to scamming Frayville, and sound like a feeble old lady. The best that would happen? Pitying looks all around town. She remembered all too well being in her thirties and forties and fifties, all too sure that she wouldn't end up that way, but everyone did. The Reaper came for all, but when he was in a mood he started with the mind.

Even if she was one day vindicated, she didn't have time to waste.

She had proof that the painting was forged, in Grandfather's sadly unexpurgated diaries that only she had read. What was she supposed to do, get a black marker and scratch out all the naughty bits? There wouldn't be much diary left!

And she was old.

Tired.

Maybe she'd go down fighting…

…but maybe, this far into her life, she'd lose.

Beth sagged back in her seat. "Fine. I'll stay home and wait for Doc."

Fox started the engine. "Good girl."

Beth's hair stuck to the seat when she turned her head. She'd have to take a bath before she could sleep just to get the police car off of her, and get an appointment with Abbie to get her hair totally redone.

The museum's outdoor lights were on, showcasing the sturdy red brick walls.

Tapper stood at the front door, holding something white to his head. A towel, maybe? Wrapped around ice? Good.

Tapper's shoulders drooped—no, his whole face drooped. He looked aggrieved and confused, as if he couldn't understand how someone could do him so wrong. His picture could go in the dictionary right next to *misery*.

His eyes met hers.

The man's mouth twitched.

That Getting Away With It smile ghosted across his face, and vanished.

A second later, the police car lurched into gear.

Beth settled back into the seat to ease her aches.

She really wanted that bath.

But maybe she'd call that art history professor from Michigan State University first. That one who'd been so insistent about Grandfather Matchpawn's diaries.

And if she had to choose between protecting her village now, for all the folks who lived here today, or protecting her long-dead grandfather, well, that wasn't much of a choice, now was it?

Informing young Tapper he was *not* Getting Away With It would be an added pleasure.

Face Less

I

Mom and Dad thought him being out in the Elephant Hill woods was "healthy." They were all about Peter doing healthy things instead of sitting in the living room watching after-school cartoons on the TV. Never mind that the woods were full of animal poo. That's all dirt was, years and years of animal poo. He'd read that in the school library during the eternal lunch hours.

At least the trail was hard-packed poo, which made it better than all the poo that was everywhere else.

He'd tried to tell Mom about all the poo, but she'd told him to stop being silly and get out there. So he'd grabbed a library book and lit out.

Slivers of sunlight slipped between the fresh May leaves, casting spears of warmth that helped burn away the boggy chill. Everyone said the ground here was too swampy to farm and too hilly to build, but Peter felt pretty sure that they stayed out because of the noxious skunk cabbage that sprouted in every muddy low spot. Fresh-sprouted like this it was the worst. The *worst*. One of the teachers said the smell was the mer-captains. Missus McGowan should know, she was, like, *forty* or something.

He could stay out here and smell the cabbage, or stay home and listen to his parents fight.

The cabbage wasn't that bad. Not really.

Maybe skunk cabbage smelled that way because it grew out of poo.

Dirt couldn't be completely made out of poo, though. No-body raked the maple and oak leaves that fell each year, or the leaves off the thorny scrubs that covered the sides of the Elephant Hills. And there were probably rabbit bones and stuff. Or did some of the animals eat bones? Something probably did.

So: leaves and poo.

But mostly poo.

The hills weren't any lonelier than anywhere else, but it beat being alone around other people. Out here, the only thing you saw were squirrels and robins. A few cardinals, spots of red against rough brown bark and green leaves. Sometimes, right before sunset, you'd see a rabbit sitting still, frozen. When he'd been a couple years younger, still a kid, Peter would sometimes toss a rock at a rabbit. Not right at them, just close enough so they'd take off and shake the whole tangle of thorn bushes covering the side of the hills.

The world kicked Peter. Peter kicked rabbits. The rabbits probably kicked chipmunks.

Today, his classmates would be at home watching TV or play-ing stupid games like baseball. Some of the rich kids, their dads had bought them real computers that played games, something called an Atari. Peter would rather bite off his tongue and swal-low it than admit how jealous he was.

He could have gone over to Tim's, but Tim was "studying for finals."

Having a friend kind of sucked, when they were busy doing stupid stuff.

Yeah, Tim and Peter played D&D a lot, and that was way cool—Tim's folks bought him all three of the books, the *ad-vanced* ones with all the levels and monsters and spells. They got him all the Star Trek and Doctor Who novels, and Tim let Peter read them right after him. But Tim's dad had a job in an office, not sweeping up the metal shop, so that meant Tim got those things, while Dad barely had money for "beer and bread and baloney."

And what was the big deal about finals, anyway? They'd always had a test on the next-to-last day of school, why would seventh grade be any different just because it was in a different building and he had six teachers instead of one? Each teacher got to give their own test? Oooh, *scary*. The only course Peter cared about was math, anyway.

Liking math did nothing to help him with the other students, but if he quit math they still wouldn't like him, so whatever.

At least Tim liked to hang out with him. Mary Felton didn't.

Not that Peter had ever tried to actually, like, *talk* to Mary Felton.

But still.

Peter peered up through the tight leaves. The sun was still pretty high, but he'd have to watch it. Once the woods went dark, the high school kids would be over on the far side of the Little Elephant, where the old Studebaker sat on rusting rims right next to the creek. They'd set up a fire pit, down on the bank where the light wouldn't show.

The high schoolers guarded their secrets like the Death Star plans.

If they caught him—

Peter's shoulders quivered and he bit his lip. He wasn't going to cry. He was in seventh grade now, almost done with seventh grade. Dad always knew if he'd been crying, even if it was just as he ran home from school where the other kids couldn't see him.

Dad saw everything.

And it drove Dad nuts every time Peter screwed up. Dad said Peter was too old for a spanking, and next time it'd have to be the belt. Peter needed to spend less time with math and D&D and that sissy stuff, and more time getting ready to hold a job. Dad told him that often enough.

Problem was, that sissy stuff made Peter happy.

Peter tried to stuff his hands in his jeans pockets, but the pockets were too snug. He was getting bigger again. Pretty soon the button wouldn't snap shut. Mom was going to have to take him to Old Sal for new clothes, and Dad would get totally tonked off.

Nobody told Peter how he was supposed to stop getting bigger.

Why did everybody else get the instructions?

If he had instructions, other kids might like him.

Heck, Mom and Dad might like him.

Peter sighed, breathing in fresh leaves and sprouting fiddle-heads with a fresh dose of skunk cabbage. The only sound was the upper leaves rustling and surging with their private breeze. The path was pretty dry for May, so Mom wouldn't yell at him for wrecking his shoes.

If he got his Tenner shoes all filthy, Mom would cry. She never shouted or cussed. She'd fight with Dad about money and the house, but with Peter she'd burst out crying and tell him he'd just wrecked his shoes, just wrecked them, and send him to bed without supper.

At least they'd save some money on the baloney budget. It'd help pay for the beer.

Maybe if he didn't get dinner, he'd shrink a little. That'd keep Dad from yelling.

But if Mom washed his shoes, would they shrink even more? They already hurt like crazy, cramming his toes in and rubbing a painful welt around his ankle.

Best to go up to the big rock and read the battered Heinlein he'd got at the library. *Have Space Suit, Will Travel.*

Peter would like a space suit.

And he'd travel anywhere. Anywhere you needed a space suit, at least.

Off to the side, behind a green canopy of skunk cabbage, something flashed brilliant red.

2

Peter knew the Elephant Hill forest better than he knew the battered castoff paperbacks crammed into his unsteady bookcase. He'd walked every path, circled every tree, climbed a few. The forest was a pungent sea of browns and greens, fallen branches shrouded in poison mushrooms and dark squishy lowlands that sucked shoes, with occasional landmarks like the abandoned washing machine or the spring-skeletal mattress.

Nothing out here shone red.

It wasn't just red. It gleamed brighter than a taillight at midnight.

The trees grew still.

The red flickered out.

Freaky. Peter frowned.

Brilliant blue flashed through the green, right from the same spot.

A swaying skunk cabbage leaf blocked it, then wobbled back out of the light.

What was it? There wasn't any electricity within a mile. And it's not like anyone had a portable TV, or a flashlight so bright it'd show up in daylight like that.

Whatever it was, it had to be twenty feet into the skunk cabbage.

Maybe it was treasure, like out of a dungeon.

Dang it, no. There was no such thing as treasure. Chests full of gems and electrum pieces didn't exist in the real world. Besides, electrum was for chumps—too heavy, it weighted you down. Take the platinum, leave the copper.

And treasure came with orcs.

Goblins, at least. Half as many hit points, but still dangerous.

The light vanished.

Peter narrowed his eyes, trying to stare right at the spot the light had been. The effort of keeping his gaze fixed on the same spot in the shifting cabbage leaves made his eyes water, but this was too weird.

There! The light hadn't vanished, it had turned green.

Camouflage?

No, that was stupid. Whoever heard of light-up camouflage?

The light had to be coming from in front of the giant maple tree right up against the Big Elephant. It couldn't be more than twenty feet, but all through the swampy black poo-dirt the skunk cabbage loved.

Maybe he could go around? There was a trail up over the top of the Big Elephant, but then he'd have to climb down that hill and all those bushes. Those scrub bushes were nasty, full of tiny thorns that you couldn't see until they stabbed right into you. He'd need, like, heavy gloves and a leather jacket and boots.

He could go get Dad's—no, someone else might come along.

Someone else might notice the light.

Peter stood still for a moment, studying the field of cabbage. The ground there was only a couple inches lower than the path, but that couple inches made such a difference.

After a lifetime of reading other people's wonders, he'd finally seen one of his own.

No, he'd *discovered* one.

And he wanted it.

Needed it.

Maybe it was worth something. If it was treasure, real treasure, he could bring it home. Dad wouldn't have to work so hard. Peter could get some shoes that fit and pants that didn't come from Old Sal. That'd be worth dirty shoes, right? Mom wouldn't worry about shoes if he brought home rubies?

Or maybe it was a machine. A weird machine. If someone lost a machine out here, something that fell off of Skylab or the Russki one—Salyut, that was it. Wouldn't that have a reward?

Last day of school tomorrow. If he showed up in ruined shoes, so what? It's not like they could laugh at him any more.

Heart thrumming in his throat, Peter stepped down onto the cabbage field.

The first step wasn't so bad. The wet black dirt squelched under his Tenner's rubber sole, but he hit solid ground right under it. The muck was more a layer of slime.

Best to get it over with, like nasty old Doctor Trembleau said when ripping off a bandage or giving a shot.

At a second step the ground tried to slip out from beneath him, but Peter held out his hands for balance. *Ha! Think you got me?* He kept his paces short, gaze flickering between the brilliant beacon ahead and the place he would step next.

The skunk cabbage and its mer-captains were awful up close, the stink thick enough to clot in his throat. The broad leaves came up to his thighs, and were covered with tiny little spines that scraped and tugged at his jeans. Muck dragged on his shoes, making Peter move carefully. A sudden coldness at his toes told him he'd found a deeper part of muck.

By the time he got to the clearing, the coldness had risen to Peter's ankles.

Mom was gonna be totally tonked off.

But he'd found the impossible treasure.

3

Peter's first thought was: a bandit's mask, but for a rhinoceros.

If the rhino bandit was done up like one of those New York showgirls.

Lines of brilliantly glittering multicolored gems trailed across the black material in delicate traceries, interweaving lines that spiraled around one another in amazing spirals, all the way out to the ridiculously outstretched wings.

It couldn't be a mask. It had no strap. It was as long as his arm.

It had three oval eye holes, but they were too widely spaced to be for real eyes. Plus the one in the middle was off-center and a little too high, like the rhino's extra eye was beside his horn.

But if it wasn't a mask, what was it?

The gems shone too brightly for the little sun that came down this far. But the mask didn't have room for batteries, so they sure weren't lights.

The mask lay atop a particularly sturdy stalk of skunk cabbage, one end hanging almost into the mud. It couldn't be too heavy. Skunk cabbage broke when you sneezed on it.

He reached out to touch one of the velvety-looking black sections, right next to a line of gems.

Not velvety—furry.

Long fur, like a collie.

Peter yanked his hand back in shock, muck squelching between his toes. Whatever the mask was made of looked thin, like felt or cardboard.

He studied his fingers. Mom would call them *acceptably grubby*, the sort of dirt you could wash off your hands before going to bed.

Okay, so it felt weird. With all those gems, though, it had to be worth something. Whatever it was, it could have sat here until the fall before someone noticed it. It's not like anyone else in the whole world was so bored (*lonely*) they'd study skunk cabbage. By the fall, it would have been filthy and rotting and vanished into the muck.

If a ray of sunlight hadn't caught some of those gems exactly right, at the precise right time, even Peter wouldn't have seen it.

The sunlight must have moved on, though.

Weird.

Peter steeled himself, pulled his shoulders back, and pinched the mask between thumb and forefinger.

The furry feeling wasn't unpleasant, only surprising. The mask sure looked like velvet, but Peter would've sworn on Dad's secret stash of Playboys that tiny soft fur tickled the sides of his finger almost up to the knuckle.

The mask wobbled. The cabbage beneath it swayed—he was touching it too hard!

Reflexively, Peter grabbed the mask before it could slip into the gunk.

The mask almost floated in his hand. Even if the mask was made of really light cloth, the gems should weigh something. It shouldn't hang in Peter's hand like a piece of stiff paper.

The wind raised a fresh waft of mer-captains.

If the limp mask was that light, shouldn't it flutter with the breeze?

He had it now. The big red ones the size of his thumbnail? Rubies, maybe? The green ones were a little smaller, but an emerald the size of his pinky nail had to be pretty pricey. Even if he couldn't sell it, someone who'd lost something like this had to offer a reward, didn't they?

There better be a reward. The smell of skunk cabbage didn't seem so bad now, but Peter felt pretty sure that that was because he'd gotten used to it. He'd brushed up against the leaves, which meant he was chock full of mer-captains.

His Tenner shoes were invisible beneath a thick layer of muck. Mom was gonna go nuts. And she'd make him wash his feet.

There *had* to be a reward.

Right now, though, if Peter was lucky, maybe Mom would have gone down into the basement to do some sewing. Dad wouldn't notice how Peter smelled, and he might not notice the shoes if Peter showed him these nifty gems really quick.

The gems were kind of weird, though. They didn't look like anything on the cover of Tim's D&D books or the tiny diamond in Mom's ring. Peter frowned and stared at the biggest one, right above the off-center eye hole. A pretty red stone, a rich red like a ripe tomato but deep, so strongly colored that he couldn't see the cloth behind it. The five facets of the gem seemed to be the edges of a hole that fell forever into redness, a square edged-pit—

Wait.

Peter blinked. His stomach gave a little twist, not as much as when he saw Mom slap Dad, but still, a real "gut feeling."

He licked his lips and tried to swallow. His tongue suddenly felt dry, though.

They'd studied shapes in math class. Math was the most interesting class the whole dang school had, and he was actually good at it. Math had definitions for different shapes, like circles and triangles and squares and stuff.

One of the things that made a square a square was the right angle. Two edges met and were perpetual—no, *perpendicular*. Sometimes a shape might have four sides, but the angles weren't right and you could tell right away that it wasn't a square. It might be a parallelogram, or a trapezoid, but it wasn't a square. If the sides weren't all the same length, it was a rectangle.

Math was behind everything in the world.

The gem had wrong math.

With his gaze he carefully studied the gemstone's cut, forcing himself to methodically study the edge of the stone.

A right angle, pointing at the mask's top edge. Another right angle pointed to the side but a little bit up. One pointed to the side, but sort of down. The fourth angle pointed the other way, but also sort of down.

Another pointed kind of up.

Five right angles.

Peter shook his head. You couldn't do that.

Maybe he wasn't looking at this hard enough.

Mister Wallerd had said that angles behaved weirdly on curved surfaces. He'd done this cool trick with putting a triangle with three right angles on a sphere. If you were really tiny and lived on the sphere like people lived on the Earth, and if you thought your world was flat, the triangle would seem like an impossible miracle. Peter had looked at the big globe in the library, and the equator and the longitudes did the same thing.

You had to know about the round to understand that triangle.

Peter turned the cloth to look at it edge-on. Was it curved?

No, the gems were pretty much flat against the cloth. Maybe a little bump, but not near enough to explain away too many right angles.

Queasy excitement rippled through Peter.

Everything obeyed the rules... except for the stuff that didn't.

Right now was when Mister Spock should show up, or The Doctor. Or even Commander Koenig with Doctor Whats-his-face, the genius with the mechanical heart. They were kind of wusses, but they knew this stuff.

A cardinal sang.

Just past the edge of the skunk cabbage patch, a squirrel rocketed up a tree.

The mud around Peter's feet felt a little warmer, as if his excitement had raised his temperature.

Almost shaking with curiosity and wonder, he shifted his grip to study one of the emeralds. It couldn't be an emerald, though, because it was cut with three right angles and one really narrow sharp point. An *acute* angle, that's what it was called. And all four sides sure looked like they were the same length.

Peter wanted to laugh and cry and scream, all at once.

Mister Spock wasn't coming.

Because Mister Spock didn't have three irregularly-placed eyes.

And it was in all the books he'd read. Aliens contacted the kids first. Kids didn't have missiles. Kids would argue for the aliens and keep the Army from shooting them full of holes. Even aliens who were immune to bullets and nuclear weapons didn't like getting bombed.

With trembling hands he turned the mask over.

The backside was impossibly black, like it was drinking in all the light that touched it. No gems, no texture, no nothing.

Weirdest of all, though—this side had only two eye holes. Even at arm's length, Peter saw skunk cabbage leaves through the holes.

And were the holes closer together on this side?

Peter flipped the mask back over. Yes, the holes were spaced too far apart for eyes. Maybe twice as far as they should be. And that third hole was just stupid, up and a little to the left.

But he could see skunk cabbage through all three of them.

His trembling had grown to shaking, but he still managed to flip the mask over again.

Two holes on this side.

A lot closer together than on the front.

Peter's breath shuddered in his chest. His pulse in his ears threatened to drown out the cardinal's trill.

Dread and delight burst out from his heart and hammered through him. Somehow, he found the strength to raise the inside of the mask, the dark side with the two holes, to his face.

The holes fit perfectly over his eyes.

When the warm furry cloth touched his face, the world came apart.

4

The inside of the mask had two holes, the outside three—but as he fit his eyes to the holes, Peter suddenly saw how they were the same holes. The two holes ran straight through the cloth to the three holes, following paths he couldn't see without the mask.

And outside the mask, everything changed.

The thick bed of skunk cabbage? It wasn't so thick. If you looked at it through the mask, it was pretty thin. There was another edge to the woods, somehow running at right angles to everything, straight out of the real world and into bizarre curves that twisted through too many angles and trees that grew sideways and these things like bats, giant bats, fluttering in the light of the extra sun that burned beneath the ground and cast a blue-green radiance up through the soil and warmed his cold feet to dry the part of the muck Peter had never seen before, where spherical worms squirmed seeking insects with too many wings. Water trickled from an impossible branch that twisted from a scaled tree, a tree that *breathed*, falling across the air to splatter on Peter's arm. Its exhalations smelled like fresh-baked Thanksgiving bread and Dad's yellow mustard and that nasty dead-flower perfume Aunt Juliette doused herself in, but somehow alive.

The world turned around Peter, like when he was lying in bed late at night and he felt the world spinning beneath him, the whirling in his inner ear shouting that the world had spun on and he couldn't catch up no matter how tightly he hung on, the whole cosmos a whirligig teacup ride from the Harvest Fair and the leering man with the broken teeth who ran it, laughing *have fun, kiddies* before cranking the dial the whole way up to see how far your puke would fly.

Peter wanted to grab hold of something. Anything.

The cabbage leaf wouldn't anchor him. Skunk cabbage tore if you touched it.

What would happen if he grabbed that wasp-yellow branch? The branch that didn't exist without the mask? Did he want to hold on to something that lived with Rod Serling?

But under all that—the worst bit?

The rabbit.

5

Peter suddenly knew that a rabbit huddled beneath the thorn bushes at the back end of the swamp cabbage, right where the ground turned up into the slope of Big Elephant Hill. It wasn't terrified. If it grew terrified at every threat to its life, its heart would burn out.

But it watched Peter with absolute fixation, a short fuse on its terror, ready to flee if Peter turned.

Nothing existed but the great big two-legs-animal. Hunger gnawed at its belly, but that wasn't important next to the threat. No time existed but now. The two-legs-animal didn't have a name. Rabbits don't name things. But the two-legs-animal had a smell, all sharp and pungent, not a hunter like the four-legs-that-bays-and-bites or the four-legs-that-sneaks-and-pounces. The two-legs-animal could strike from a distance. It could kill without approaching.

The rabbit didn't have a name either.

But it knew it was *this* rabbit.

And all *this* rabbit wanted was to eat another meal and return to suckle its young, to warm them with its mate.

Its only hope was stillness.

But now the two-legs-animal had opened to *this* rabbit. The two-legs-animal mind felt so huge, so free of meaning. Impossible. Incomprehensible ideas, like *future* and *past* and *imagination*, burning through a brain physically incapable of understanding any of them.

Terrifying.

Peter couldn't help remembering the time he'd pitched a rock at a rabbit, just to see it run. Just to make something notice him. Fear him.

Shame flooded Peter.

In the vastness of Peter's mind, *this* rabbit felt the memory.

It didn't know shame.

But it knew rocks.

Without past or future, the rock was now.

This rabbit tried to bound up the hill, but kicked at the wrong angle, leaping off the hill and into that extra direction. Not the hill any more, it was a slope, a bend, a tunnel, *this* rabbit kicking at something that wasn't there, tumbling and falling into the sky, plunging into the ground and the blue-green sun, screaming—

Peter slammed his eyes shut and wrenched the mask from his face.

Hot stinky air burned in his lungs and fresh tears ran down his face, but the rabbit's thoughts vanished from his mind as quickly as it had appeared. He still felt *this* rabbit's horrified, uncomprehending terror at falling into impossible dimensions, things the tiny rabbit brain could never hope to comprehend, the rabbit's absolute awareness that Peter could kill it if he noticed it. The world wobbled around Peter and he slumped to his knees, the nasty muck instantly soaking through the well-worn denim, the cloth uncomfortably tight with this last year's growth, his shins suddenly all slimy and cold.

The sun, the yellow sun, shone overhead, but the air itself felt chill.

Peter's heart felt colder.

This thing… was dangerous.

He needed the Doctor and Obi-Wan Kenobi both on this.

Peter fought to control his breath, letting his pants soak up the muck and the tears run down his face.

The arm of his T-shirt was wet where the tree had trickled water on him.

If it was water.

Peter grimaced and tried to pull the shirt sleeve closer to his nose. It smelled yeasty.

The impossible tree's breath had smelled of bread. Bread and cheap carnival mustard.

It had drooled on him.

Hopefully it was drool.

Had an alien tree peed on him?

Impossible.

But real.

Peter needed a few minutes to get his breath back. Despite how hard he willed his shoulders to stop their humiliating shaking, they wouldn't still for a couple more minutes. With the back of his empty hand he scrubbed the shameful dampness from his cheeks. Maybe the mask's gems would distract Dad from the tear tracks.

Dad would tell him *man up* right about now. When things were hard, Peter needed to *man up*. A seventh grader wasn't a baby anymore, even if he couldn't drive or drink or do all the man things yet.

The vision had left him more tired than the time last year Mom and Dad had started punching each other and he'd tried to walk the sixteen miles to Grandma's, humping along a suitcase with a change of clothes and his favorite books. This time he felt like he'd joined the high school running team, and somehow made his body dash quickly enough to win the marathon. His every muscle felt worn thin.

Someone had to know about the mask.

Maybe the government had a secret department for this stuff, like the Blue Öyster Cult song said.

But unlike the song, he needed to report this.

He'd get the mask home. Ask Dad to call.

And there still had to be a reward, right?

Especially if it was from the Salyut or something.

Even if there wasn't a money reward, maybe the FBI would tell his parents that he'd done good. Maybe he'd be a hero—after all, if Peter left this thing out in the woods, any idiot could find it.

But the tricky part would be getting it home.

The woods weren't bad. But he had to get past three blocks of houses before getting home. Anyone who saw him walking down the street with a bunch of rubies and emeralds and stuff? An adult would call the police. If anyone was going to call the police, it should be Mom and Dad.

If a classmate saw him? Or one of the high school students?

They'd take it. The other kid would get the reward, and Peter would get a black eye. And the belt, for getting the black eye.

Peter held up the mask in both hands. It wobbled a little in his hands, but seemed straighter and stronger than anything so light should be. It was only about six inches wide. Maybe he could fold it.

He held the middle of the long mask to his sweaty T-shirt, grabbed hold right next to it, and pushed the cloth.

The whole world twisted.

Not in the same way it had when wearing the mask. That twist had been to add something. This twist made a sickening wrench in Peter's stomach. He could see light bending away from him like the mask was a rock in a stream, leaving only a cold darkness that sank into the middle of his chest. His sinuses burned, and he belched something bitter and vile.

Fighting to keep from spewing all over himself, Peter relaxed his grip. One hand clamped the mask to his chest, the other went to his gut.

The world returned. His stomach let out one last complaint and settled down just short of puking.

Maybe the mask *could* bend.

But it really, really *shouldn't*.

When he could stand straight again, Peter held the mask in front of him. It looked harmless enough, like something that might be worn in the Thanksgiving Parade on TV.

Could he put it under his shirt? No, not without bending it. And he wasn't doing that again.

Finally, he tucked one end in his sweaty armpit and let it hang down his side, gem side facing him. He held the arm flat against him to hold the mask there. People might glimpse the gems around the edges, but maybe not.

Feeling like a rabbit watching for the fox, Peter set out for home.

6

Out in the home-lined side street, the sun felt a whole bunch hotter than it had in the forest. It burned down from the rich blue sky, driving a warm breeze before it. The heat attacked the stinking mud that engulfed his shoes and caked his pants, drying the outer layers to flakes and clots. It wasn't so bad the first block, with the dirt road, but once the sidewalk started he left a black trail. He felt pretty sure it smelled terrible, even if his nose had gotten used to it.

A mom hanging laundry on the spinning rack next to her side door paused, clothespin pinched between her teeth, to disapprovingly stare as he trudged past. A toddler at her feet ran back and forth with an upraised teddy, shouting "Super bear! Super bear!"

With the gem-laden mask clamped under one arm, Peter felt too nervous for the kid to annoy him.

But when he'd barely gone past and the mom said, "Here, honey, be careful, you'll get dirty," hot shame threatened to burst his face into flame.

He had to get home.

His cheek itched. He scratched with his free hand. Bits of black dirt flaked away, joining other bits on his T-shirt.

It wasn't just wrecked shoes. He'd wrecked his shirts, his pants, probably his underwear too.

Mom's going to kill me.

No, don't think about that. Think about the fourth dimension, at right angles to everything.

Remembering those spherical worms, perfectly round but squirming through an extra angle, made the concrete snag Pete's feet. He almost fell, but managed to catch himself.

If he tripped, would he fall through the ground and into the blue sun? Even though he couldn't see it?

The thought made him want to throw up, but his hollow stomach only burned and knotted.

Across the street, on the shaded porch of one of the older homes, nasty old Grandma West—not Peter's grandma, just a general grandma—peered at him through narrowed eyes. Her lips pursed even tighter when she caught Peter looking back. She was probably wondering if Peter was drunk, or if he'd been visiting Mary Jane like some of the older kids.

He didn't even *know* anyone named Mary Jane. How did everybody else meet her?

Peter's heart seemed to rattle against his skinny ribs, and though the sun was drying the mud on the outside, his own sweat was softening it on the inside.

This wasn't good. He couldn't freak out. Not now.

Who knows what Grandma West would do with the mask?

Peter didn't know how to sneak down the street—

—no. Wait.

He *did* know how to not be noticed.

Put aside the impossible right angle away from everything. Forget the blue sun and the flapping batlike things.

The rabbit.

He'd plunged into the rabbit's soul.

The rabbit knew how to not be seen. That wisdom had been hard-wired into it like in Tim's old mechanical calculator. It was designed to hide.

That awareness.

Peter stopped trying to walk and focused on stilling himself.

His heart still thrummed, but remembering that tiny point of awareness drowning in his mind helped slow it.

Better.

Rabbits didn't know future or past. They only had now. They didn't distract themselves with what would happen or what had happened. *This* rabbit paid attention only to what was around it.

Peter closed his eyes.

When he opened them again, he looked out with a rabbit's soul.

Take a step. Know that the ground was solid, because what else would it be?

Grandma West? Not a threat. She wouldn't come after him. Not if he walked smooth and steady home. She'd think he was just a dumb boy who'd fallen into the mud.

Expand his attention.

A car engine growled behind Peter. One of those new AMC Hornets, bright orange paint and nearly idling, but with its big engine announcing the owner was a threat.

But Peter was on the sidewalk. The driver wouldn't run him down.

Up on the next block, on the other side of North Maple: Spencer Nordeen and his posse of high school bullies, hanging out in their front yard around the old Mustang they were always tinkering with. They'd run him down if he set foot in their space.

He could duck down North Maple and run down the alley. Missus DeWalt might be in her garden trimming the tomatoes or whatever it was she did, but the worst she'd do was yell at him. Even if Spencer heard, he wouldn't bother to chase. The only thing he had to worry about was Mister Dexter's beagle.

Peter was a terrible runner. He'd go a few yards and then his side would knot up. The gym teacher always yelled at him to walk it off, but that never worked.

No, that's the past.

Listen to the rabbit.

The rabbit knows how to run.

How to return to the burrow.

Step by step, rabbit wisdom brought Peter safely home.

7

Maybe a rabbit didn't worry about the future or the past, but Peter sighed with relief when he slipped through the busted section of fence into his back yard, the mask still clutched under one arm.

Peter's family's house was the smallest on the block. Dad had worked on the back porch all last summer, but somehow it still sagged in the middle despite all the braces and lumber he'd nailed up underneath it. Some of the gray shingles had blown off last winter, but Dad had nailed dark black ones in their place. The black ones weren't quite the same size as the old ones, and Dad hadn't been able to cram them in as tight as the others. Peter felt pretty sure that if Dad had let him get up there he would have been able to get them all the way in, but Dad had said no way. The shingles looked crooked, but Dad said they'd keep the rain out.

A couple of the boards on the back wall had slipped, exposing wooden studs beneath. Dad said that was this year's project, and that he wanted to get some of that blow-in insulation while he was at it. Peter was pretty sure he'd seen a fat red squirrel disappear into one of those gaps, but if he mentioned that to Dad he'd yell.

The one kitchen window that still worked had been knocked open and propped with the brick. The smell of garlic from the garden drifted out, mingling with the thick aroma of the Creeping Charlie that covered the back yard.

Was Mom making spaghetti? Of all the nights to be sent to bed without supper!

No, Peter had a treasure. Whatever the mask was, it wasn't like the time he'd brought home the stray Rottweiler and Mom had gone all Vader on him. He'd get dinner.

If Mom was cooking, the fight was over.

So why was Peter suddenly so worried?

Not afraid. Worried.

Peter kicked his feet against the pyramid of old cinderblocks at the back of the yard, trying to knock the last chunks of swamp cabbage muck off his shoes. Each impact sent slivers of pain up through his cramped toes and scraped his heel, but what else could he do?

When he was done, the blue Tenners were still as black as the roof patches. Sticky mud choked the laces. If he wore those into the house Mom wouldn't just go Vader, she'd be full-out Dalek. He trudged up to the door, dragged them off his feet, and peeled the equally filthy socks off after them.

His feet were filthy, but only with what had filtered through the canvas shoes and cotton socks. It wasn't a chunky, crumbly filth, like on his pants.

Would Mom be less mad if he took his pants off outside the back door?

No, that was stupid. That was sixth-grade thinking, not seventh-grade.

Instead, he brushed a hand against the drying muck covering his shins, trying to get the loosest parts off.

Despite all the muck, the mask was still clean. The gems

gleamed in the sunlight—no, even in the sunlight, they still shone too brightly. The velvet darkness of the reverse side was as pristine as when he'd picked it up.

Dad would know what to do with it. He'd know who to call.

"Peter?" Mom called through the screen door. "That you? Wash your hands for dinner."

Ready to burst with a bubbling stew of excitement and worry, Peter pulled the creaky screen door open and stepped into the kitchen.

Mom stood right over the stove, her favorite wooden spoon in the big dented saucepan. She looked flushed and her eyes drooped a little, but she didn't have a fresh red mark on her face so she was just tired. That was okay. Everybody got tired. And yes, it was spaghetti sauce. She had the big pot on the crowded counter, wedged in between the coffee maker and the blender, ready for a load of water.

Peter had to act quick. "Look what I found, Mom. It's gotta be worth a fortune!"

Mom's gaze flicked up, back at the sauce, then flashed to focus on Peter. "What did you do to yourself?" she shouted.

"There's got to be a reward," Peter said desperately. If he could get Mom to pay attention—

Mom dropped the spoon in the sauce.

Peter's stomach knotted so hard that he farted.

"I work my fingers to the bone to keep you in clothes," she said, "and this is what you do?"

"What's going on, Molly?" Dad yelled from the living room.

"Your son is—I have had it, I have had it!" She looked down at the sauce. "And now you've made me drop my spoon in the sauce, it's even more of a mess. I have just had it!"

"But Mom," Peter said.

"Don't you 'But Mom' me!"

Heavy feet tromped across the floor, the vibration coming up Peter's legs. He had a last chance.

"To the bone!" Mom said. "How am I supposed to clean those?"

Dad stormed into the kitchen.

Dad's face was red too, but Pabst-red. He'd stripped out of his uniform, leaving him in the stained sleeveless white T-shirt and the old jeans he wore around the house. "Can't a man get *any* goddamn peace around here?" he snarled, then saw Peter and froze.

"I found this," Peter said desperately. "There's got to be a reward."

"You talk with him," Mom reached for the utensil jar, hand scrabbling through it. "I can't handle this boy, I just can't."

All Peter's thoughts about the mask's wrongness, about calling the government or getting help, dissolved in his father's bleary gaze. Instead, he raised it like a banner. "There's rubies and emeralds. Someone'll pay a reward, I know it."

Dad's lips twisted in a snarl, and his bellow shook the window glass.

"What did I tell you about that sissy stuff!"

Dad launched himself forward, almost knocking Mom aside to snatch the mask from Peter's outstretched hand.

Before Peter could shout a warning, Dad brought his hands together to crumple it.

A pain like a hundred-penny nail pounded through Peter's head, and the world shattered.

8

When Star Trek or Doctor Who wanted to show alien dimensions and cosmic weirdness, they made the TV all fuzzy and wobbly. Sometimes they shook the camera and told the actors to stumble to the left together.

The bent mask wasn't anything like that.

Instead, Peter thought he understood how the rabbit had felt.

The kitchen had grown not only a fourth set of right angles, but a fifth, a sixth. Their three-dimensional stove at one moment seemed flat, spray-painted on the floor, then convulsed into a full array of extra sides, more than Peter could hope to count. He could see Dad's gaping mouth and the bald spot on the top of his head and the worn-out seat of his favorite jeans and straight down Dad's hairy left ear into his brain.

The sight made Peter's brain hurt even worse.

Mom screamed, but it sounded like something from a monster movie, with all these extra voices around it. She'd somehow screamed *before* she screamed, the sound echoing around the extra dimensions and returning before she opened her mouth.

Everything seemed too close. Peter suddenly saw he could reach past the stove, through the stove, and touch the fridge. The far side of the fridge. The little rickety laminate table. He could touch *inside* the table if he tried.

Spaghetti sauce sprayed through the air, the family saucepot tumbling end over end, not through the air but through the not-air, towards the blue-green sun beneath the earth. It wasn't beneath the earth now, it was beside it, around them, its position twisting as Dad's strong hands twisted the mask. The impossible trees were back, their branches thrashing like old Mister Glocker when he'd had his seizure in church. The bat creatures he'd seen before all flailed, scratching at the air to escape.

Peter's every instinct screamed to run, but the memory of the rabbit falling into unseen dimensions stopped him cold.

Spaghetti sauce spattered his face, garlicky and oh so hot!

He shouted in surprise, but kept his feet still.

Dad, though—

Dad looked like he'd discovered a live rattlesnake in his burger. His mouth was stretched impossibly wide as he screamed through alien dimensions. He held the mask in two shaking hands, six inches away and a million miles past the moon. In some directions the mask was a crumpled mass: in others, the directions most wrong, it lay as flat as ever.

The alien blue sun quivered.

The grimy tile beneath Peter's bare feet quivered along with it.

More shouts and screams came from somewhere.

A car horn blared, and didn't stop.

Peter's fear erupted into terror. Was Dad starting an earthquake?

No, the whole *world* was bending.

A volcano? Right here?

"Dad!" Peter couldn't make his voice any louder, not without screaming. "Dad! Hold still! Straighten it out! Stay right there!"

The sky thrashed.

Dad wobbled.

One of his big shoes left the ground.

And came back down on the wrong side of everything.

Dad still had three dimensions—but one of them was perpendicular to the kitchen, to Peter, to Mom, to everything.

Dad flickered like the bat-creatures.

Horror filled Peter.

Through the incomprehensible chaos, madness his brain refused to accept, he understood that if Dad took one more step, or lost his balance, he'd fall into forever.

An awful voice in the back of Peter's head whispered: *let him fall.*

Dad drank. Dad hit Mom. Dad yelled at Peter all the time, telling him to toughen up and be strong when all Peter wanted was time with his friend. It wasn't even about the books or the D&D, although that was pretty cool, it was about having someone who wanted to hang with him and Dad didn't understand that at all.

Maybe he and Mom would be better off without Dad.

For just a breath, Peter felt more afraid of himself than of the world coming apart.

But no.

It didn't matter if Dad was a good guy or not.

Peter couldn't let him fall sideways into forever.

If a starship captain would risk himself for the lowest crewman, how could Peter not try to save his dad?

There was only one way.

Peter's heart beat so fiercely it made his vision throb and his tongue burn.

But he reached through a dozen wrong directions.

Put one hand on the edge of the mask.

And pulled himself across twisted dimensions to put his face against the black velvet eye holes.

9

The blue sun still shook, its radiance burning up through the floor. Peter's cheek burned where the boiling spaghetti sauce had left its mark. And he would bet his Star Trek photonovel collection that Captain Kirk's stomach *never* hurt this bad.

But the mask's eye holes, drawing that extra dimension into his eyes and his hands, somehow slashed away a layer of madness.

The bat-creatures still flapped frantically. Peter's toes still instinctively clutched at the tile floor, as if he was a bird and could anchor on a branch. Everything looked twisted in a way that made his instincts shriek in revulsion.

Dad still stood with one foot at right angles to reality, but he'd frozen in place.

Mom had frozen too.

Oh my God. Had the twisted mask broken *time* now? How was he going to put the clock back together?

No, Peter realized.

They'd frozen because they were—

It didn't matter that Peter was a weird kid 'cause he had enough of him *inside that he knew Peter was his like he knew that broken and paralyzed knuckle on his left pinky was his, big brown eyes so full of things the kid couldn't explain, and he couldn't blame the kid because he was too damn young to understand what he was. Kid still thought his dick was just something to piss with.*

—inside each other, just like the—

She worked so hard to make what little they had nice but there never was enough money, she skipped breakfast and lunch to buy soap and there still wasn't enough to get Peter a new pair of shoes even though his feet were fit to burst through the old ones and you couldn't tell a boy to stop growing, that's what they did, and Al just kept buying beer every night, might as well flush dollars down the toilet.

—rabbit. Peter tried to shout *don't move*, but—

The goddamn noise wouldn't stop, screeching in his *head until* he *couldn't read, couldn't barely think, couldn't hardly balance the checkbook, except* he *didn't really balance it because the bank account never had as much as it should. The only thing that shut up that horrid racket was beer, but some days* he *needed one and some days a dozen wasn't enough and* he *was always guessing and missing. No matter what* he *wasn't going to end up like Uncle Dan, with doctors pumping him full of drugs and stirring his brain with an electric needle until they locked him up and let him drool, and* he *wasn't going to end up a goddamn alky,* he'd *trip and fall into the sixty-ton steel tulip press first, get Molly and Peter the insurance money, the company had all the best insurance, but* he *had to toughen up the boy first because the whole goddamn world beat faggots with baseball bats and Peter would be so fucking alone once Molly died and he had to be able to stand up for himself, had to be able to break a jaw when some asshole needed it.* He *loved the boy too goddamn much to leave him unprepared.*

—they'd already heard the words in his brain, they knew he'd seen the rabbit falling into forever.

Peter raised a hand, pressing the mask to his face.

Slowly, carefully, Dad relaxed his grip.

The mask flattened.

Peter pushed harder, pinning the mask to his face.

Such a smart boy. He must have gotten that from her *mother. It had been years since* she *picked up a pencil for anything other than a grocery list, and Peter was worth it, so utterly worth it, but every day* her *eyes caught on something and* she *burned to sketch it, to snatch the box of watercolors from the back of the closet and make it last forever, but there was always the laundry and scrubbing the floor and* she *just couldn't keep up, not with all the work of running a house. Peter needed to go to college, but* she *didn't have the faintest idea how you even did that, the counselor at her high school had offered to help her get into an art school but* she *knew artists starved and* she *loved Al with every shred of her soul so they'd married and this was the best happily ever after* she'd *ever have and it had no room for drawing or art or even painting the wall a nicer color than the off-white.*

As the mask flattened, the shaking stopped.

Without the whirling chaos, the blue-green sun shining from below the earth seemed natural. One of those breathing trees rose up through the living room, but not really through, with freshly broken branches steaming yellow haze that stank of licorice and roses. Bat creatures whirled sideways-overhead, an agitated flock, but two of them began circling closer towards Peter.

The pain in Peter's head swallowed everything. His spine hurt like a line of electricity and his eyes burned and watered. Just like the books he loved said, his brain wasn't strong enough to stare into the reality outside reality.

In the stories, the effort killed people.

Peter couldn't help wondering if those stories were really made up, or if some writer had told people that he'd made them up rather than admit the truth.

But he had enough strength to slide his empty fingers up the mask and touch his father's heavy, calloused hand.

His father grabbed him back, fiercely enough to hurt.

Peter knew Dad wasn't trying to hurt him, though.

The black bats fluttered closer.

Dad had bent the mask. He'd trashed the bat-world, too.

The bats wouldn't be happy.

Sudden tension thrummed through the headache. "Your right foot," Peter's throat hurt. His voice sounded hoarse. Had he been screaming? "Put it right—no—yes, right there."

The bats pulled their wings in and dove.

Peter didn't tell Dad to hurry. Dad knew that. Peter was too scared to feel embarrassed. "An inch left—no, my left—yeah."

Dad nodded.

Mom said, "You can do this, Peter."

Peter's eyes flooded with tears. He didn't have time to cry, the bats were getting closer. "I'll tug in three... two..."

Dad tensed.

Peter braced his feet on the tile. At least he'd taken the socks off.

"One!"

Peter yanked.

The world gave a little twist.

Dad tumbled back into the proper three dimensions. He staggered two steps and cracked head-first into the crudgy old refrigerator. Metal ponged into another dent.

Mom laughed.

Dad swore.

Peter felt their joy and relief without the sounds.

The bat-creatures extended their wings, braking against the air. They weren't really wings, but more some sort of—liquid, maybe? Something that flowed and shimmered. They skidded to a halt a little more than an arm's length away, wings twitching and shuddering to maintain their flight.

Peter reached up to grab the mask, ready to yank it off his face and banish the vision. Leave those flapping monsters back in their dimension.

They didn't come any closer, though.

Peter's headache grew even worse, but he couldn't look away.

Mom and Dad, they wanted him to take the mask off, even as they knew he wouldn't. Not for another moment.

One of the creatures was a deep velvet black, its surface absorbing all the light that struck it. Its skin, if it had any, lacked any features. It might as well be a hole cut in the fabric of space.

The other, though, was more of a gray. Its surface was kind of mottled, with intertwined lines of pits running from the tips of the irrational wings to its main body.

Realization hit Peter.

If Peter's mind had stunned *this* rabbit, what would a four-dimensional or five-dimensional mind do to Peter?

He'd wanted to tell the rabbit to not worry, that he'd never throw another rock.

What were the bats trying to say?

The gray bat edged a few inches closer. One wing fluttered, but the other grew still.

The pits in its surface ran in intertwined lines. They had shapes.

Peter peered through watering eyes.

One of the biggest pits was all right angles, but had five sides.

Relief made his stomach sag.

Carefully, he turned his head so that one of the masks' outstretched wings went in a direction he couldn't point.

Mom gasped.

Peter closed his eyes.

Something tugged on the tip of the mask.

An almost-recognizable emotion sifted through the headache. Gratitude? Sympathy? Affection?

The bat-creature drew its lost mask back into the alien dimension.

Peter gasped as the headache evaporated.

Reality snapped back.

Something wet and liquid hit the floor.

10

The kitchen was a disaster.

No, the *house* was a disaster.

Shattered glass from both windows lay everywhere. Glass slivers embedded in the plaster ceiling dangled. The countertop appliances lay tumbled and broken against the back wall, like someone had picked up the whole kitchen and tipped it sideways, but the table had slid the opposite way and collapsed. Through a crack in the wall as wide as Peter's head, he saw the neighbor's new Cadillac, all four tires flat and windows busted.

That liquid sound? Somehow the spaghetti sauce had migrated from the pan to a perfect circle on the ceiling, right next to the dome light. Most of it had splashed down on the tile, but remnants still dripped tomato and garlic.

The stove had been shoved back a foot, somehow inside the wall. Not breaking through the wall, but embedded. At least the burner had gone out.

The whole place stank of mer-captains. The gas line must have broken.

The Death Star would have done less damage.

Mom sat on her butt with her back against the kitchen cupboards and her legs spread out in front of her, head hanging loose. How had she gotten all the way over there? And how had the good silverware from the box in the attic gotten scattered all around her?

Most worrying, her face was slack.

Peter had seen Mom angry. He'd seen her with a big smile, laughing.

Seeing her with her jaw hanging open and her eyes staring at nothing trickled animal fear through him.

Dad was pulling himself off the floor, busted glass crunching under his knees. A couple of fresh scratches on his face and arms leaked traces of blood down his undershirt.

The undershirt had lost its stains. It had a couple new tears, but the yellows and browns of age had vanished. Had something ninety degrees off reality sucked the stains off the cloth? Or had Dad just left the stains on the other side?

Peter's body felt like he'd lost an argument with a whole bunch of high school kids. His teeth hurt. Yeah, okay, his arms and legs hurt too, but how could your *teeth* hurt?

Dad's sudden phlegmy breath sounded like the neighbor's air conditioner coming to life.

Mom's whole face twitched. She blinked. Her eyes softened, and she focused on Peter.

Peter hurt, yes, but suddenly he felt this terrible knot in his throat like a fist. Mom yelled at him, yes. She'd told him that she worked hard. He'd been afraid to say anything about his shoes, but—she knew. She'd always known. And now he knew just how hard she'd worked. Skipping breakfast? Peter would go crazy hungry if he didn't get breakfast, or lunch, let alone neither!

But some things were too big to say.

He couldn't fit the words out through the little narrow crack in his throat.

Nobody moved for a second, in excruciating paralysis.

When the stretching silence threatened to snap Peter in half, he blurted "You know, Mom. I'd really like a picture of my D&D fighter. Maybe if you showed me how to do my own laundry, you'd have time to draw me one?"

Mom blinked.

Peter didn't dare breathe.

Somewhere outside, a distant siren warbled.

A laugh ripped its way out of Mom's gut. Not a fake laugh. An honest laugh, like something was really funny.

Peter felt a fresh surge of dread. Had he messed up?

"Honey." Mom wiped an eye. "Honey, I'd love to do that."

Peter's fear drained.

Mom raised her arms.

Peter ran forward and let her fold a hug around him. A hug in the proper three dimensions.

"There's paper at work," Dad said. "A bunch of paper they just throw out. I'll bring some home."

Mom quivered, then her hand jerked off Peter's back. "And you!"

Peter looked over his shoulder to see her jab two fingers towards Dad. "I'm not letting them stick a needle in your head. I will *burn* that doctor to the ground before letting them hurt you. But if there's a medicine that can make that horrible racket in your head stop, you're getting it."

Dad leaned back like he'd been slapped. "What if—" His face hardened. "They can't. They couldn't."

"Then—" Mom stopped. Her voice got softer. "If a beer really is the best thing for it, we'll find a way to make it work. But you deserve better." Her words turned hard again. "Your job has insurance. And we will goddamn well shitstain use every cocksucking part of it."

Peter leaned back in shock. You'd hear President Carter launch the F-bomb at the Russkies on TV before Mom said "darn."

Forget seeing an alien universe—Mom had *cussed*.

Not well, sure, but *hard*.

Dad looked as shocked as Peter. His jaw worked for a moment, then he carefully walked across the busted glass and the smear of spaghetti to kneel next to Mom and Peter. He licked his lips. "I don't deserve you," he said. His voice grew tight. "I never have. And I'd..." His face lost a little color. "I'd rather have you than one of those magazines any day."

Mom's face froze again.

Peter felt puzzled. He'd shared Mom's head, and Dad's—but whatever had happened, Mom and Dad had had their own sharing.

He decided that was okay. Peter knew what he needed to know.

The siren grew louder.

Then Mom flung an arm out, grabbed Dad, and yanked him onto his knees so she could hug him too.

For the first time in forever, Peter found himself pinned between his folks. Dad's chin had the top of his head jammed to one side and the side of his nose was stuck against Mom's head, but the weird fluttery feeling that sparkled through him made wheezing through one nostril okay.

"Listen to me," Dad said.

Peter couldn't imagine doing anything else.

"You will eat three meals a day," Dad said. His voice was soft, but carried a weird kind of menace. "Either we all eat, or none of us do."

"You can have my lunch," Peter mumbled into Dad's chest.

Outside their universe, someone shouted.

Mom quivered. "Okay," she breathed. "We'll figure that out. Somehow."

The siren was closer. A fire truck. It had to be on their street now.

Dad loosened his grip. "I better go talk to them."

Mom eased her arms as well, letting Peter pull back, and studied the devastated kitchen. "What are you going to tell them?"

One hand on Mom's shoulder, the other on Peter's, Dad said, "I don't know."

"You have to say something!" Mom said.

"I mean, that's what I'm telling them. I'll tell them I have no fu—no clue how this happened, but it wasn't anything we did. I sure can't explain it." His gaze fixed on Peter. "And I don't think you *should*, okay?"

Peter didn't know how he'd even *try* to explain. "Okay."

"Wait here," Dad said, rising to his feet.

"Dad," Peter said quickly.

Dad froze mid-step, looking down at him.

Peter licked his lips. Maybe he could say this later, but the longer he waited the harder it'd get. "There's a girl. Her name's Mary. Mary Felton. But she doesn't even know I'm in her math class."

Dad wobbled on his feet.

Then he fell back to his knees, seizing Peter in both arms and squeezing the air from him. "Life's hard enough, boy," Dad murmured into Peter's hair. "I don't want it to be any harder for you than it has to be."

Dad only broke the hug long enough to grab Mom and pull her in too.

The siren reached a peak and trailed down.

The world was huge, and complicated. Mom and Dad didn't have the instructions either. You couldn't face everything.

But maybe together, they'd need to face less of it.

Waiting for the firemen in the ruins of his home, Peter felt happier than he'd ever been.

Drag Air Through Fire

|

I'd transformed a ramshackle century-old wooden horse barn into the most advanced applied physics laboratory in the world.

Maybe the world would even survive it.

At least I hadn't needed to install a furnace. The dozens of computers generated endless waste heat. Industrial capacitor banks filled half the floor, each bank looming like a Costco four-pack of coffins and radiating its own warmth. The buzzing cyclotron more warmth. Even the phalanx of glowing electron guns surrounding the fifteen-foot copper pentagram laid over the only flat concrete in the place fought the chill. With the spray-foam insulation over the gaps in the walls, the barn remained above freezing even in Minnesota's unspeakable winter. Not too warm—I didn't want Jane Doe's corpse to thaw out too much.

All that electrical smell added a modern edge to the century of horse by-products saturating the walls and floor. A scent you wouldn't find in any other cutting-edge lab in the world.

Next month's credit card bills would be unspeakable.

Not to mention the power bill from weeks of charging all those capacitors. Batteries would have been cheaper, but capacitors are optimal for instantaneous discharge of precise amounts of stored energy.

The three-foot-wide digital countdown clock mounted above the barn's nearest stall showed eight minutes and forty-three seconds to temporal-spatial transcursion. Thirteen seconds ahead of schedule. Good.

Those massive bills would appear only if the universe still existed in eight minutes and forty-four seconds.

Despite my aches and bruises from all the physical labor and the way my skull throbbed from the continuous flood of computer noise and my burning sleep-starved eyes, I felt like a small boy on Christmas morning. No, not the tedious holiday of empty consumerism accreted around an empty religion dreamed up by primitive monkey brains. I mean the actual day of the birth of a Savior, except the only one it would save was Phoebe.

And, indirectly, me.

I'd scheduled nine hours of sleep last night. It was the rational decision. But the prospect of salvation or obliteration overwhelmed even *my* reason. After months of work, after ridicule and imposed psychotherapy and rejection and being fired from the think tank and scrounging resources from disused factories and third-hand dealers and the occasional outright theft, after busted bloody knuckles and torn muscles and living on instant ramen and bad oatmeal until three of my teeth imploded, my endless checklists were finally down to the last page.

Next item: pee.

Not even ten AM, but my flannel shirt already stank. Tired-sweat, excited-sweat, the reek of a man who'd chosen love over his friends, his teeth, his hair and health.

But Phoebe would be so thrilled to see me, she'd overlook it all.

Or the universe would unravel.

I'd judged the risk of a new Big Bang to be acceptable.

I spent three of those extra seconds staring at the framed photo standing next to my primary monitor.

Phoebe and I. Heads tipped together, smiling. On a Paris dinner cruise down the Seine.

Our last—our *most recent* photo.

After Paris, we'd returned home to Atlanta. I'd picked back up at the think tank with people who were sort of like me, only less smart, and Phoebe had sunk back into the destitute inner-city firetrap of Peachtree Hill Community Mental Health Center.

My Phoebe cared about people that nobody else cared about. The homeless. Mentally ill who wandered the streets losing arguments with invisible fairies. People whose families had given up on them, people whose brains didn't even reach fruit level, Phoebe cared for them all.

Not because she had interests in common with them, or they worked together, or were tied by the accidental bonds of unspeakable trauma or shared genes.

She cared because she thought people deserved it.

Even people like me.

She was the best person I'd ever known.

And she called me on my bullshit. She made me be a better person, because I wanted to be worthy of her. She gave me a reason to be human.

A tear blurred my vision.

I wiped the traitor away. *Break down ugly crying* didn't appear on my schedule for another two hours. My monkey brain would have its chance, but not now.

Now was about the logical brain. Half my colleagues pretended to understand my work and the others comprehended only slices of the whole. My logical brain worked better than anyone's.

And in the last three years, I'd invented whole new realms of physics. Realms I could never claim credit for, because some fool would attempt to implement them and unravel spacetime.

But I needed them.

No—*Phoebe*, the only person in the world who thought I was worth something just because I was me, needed them. Our marriage wasn't about equations I could solve, cosmological mysteries I could neuter, or shattering other theorists' malformed theories.

I loved her, because how could I not?

I had no idea why she loved me. I feared exploring that question. I might persuade her that she didn't.

I had no time for maudlin introspection. I willed my jackhammering heart to slow and kicked my shoes off. As they said in the movies: *go time*.

Phoebe needed an action hero, but only had me.

No.

Action heroes had failed her.

She needed *me*.

Some thirty feet away, in the shadows of the unsafe hay loft, the barn's man-sized door groaned.

I grimaced. That latch came unstuck every time a westerly wind exceeded eight and a half miles an hour—

A figure in a massive fur-hooded thigh-length parka trudged inside.

I froze.

I'd hung NO TRESSPASSING signs and the culturally-respected *I will shoot you* signs. The driveway onto this isolated chunk of land had a heavy gate and a heavier padlock.

But last night I'd opened the gate. Phoebe might need the ER in a *real* hurry. And some infernal neighbor had taken that as an invitation—

The intruder tugged his hood down.

The dark brown face paralyzed me.

I'd left Atlanta specifically to escape Aaron Smith.

2

I'd grown up with Aaron. We'd been best friends, bonding over mutual alienation. Boys in the 80s, especially black boys like Aaron, didn't dare apply the word *gay* to themselves. I was so nerdy that the nerds rejected me. We'd discovered D&D together, saw the last real Star Wars movie and loathed the Ewoks together. I didn't understand his obsession with comics and history, he didn't get my fascination with math, but in junior high he kept me company studying his Latin while I devoured multivariable differential equations. He hunted deer every fall, I taught seminars.

For the last three years he'd insisted that I needed to waste time eating and exercising when what I really needed was solve the nearly endless problems involved in breaching space and time.

Swearing is for the monkey brain, but a heartfelt F-bomb pushed at my teeth.

Aaron's eyes went wider than mine had when my first fusion reactor finally worked. He absently stepped backwards to shove the door shut behind him while taking in the humming computers and the massive capacitor banks.

My mouth instantly parched, and the knot in my gut clenched even tighter.

I should have guessed that Aaron would never quit looking.

I tried to lick my lips, but my tongue was sandpaper. "You found me."

"You didn't make it easy, dude." Aaron's voice might have filled out with the years, but his vocabulary hadn't changed.

I glanced at the timer. Seven minutes and fifty-one seconds. "Listen." My pulse felt like a hummingbird in my neck. "I'm rushed right now. Give me fifteen minutes and we can talk all you want." Or the universe will unravel all the way back to the beginning of time and we will never exist. Problem solved.

Aaron's eyes caught on the countdown timer. "Paul. You look like shit."

My lips twitched to chide him for cursing, but no—I had eight and a half minutes of tasks, and seven and three-quarters minutes to perform them.

My finances would implode in days. I would have no second chance.

And I certainly looked… unwell.

Aaron pulled his hood the rest of the way back so he could swivel his gaze all around the barn. His nose wrinkled, but I don't think he really noticed the smell. "What is all of this?"

"I'm processing public gravimetric, astronomical, and weather data in real time to precisely track the Earth's position relative to its historical placement in spacetime." My answer surprised me— not the factualness of it, but that I answered at all. My monkey brain felt desperate to explain, to be understood, but—no time! "Go. Away."

Aaron stripped off his gloves, a refusal as blatant as a shout. "I'm not leaving. You've been a wreck ever since Phoebe died."

She is not dead. I just haven't saved her yet.

Merely getting in the suit and harness took four minutes.

"And this mad scientist gig?" Aaron waved a hand. "Running away? To an old barn full of what the hell?" His voice got softer. "This is real bad, buddy."

I stood, concrete floor icy beneath my soles, and dredged up my best body language. Gaze straight at Aaron. Chest out. Chin up. Breathe a little quicker, a little deeper. Ready to fight.

Aaron rolled his eyes before I could open my mouth. "I got you that book. Remember?"

I grimaced. One Saturday in that hideous first year of college, we'd had a heart-to-heart conversation. The next week, I'd opened a mysterious package to discover the first edition of *Nonverbal Behavior in Interpersonal Relations*.

He'd bought himself a copy too. So we could discuss it.

It had helped more than I'd ever been able to say.

I dropped the pretense, deliberately draining all emotion from my face.

"Don't think going all Vulcan will help you, either," Aaron said. "You helped me when I didn't want help. And I'm here for you. That's what friends do." His eyes flicked to the timer. "We watch out for each other."

His monkey brain was in charge. Reason would not shift him.

I was scheduled to be getting dressed—the pee was cancelled. The complicated silver fireproof suit I'd need to wear during transcursion was laid out on a table on the other side of the open space. Ignoring Aaron, I walked over and grabbed a shining silver glove.

"All this?" Aaron stepped closer and waved a hand. "It's how Doc Ock got that way. I'm not—*fuck*!"

I followed his gaze. My spirits plunged even further.

Even as someone who had known me my whole life, Aaron would find the transcursion loop... disturbing.

If I could have constructed the device in seven dimensions I would have gone with a simpler, less superstition-soaked (and less energy-hungry) cube, but as we live in only three, I chose a circle of copper wire. I needed additional energy guides, five evenly intersecting wires of equal length.

All completely rational. Math dictates engineering.

But even I was *perfectly* well aware that Aaron would see only a pentacle of braided copper wire laid out on the barn floor. The surrounding ring of meticulously aligned electron guns salvaged from antique tube televisions, all glowing and buzzing with accumulating energy, wouldn't help.

Poor Jane Doe's cadaver, tucked neatly on an equipment-laden hospital gurney right in the center, made it a scene straight out of one of his horror comics.

3

The energized mathematical matrix composing what we perceive as space-time constantly changes. Transcursion requires precisely imposing energy on a sub-matrix—

Too complicated? Very well. The Sun had moved one and a half billion miles in three years, and I needed exact—

Even simpler?

Fine. *Time travel.* That's incorrect in almost every detail, but maybe most monkey brains can accept it?

When the timer hit zero, the barn's equipment would shove megawatts of precisely tuned interference waves into the transcursion loop. They would pop myself, Jane Doe, and all the equipment strapped to the gurney back to that critical point of space-time. Rescue Phoebe. Return up to six hundred pounds, including the equipment, to the exact same millisecond I left in.

The loop looked like a pentacle for perfectly sound engineering reasons.

I should have hung a *Welcome, Satan!* sign to complete the view.

Aaron's face blanched. "Paul." His gaze swiveled up to my face, then back at the transcursion ring. "What... are you doing?"

His hand fumbled at the side of his parka, right over his belt.

The only thing between success and Aaron calling 911 was his down parka.

"I didn't kill her!" I said. No, too loud, it made me sound defensive. The implacable cold rising from the concrete slab through my socks and into the tiny bones of my feet wasn't helping.

Aaron dropped his gloves and snatched at his zipper. "Listen. Paul. Whatever's going on. I'll help you, you know that, right? I'll be right there with you, the whole way."

Go above and beyond for a friend one time, and they never stop trying to repay you. "I bribed someone at the morgue." Keeping my head turned towards Aaron, I fumbled at the gear piled on the table. If I'd had enough space I would have laid everything out side-by-side, but I'd run out of money and settled for stacking gear in reverse order. And right now, the bulky silver fireproof suit was between me and the Taser.

My risk assessment had included the possibility of an interloper, but I had foolishly assumed it would happen during transcursion. Brilliance is not prescience.

"Why?" Aaron got his parka unzipped.

I finally got the precious fireproof suit free of the table and dropped it on the floor, helmet and all, so I could scrounge in the tool belt. "Because they found the remains of six bodies. It's vitally important that the body count match up, even if some of them were never claimed. The universe demands observed consistency, or we'll paradox out and everything unravels all the way back to the Big Bang. And this poor lady is about Phoebe's size."

Hand at his belt, Aaron froze again. "Paul. Dude." I watched him swallow. His breath stopped. Shock and surprise. "Listen. Phoebe is dead."

I could see him scramble for understanding.

Extraordinary proof that you can't understand is mere lunatic rambling. Years before I'd helped Aaron figure out how much mortgage he could afford. There's no way he could follow my math.

And how many minutes remained?

"She's been dead since—" His voice trailed off.

I glanced up from my search.

He was looking at one of the columns supporting the hay loft. If he'd had any doubt that the bundle wired to the wood was an explosive, I'd left the label on.

"Buddy." Aaron swallowed. "Why... do you have Tannerite..." His gaze flicked around the room, then settled back at me.

I kept digging through the gear. "A dead man's switch. If I fail to disarm it by ten-fifteen AM, the whole building goes up."

Aaron's calm shattered. He snatched his phone off his belt. "Killing yourself won't bring Phoebe back!"

"No." Near the bottom of the gear, my searching hand finally found the Taser. "But this equipment is too dangerous. Abandoning it would be irresponsible."

Aaron raised his phone.

I turned and fired.

4

Seeing me raise something that looked like a handgun made Aaron's jaw drop open in surprise. Then the darts plunged into his gut.

I couldn't help wincing as his eyes bugged and his shoulders locked up. His whole body trembled and he crumbled to the ground, limp as a sleeping cat.

A Taser is much less harmful than a bullet, but pumping that many volts through someone is inherently risky. I couldn't help watching Aaron shudder for precious seconds, until I saw his chest heave and gulp in air.

A strand of my tension dissolved.

I hadn't killed my oldest friend to save my love.

Of course, if I had made a mistake in my math, he and I might never exist.

Aaron gurgled. Was he trying to speak?

I glanced at the timer.

The timer read—three minutes and nine seconds? Shock gave me my own gurgle.

I'd timed myself getting into the suit. It needed four meticulous minutes.

Aaron had ruined everything.

My logical brain could only whisper *too late*.

I'd failed Phoebe.

Fortunately, my monkey brain doesn't listen to reason.

I flung my rear onto the bench, wrenched the suit over to me, and jammed one foot after the other into the legs. My pulse sounded a drumline in my ears. The suit had started out a size too big and had gotten even roomier thanks to my total lack of appetite. I had to cinch the waist belt extra tight. My arms slipped down the sleeves on their own.

For clothing meant to reflect heat and repel flame, the suit was uncomfortably warm. My frozen feet instantly began to thaw, and fresh sweat broke out over all my skin.

I'd meant to drain a bottle of water before transcursion. No time. Dehydration wouldn't kill me. I started tugging the complicated layers of zippers into place.

"I'm sorry." The words surprised me even as I spoke.

Aaron's arm flopped. Even I could see the frustration in his gritted teeth.

"The taser will wear off in a couple of minutes." I picked up the oversized helmet, shaped just like a giant Tupperware cake cover. "I used a hundred pounds of Tannerite, so you'll want to get some distance."

"Not..." Aaron choked.

"Yes, get away."

"Without." He gasped. "You."

"I'll be back instantly," I said. "Or I'm—" My voice caught. I had to will a deep breath. "Or I'm with Phoebe. And that's okay."

The helmet slipped right over my head and strapped right into place. The heat of my breath instantly reflected back at me, as the droning chorus of computers faded.

Fifty-eight seconds.

Forget the Taser, no time to rewind the wires.

Forget the safety harness.

Tugging the gloves on, I staggered to the transcursion circle. I had planned one minute to make my way between the precisely arrayed electron guns. I didn't have time to methodically weave my feet through the maze.

Fortunately, my monkey brain had paid attention all the times I'd picked my way through.

I crossed the outermost copper wire at ten seconds.

Nine. Eight.

My gloved hand closed on the edge of the gurney.

Seven.

I snatched at the air tank's metallic hose.

Six.

Metallic hose hissed between my hands as I struggled for the connector at the end.

Five.

I'd logically decided that I might need ten feet of hose. Now I cursed nine of them.

Four.

The hose's suit connector was a hard lump in my hand.

Three.

I jammed the connector to the suit's air intake and twisted.

Two.

One.

My monkey brain filled my skull with screaming.

5

I could see the table of computers and my countdown timer hanging above the barn stall, paralyzed at 0:00:00, and at the same time choking-thick, greasy black smoke completely blocked my vision. The fireproof suit rippled around me, all at once buffeted by northern Minnesota's chill and an Atlanta inferno.

It wasn't superposition. I saw them both, in full detail, simultaneously.

I stood on two different decrepit concrete floors. Both were badly cracked, but one had been patched. My right foot was a fraction of an inch higher than my left, and at the same time on even ground.

Neither my monkey nor logical brains had evolved to process any of that.

An endless instant later the impossible sensation faded, leaving me gasping bottled air.

A faint wisp of smoke had already slithered into the suit, stinking of grease and burning plastic and unidentifiable awfulness. My heart seemed to rattle around loose between my ribs. My stomach burned and, yes—I'd anticipated correctly, I suddenly needed to pee.

The helmet's lights revealed only hungry, roiling blackness.

My face ached with a grin for the first time in years. I'd done it.

And the gurney had come with me.

The transcursion inversion device was far too heavy to carry, so I'd strapped it to the gurney's bottom shelf. When I triggered it, anything attached to it would have its temporo-spatial matrix cross-energized to—

Fine. It was a retrieval device. Hit the button and we returned to the barn. You do understand that's not what really happens, don't you?

If I'd arrived before the fire, someone would have seen me. Observed inconsistency would have undone everything.

If I'd arrived too late, Phoebe would die.

But this thick black smoke was exactly what the footage from the party store across the street showed at the very beginning of the fire. People would be scrambling for safety.

Poorly stored old oil had had caught fire in Peachtree Hill

Community Mental Health's big indoor garage at two in the afternoon. The blaze had passed through a cabling hole cut through a concrete wall into the administrative office, where the fire became unstoppable.

But the vans had all been in service, ferrying patients to and from appointments. The garage was a large, empty space where I wouldn't be seen arriving, but could be confident of not arriving inside a wall.

At this moment twenty miles away, a younger version of me—one with a comfortable layer of fat on his ribs and a complete set of clean teeth—was in a meeting at Novex Research, politely but inexorably ripping a coworker's proposal to shreds. That poor fool had no idea what was coming.

Smoke obliterated all sight.

Fortunately, I'd watched a whole series of firefighting instructional videos.

The heavy suit made sinking to my knees cumbersome, but I kept one hand on the gurney for support and ignored my protesting knees and spine.

As expected, a pool of clean air hugged the floor.

The garage looked totally different from an infant's height, and on my rare visits I'd never studied the bottom few inches of the walls. After a moment, though, I made out the metallic shine of the aluminum rollup doors.

If I rolled up those doors, the air would clear. Clear air would help me find Phoebe.

In the weeks following the fire, though, I'd spent ages studying the photos. The doors had remained closed until they melted. I was counting on that fire scouring away any evidence of my presence and maintaining observed consistency.

Indecision stole a precious second.

Adding more air to the fire would make the building burn more quickly.

I only had moments to find her.

Stick with the logical brain's plan. Let the monkey brain implement it.

I stood and, entirely by touch, dropped the rails on the side of the gurney. I'd planned to drop Jane Doe right here. Getting her on the gurney had been a sweaty challenge, but I'd thought that dumping her off would be comparatively easy.

Here in the moment, though, I couldn't callously shove her off. Despite the mass of the bulky suit, I found myself clumsily digging my hands beneath her shoulders and knees and heaving to try to set her gently on the floor.

Jane Doe had lain unclaimed in the morgue, unwanted and unloved.

But right now she was helping me save Phoebe, and despite myself I couldn't help loving her just a little for it.

She deserved better.

The second I hauled Jane off the gurney, her feet slipped free. I winced at the double thud they made against the ground, but at least I was able to ignore the pain in my lower back enough to ease her head to the concrete.

The person that Jane Doe had been was gone. I knew that. What I had brought was only remnants.

I whispered "Thank you" before rising to my feet.

Then I raised one hand protectively before me. Seized the gurney with the other.

And tromped towards the inner door, and the fire's growing growl, as quickly as I dared.

My lower back burned. The checklist had called for me to wear my back brace under the fireproof suit, and giving Jane Doe that last breath of respect hadn't done my already marginal spinal discs any good. My body threatened to revolt every time I knelt to reorient myself.

Phoebe needed me.

I'd made a simple harness to drag the gurney after me, but hadn't had time to slip it on. Dragging two hundred and sixty pounds of gear on tiny aluminum wheels loosened my arm in its socket, but I snarled and marched.

I found the cinderblock wall, followed it to the door, and emerged into a hall of flame.

6

The smoke in the hallway was thin enough for the lights on my helmet to seep through, revealing lines of haze being sucked up into the ceiling and probably through a fresh gap in the roof up into the sky. Flames licked up the walls—this old building had been treated for fire retardance, yes, but enough heat sets anything ablaze. The fraction of the heat penetrating my fireproof suit threatened to bake my muscles on my bones. Smoke seeped through it somewhere, probably where the helmet or the gloves met the body. I hadn't had time to double-check the zippers and seals. I had never smelled such a hideous industrial stench before. Even with bottled air, my eyes watered and every breath threatened to rip a cough from me.

I willed my lungs to ignore the chemical burn, inhaled, and bellowed Phoebe's name as loudly as I could bear.

The only sound was the growl of flames, muffled by the suit.

I hauled myself forward. Phoebe usually worked out of the three treatment rooms on the left of this hall. She'd often complained that she didn't have time to pee at work, so my monkey brain desperately hoped she was in one of them when the fire started.

The first door stood open. The helmet light showed an unoccupied treatment room. I left the gurney in the hall, easing my shoulder for a few seconds as I stepped in to check the floor behind the exam table.

Nobody.

I grabbed the gurney with my other hand, heaved, and staggered forward. The smoke was in my head, making my brain wobble.

I bellowed Phoebe's name again, ending with a chest-wracking cough.

From behind the second door, someone shouted back.

I froze for a split second. Had that been her?

Was I going to find another victim, and walk away?

Phoebe made me human. The murderous fire might make me cruel.

My feet and fingers throbbed with the heat.

Something, somewhere, crashed down hard enough to shake the air. The garage roof? A wall?

I wrenched the door open.

My heart stopped.

Inside the treatment room the love of my life crouched in a tiny ball, as far from the burning door as possible. Her treasured face held a mix of stunned fear and miraculous hope.

As I had inferred, the fire had trapped Phoebe.

I'd never considered that she might have a patient huddled right next to her.

Of course she wasn't alone. Phoebe cared for everyone. If she'd been with a patient when the fire trapped them, she'd stay with the patient. That's who she was.

That's part of why I loved her.

But I'd calculated the transcursion for six hundred pounds. With two hundred and forty pounds of equipment, that left three hundred and sixty pounds of people.

The patient huddled under Phoebe's arm had to weigh a hundred pounds.

We were way over mass.

And if I could take them both?

I'd only brought one body. We'd lose observed consistency. Paradox, and unraveling.

7

Waves of heat buffeted my back, washing past me into the treatment room. Phoebe raised an arm to cover her face, hand clenched into a fist to try to protect her fingers from the searing flames behind me.

"Pheeb," I coughed. "It's Paul."

She glanced back up, her streaked face already red. Blisters had already started to cross her forehead. My soul clenched—yes, yes, there's no such thing as a soul, but right then I had one and it knotted up tight. A cough shattered her voice but I made out "Paul?" before she huddled back down.

I dragged the gurney the last few feet into the treatment room and my hands fumbled at the oxygen tank. Fortunately I'd arranged this equipment yesterday, and her air mask was exactly where I expected it. Even with both of us breathing from the one tank, I'd brought enough air for thirty minutes.

Another massive thud jolted the room.

Somewhere, the top of the building had collapsed.

Air wasn't the problem. If heat didn't kill Phoebe, the roof would. She wouldn't last three minutes.

Phoebe took a deep drag on her air mask as I yanked a silver fireproof blanket off the gurney. By the time I got it over her, she'd passed the air mask to her patient.

My monkey brain screamed *That air's not for you, asshole!* I choked the words down. Instead, I yanked out the spare fireproof blanket and threw it over the patient.

I'd abandoned my career, my health, everything to find my Phoebe.

I'd stretched my brain. Solved the unsolvable. Invented whole new types of physics, and the new mathematics to conquer them.

Nobody else could have done it.

And once again, the human element had tripped me up.

It didn't matter if the patient was a hopeless drunk, an addict, schizophrenic, whatever. Phoebe wouldn't abandon them.

Phoebe was Phoebe.

And being with her, if I wanted to be with her, I had to be a better person.

We had to get this patient out of the building before I hit the button and took us home.

The floor shuddered.

Debris rained down in the hallway, and I felt the fire suck the room's air away.

No. We weren't getting out that way.

I'd studied building fires for hundreds of hours. But I hadn't understood their ravenous, implacable force until now.

The hard truth was, we weren't getting out at all.

If I died here, the investigation team would find eight bodies. Not six. The inconsistency would unravel the universe, but so what?

And right now, before that unraveling, Phoebe huddled helplessly just short of burning.

I had one thing that could ease her pain.

I drew one last breath of mostly clean air.

And lifted my helmet.

8

Alien sensation hammered my face. It wasn't heat. It was something on the far side of heat, something my nerves didn't know how to interpret. Humans hadn't evolved to be so close to so much flame. My eyes seemed to steam and shrivel. The heat punched the air right back out of me, but I managed to gasp "Love you Pheeb" with my last clean air.

Phoebe raised her head just enough that I could see the shock in her teary eyes.

I'd hold that vision in my soul as long as I lived. One minute. Perhaps two.

I dropped the helmet over her head, pulling the giant flaps down over her shoulders to give—well, not a seal, but blocking out at least some of the smoke.

With my lungs empty, the smell hammered into me. The suit had kept the worst of it out, all molten metal and plastic and something that had to be roasting flesh. My body wanted to gag, but I jackknifed forward and clenched my gut.

Phoebe's anonymous patient jabbed the oxygen mask at my face.

Right then, I understood.

I understood why Phoebe cared so much. This person didn't know my name. Maybe they'd lost a loving home, or never had one. They weren't even the bottom of the social pyramid, they were the gravel beneath it.

And they'd shared their last breath of air.

With a stranger.

A person that probably nobody ever even missed offered me air.

My logical brain screamed for the gasping monkey to shut up.

Six bodies had been recovered from the fire, yes. Some had never been claimed.

How many people were in the building right now?

If this patient disappeared right now—would anybody notice?

Had the fire investigators really searched the rubble? Or had they walked through the smoking ruins, gathered what was on top, and written it off as a loss? Did scorched and crumbling bones still lurk beneath the rubble?

Could I get away with taking them both? That was purely my monkey brain, scrambling for any path to success.

If I tried and was wrong, the universe never would happen.

But if there was even a chance I could save Phoebe—

We needed the retrieval mechanism.

But we didn't need the gurney. The heavy suit.

The massive air tank.

Ditching all that might—*might*—get our mass down enough.

The rest was human nature.

Nobody cared about this place.

I was going to assume that the inspectors hadn't *really* searched the rubble. That they hadn't counted all the bodies. That taking an extra person was already part of the historical record. Not because I reasoned it to be correct, but because I *needed* it to be correct.

Logic be damned.

I sucked a double breath of air, held it in, shoved the mask back at the patient, and whirled back to the gurney. My gloved hands fumbled at the oversized buckles on the leather straps holding the retrieval device to the gurney, but I managed to undo them both before the air gushed out of me.

The patient's eyes were clinched almost shut, but when I looked back they shoved the mask at me.

Another desperate double breath and I flopped onto my seat. The steel case holding the transcursion reversal gear weighed over a hundred pounds, but my blistering face and scalp drove me better than any goad. Bracing my feet against the gurney's bottom shelf, I seized the case and heaved it towards me.

My back exploded in agony.

I pulled harder.

After a moment's hesitation, the retrieval device slid off the shelf and crashed down excruciatingly onto my shins. I couldn't help the gasp of pain, and sucked in horrific smoke.

In moments, one way or another, we wouldn't need air.

But I'd cut out the mass of the gurney and the massive air tank.

My eyes burned so horribly I could hardly crack them, but my waving arm found the outstretched air mask. A desperate gulp of barely tainted air, and I attacked the zippers holding the top of the suit closed. By the time I had the jacket ripped away and let the heat assault my torso, my head spun like I'd spent a year on a carnival ride. I still managed to grab the proffered mask for another breath.

Not many people get to take two last breaths.

The patient reached for the precious mask. Their turn.

We couldn't take the mask. It was attached to the air tank. Too heavy.

I flung the precious mask off towards the gurney and flipped up the plastic cover protecting the reversal unit's activation switch.

I found the patient's hand in its quest for the air mask, took it in mine, and guided it to one of the straps on the reversal unit. "Hold it!" I shouted.

Skin past burning, blisters forming everywhere above my waist, head reeling and eyes useless, I still had to do the hardest part.

I seized the fireproof helmet and ripped it off my love's head.

Flung it into the fire.

Grabbed her arm.

Were we over mass?

Would I leave an extra body?

Had I caused inconsistency, unraveling this little piece of the universe and taking the rest with it?

Phoebe was worth it.

With my free hand, I hit the button.

That horrible double perception devoured my mind.

9

A voice drifted from somewhere distant. "What the hell?"

I needed a breath, a blessedly clean breath that still left me coughing and choking, to identify Aaron's voice over the wavering hum of too much electronic gear.

I was lying on bone-chilling concrete. It felt wonderful on my burns. And my lower back was agony.

Two people coughed nearby.

I'd recognize Phoebe's cough anywhere. Somehow, I'd gotten away with it.

The voice said, "What—did you just do?" Aaron.

I'd tased him only three minutes ago. The eternity I'd spent in the burning clinic didn't count. He hadn't had time to recover.

My eyes didn't want to open, and my breath broke up in its own cough, but I managed to gasp "Aaron." My voice sounded unrecognizable.

"You total—dick."

After another round of coughs, I pried one eye a hair open. The horse barn's ceiling looked fuzzy and liquid, but I knew every one of those cables strung through the rafters. The all-pervasive fire stink drowned out the smells of ancient horse. My mouth tasted of cinders. I had ash and soot and tender burns over every inch of my hide. Dozens of cinder holes punctured my flannel shirt and jeans.

My vision cleared enough to make out the bundle of Tannerite wired overhead.

Dead man's switch.

My body ached to lie on the soothing concrete and gasp until my lungs cleared. Instead, I hauled myself to my knees. When I tried to stand, the flare of pain in my back stopped me. Gritting my teeth, I crawled as fast as I could. I toppled a trail through the electron guns surrounding the loop, but their alignment didn't matter anymore.

At the computer cabinet, I reached up and flipped the dead man's switch to "off" and tugged out the wires. The status lights lit up on the computers stacked everywhere as drives began scrubbing themselves. My logical brain reminded me I'd have to sell everything to even dent the bills.

Worth it.

Aaron shoved himself up onto one arm. "That light—"

I saw the moment his gaze caught Phoebe.

I tried to enjoy how his jaw dropped, but my monkey brain already had me turning.

Sprawled in the center of the transcursion loop beside a stranger, skin blistered and reddened and gray with soot, Phoebe peered towards me.

My heart froze.

Phoebe blinked. "Aaron? Is that you?"

My frozen heart shattered. I'd saved her, and she didn't even—

No. I'd lost weight. I'd even lost a few teeth.

She didn't recognize me anymore.

"Pheeb," I breathed. "It's me."

She blinked. "Paul? But—"

Then I was on my knees in front of her, filling my soul with a face I had only hoped to see again. I ached to take her in my arms, but with those second degree burns she'd be in agony once the endorphins wore off.

I'd hold her in the hospital.

I'd make it up to Aaron, somehow. I'd pay the bills. I'd deal with the messiness of human nature and hold my secrets.

Phoebe said "Paul? What—"

Before any of that, I had to soak my heart with her. Be human again. She'd have so many questions. How would I explain we were in a Minnesota winter and not a Georgia summer, that three years had passed, that I'd spent her life insurance saving her life?

She coughed. "Why'd you shave your head?"

Monkey brain started to laugh.

The laughter devolved to sobs. Two hours ahead of schedule.

Whisker Line

I

Hands sweating, Aleksander reached over the shining metal cart to offer the young lady his dollars. She smiled and gave him an apple the size of a frag grenade, impaled on a wooden spike and drenched in caramel. Mister Counselor Henders said that the apples were best now, when the leaves on the maples and oaks changed color—trees, in a city! These people cut holes in the sidewalk to plant trees! They left this open plaza just to have a place for people to see trees and sell apples and sit on benches and drink their weak coffee.

He'd seen trees half a lifetime ago, before the war made everyone horrible. But never in the sidewalk, right next to long cars and gleaming signs and woven wire drums just for trash. You could have so much food that you didn't want it all, and the city put out special cans to put it in where men got paid to take it away and bury it.

You didn't bury food. You stashed it, back in the most twisted corners of the dark tight tunnels where nobody else could get it.

Months in this city, and still Aleksander thought: so much food!

A city so grand, so incredible, they even gave it a name starting in New. *New York*.

The young lady didn't look at his face—no, she looked, but she didn't stare. She didn't even look away to spare him the shame of being seen. She was maybe a year younger than him, in a tightly curved black T-shirt and a round white hat, and she looked right at him.

I have a face now, Aleksander reminded himself. The burn scars? Gone. *They gave me a face. And a new leg, of metal!*

The lady gave him a caramel apple and a smile. So much food, but the smile was the best.

Tears glimmered at the edges of his eyes. He could eat fresh apples—the doctors had given him *teeth*.

A chubby homeless man sprawled on the sidewalk across the plaza, near the bustling six-lane boulevard, leaning against the brick wall next to the bus stop. The man had the face he'd been born with. He had family, *human* family! How was he homeless? But people tossed their change into his upturned filthy blue baseball hat!

These beautiful, wonderful people, so much bigger than him but so giving. You have to take care of the small ones, they'd told him. And they were so big, everyone was small. Even the buildings around the plaza—fifty, a hundred stories of glass, that caught the autumn wind and forced it to run through the trenches of the streets. So big, they changed the wind. So big they needed names.

No more hiding in the tunnels, scrabbling along on two hands and a knee. No more sleeping as the accepted but deformed member of the Family's furry, frightened, slowly shifting huddle, rich with the comforting stink of urine and pellets, one ear of each head always perked for the sounds of boots or blasts or the million other deaths. He slept in a bed now, in his own room, a room with a dresser and even a tiny rug to keep the morning chill off his bare feet. He had a tall dresser with space for clothes for a horde.

He'd shoved and dragged the dresser in front of the window, though. Who could sleep near a window?

Aleksander thought his heart might burst with frenzied joy. They'd taught him English and given him a face and a job moving boxes at a store, a store full of food and tools and drink, so much *clean*. Clean clothes, every day!

The doctors couldn't fix the scars nobody could see, though. Mister Counselor Henders said that he didn't need to watch for storm drains any more, but he did. Aleksander stayed aware of the storm drains (two, one six meters north, another ten meters south) and manhole covers (one, in the middle of the road). The tunnels led to the Family.

Nineteen years old, and he had everything a man could want. But he would always know where the nearest drain was. He'd always help the Family.

Aleksander raised the stick, breathing in the impossibly sweet smell of the caramel, and plunged his new teeth in. Juice ran down the edges of his mouth.

Too much apple.

Once he'd eaten his fill, his friends would thank him for it.

Mister Counselor Henders wanted him to move boxes? He'd move boxes. He'd move mountains. He'd give them the leg back, teeth back, the *face* back, if someone needed it. Anything.

On the other side of the plaza, thirty floors above the rushing river of cars and flowing course of people, one of the smaller but still fabulous glass buildings exploded.

2

Knives of glass rained from the sky, pelting the plaza, accompanied by a soundtrack of cars colliding and screeching tires and horns bellowing ignorant outrage.

A decade of bloody instinct made Alek fall to a crouch and scuttle around the metal pushcart on his hands and one leg. His palms and fingers had grown soft, and the pebbled cement left scratches and scrapes.

The young lady apple seller screamed. Alek's throat tightened—she'd attract snipers! Didn't she know?

The smart thing to do would be to shove her out of cover, away from him.

Right after the war started, when his first family's home had become a crater and the soldiers started shooting everyone, Alek and his brother and his two sisters had hidden in a wrecked limousine. He couldn't stop screaming, even though Pavel put a hand over his mouth and begged him for silence. The screams had kept boiling out of his guts. Pavel had finally shoved Aleksander out of hiding, so the soldiers would find only him and not all four children.

Pavel had been smart. Alek lost a leg, his first family, because he couldn't shut up and hide.

Alek should shove the young lady out into the carnage. Let her take their wrath. Whoever's soldiers "they" were.

Alek clutched her denim pant leg and yanked. "Down!"

A blade of glass hit the concrete two meters away and shattered.

Alek knew all the kinds of screams. The shrieks of mindless terror. The horrified shout of violated flesh. The anguished cry of seeing a loved one churned into ruin. He heard them all now from countless throats.

The young lady still stood, barely taking a breath before screaming her fear again.

Alek pushed the back of her knee, breaking her stance, bringing her tumbling to the ground. Air burst from her mouth and her lips gaped like a fish. He crawled forward to lay a finger across her lips and frantically shake his head.

Understanding appeared in her watery blue eyes, and she nodded as she fought to capture her breath.

Most of the glass had fallen short of the pushcart, but the worst was coming. No bullets—not yet. Keeping as low as possible, Alek reached up on the cart, seized one of those limitless bottles of clean cold water, drenched his shirt, and pulled the collar up over his mouth and nose. He splashed the rest of the bottle over the young lady's tight black cotton shirt and yanked her shirt up, exposing her taut pale belly and perfect bellybutton.

The last thing he saw before the blanket of smoke enveloped them was her outraged glare.

Destroyed buildings sent out a thick, black cloud of insulation and burnt wiring and ashes and all the dirt that built up inside them over decades, full of asbestos and fiberglass and all the horrible things the builders hid away inside the walls, ground up and burned up and dissolved into the air. This cloud stank of burning tar and insulation and hot metal. Alek thought he caught the burned-pork-fat of dead people as well. The wet shirt caught the worst of it, but he still gagged and coughed at each breath, eyes instantly flooding with protective tears.

Alek felt the young lady convulse and choke, then her hands clutched her water-soaked shirt over her face. Joy flickered in his heart—he hadn't pushed her out, he'd helped her.

Maybe he had saved her.

He couldn't do anything more for her, though.

Everything that Mister Counselor Henders had told Alek sloughed off, like an oversized jacket snagged by a soldier. He didn't go for the police. He didn't call for help.

Police would come. Soldiers would come.

It was starting again.

The storm drain at the edge of the road. Probably five meters north now, not six.

The stinking cloud burned his eyes, so he shut them.

Fumbling behind him, he seized two more caramel apples and set out for safety.

3

Mister Counselor Henders had not been happy to hear that Alek had investigated the drains, and had made Alek promise to not go exploring. "You're safe now. The sewers and storm drains are more dangerous than the street. Believe me."

Alek had tried to believe. He'd *wanted* to believe. They'd given him a face, a leg. Teeth. A life in the sunlight and work that needed doing. But he'd seen that the manhole covers locked with a special wrench, but the storm drains needed no such help. The steel drain grates were too small for a man and too heavy for a child. Alek had lots of practice with drains, though, and he wrenched the cover aside as easily as another man might walk across a room. Getting the cover back in place from below took more strength, but it had to be done.

An open drain was an invitation for a grenade. Or a dog. You could out-crawl a grenade, if it bounced the other way, but never a dog.

Alek felt safer in the concrete tunnels, on a squishy waterlogged bed of mulched leaves and plastic wrappers and dog leavings and stubby stabby straws. The choking cloud from the exploded building filled the tunnel, forcing him to keep the neck of his wet shirt stretched over his face for a little scrap of protection. Between each thumb and forefinger he clumsily clutched a spear of a caramel apple. They made his crawling clumsy, but he needed them. But his leg, the new leg, slowed him down. Even as he thought *this was a gift*, he stopped long enough to unbuckle the leg and abandon it. He had no time for anything that wouldn't keep him alive.

He crawled straight down the meter-wide shaft, ignoring the side tunnels, dashing from one narrow shaft of light to the next, hands and knee squeezing moisture out of the compost until his arms turned black to the elbows and his jeans dragged their own swamp, gasping for oxygen through his wet shirt. He crawled as fast as most people could run. When the air finally grew clear and rich with the million smells of decay, he stuffed the apples inside his shirt and crawled faster, until his exhausted collapse in the safe darkness between access plates.

Alek curled on his side, arms clutching his knee, trying to sink into the inches of decomposing leaves and sticks and plastic that made the floor. Concrete hugged him on all sides, almost too close for him to move. Now that his chest could suck one lungful of clean air after another, now that the screams had faded until he could only hear them inside his skull, now that the glass had stopped falling and the cloud was already breaking, Alek stopped and let his heart shatter into a billion glittering falling shards.

A year before, the last time he'd been in a tunnel, it had been a sewer. The new soldiers, the strange ones with the blotchy gray uniforms, had seen him. They'd baited their trap for him with a huge loaf of bread. Alek should have known better, but he'd been hungry. After years of war, the Family hadn't been able to scavenge enough to eat. There just wasn't enough food in all the city for the humans, let alone the Family.

If he could have taken that loaf of bread back to the nest, he would have been a hero.

Instead, the new soldiers had shot him with wires. He couldn't make his leg move, or his hands. They'd caught him and tied him up, these strange soldiers with tears in their eyes. Soldiers did not cry. They'd taken him in and taken him to this new land and given him gifts.

We are here to help the weak.

Our home has no war.

You will be safe.

The strange soldiers hadn't lied. Mister Counselor Henders had not lied.

They'd merely been wrong.

War was everywhere. And now it had come for these kind people.

Alek shuddered and sobbed silently in the dark as his fresh hope died.

And the Family smelled his need.

Tiny feet scuttled along the edge where the mulch met concrete. Two chubby teardrops, long hairless tails held high for balance, fur made greasy on their foraging expedition through the tunnels. Soft round ears perked high, moving independently to track every drip of water on concrete and beetle scuttling on compost. Tiny soft three-part noses with flowing whiskers that reached and touched and investigated and understood.

Every city had rats. Even in this one that had seemed so impossibly clean, so bright in soul, rats made homes in the tunnels and inside the walls and on the top floors of the tall buildings.

Alek made himself lay still. They were Family, but not a part that he knew. He didn't want to scare them.

He needed the Family. They were all he had, now.

Soft whiskers, almost vaporous, brushed his face, his tears. He could smell them—and now, with them so close, he could smell himself. Through them, through the touch of their tiny fingered paws and ghostly whiskers, he smelled his own stink of fire and fear and food. Even with his eyes closed, he knew who they were—the larger girl, almost gravid but still scavenging, and the younger one, barely old enough to be let loose from the nest. The touch of a whisker and the brush of a paw touched the heartbreak flooding his mind and filled him with the humid warmth of the nest, the churn of family, the tiny squeals of the bare pups.

Alek had used that ability constantly, every day for years, until the strange soldiers had trapped him. He'd learned the trick as a child, or maybe he'd been born with it. Or maybe it was a gift of heartbreak.

The Family knew heartbreak. Heartbreak was the Family's world, even in this unfathomably rich land. Pups and mates died. Even though this city had so much food, the girls told Alek how some of it was bad and made you bleed from the mouth and nose if you ate it. The Family didn't have words, but they had feelings, so many feelings. They had hope, and fear, and joy, and despair, and all of those feelings wrapped themselves through his mind.

He was back with those who could never hurt him. If anything, he could hurt them. A careless motion and he might crush someone. But he never did—their every touch filled his soul with their presence, their warmth, their love.

Moving slowly, so as to not startle his new Family, Alek straightened his leg enough to expose his stomach and free the offering he'd brought. Two caramel apples, warmed by his stomach, each bigger than both of the girls together.

The girls leaped, teeth snagging into caramel, digging for the sweet apple beneath. Alek felt their glee as they devoured all they could, eating until their furry tummies bulged. Finally each seized an apple with their overextended jaws, but the apples were too heavy for one to move.

Alek's hand brushed the larger girl's back.

They released their grip and sat back. He could feel them in the saturated darkness, crouched expectantly.

Alek wrapped the apples back in his shirt, rolled to his knee, and followed the girls to the Family's nest.

His nest.

His true home.

4

The Family welcomed him. They accepted his delicious gifts, enveloped his mind, treated him as one of their own. Nestled in the smells of pellets and urine and babies and life, they welcomed him with soft whiskers and grasping paws and smooth fur and quick, tasting tongues. Alek lay on his back in the lightless tunnel of crumbling concrete and let them greet him, sinking into the pack's thoughts even as they soothed away his.

Thinking hurt. Hope hurt. The shattered, glorious life he'd had was gone.

But letting his soul dissolve in the Family eased everything.

The Family told him everything, passing raw wisdom from whisker to whisker. Humans wrapped the world in words—they'd call this place an abandoned drain tunnel. The Family knew dissolving concrete beneath scrabbling paws, the smell of old lime, the tick of nails against plastic pipes. They passed along the smell of a scrap of soft stolen wool or the crinkle of a plastic bag. And the food! The Family were master scavengers, eating part of everything they found and dragging the rest back to the nest for later. They had nuts, scraps of pizza crust, forgotten sticks of fried potatoes. The Family was fed, and dark, and safe.

And now they had the delight of a caramel apple vanishing into hundreds of squeaking mouths, the whole colony clamoring for their bite.

Alek tasted every snatched morsel, every hint of caramel licked off of upraised paws. He felt juice and sticky caramel on whiskers. The knowledge flowed through the Family and into him, and his fresh loss flowed out until it stopped.

Wordlessness was better. Wordlessness hurt less.

They'd told Alek of the tunnels, of the maze they lived in. Most of it he couldn't enter—the cracks were too tiny, and you needed a rat's nearly-liquid body to flow into the most sacred chambers, where the pups lay in tight clusters beneath proud, tired mothers, and where the older rats curled up and slept in great warm piles of comfort. The boys, who lived to eat, sleep, and make more Family. The warm comfort of belonging, even if life was hard and too short.

Finally Alek's heart felt empty. His breath grew still and calm. Home. Safety.

The whisker line told so much about the world, but Alek couldn't use all of it. The Family was all smells. They found their way by smell, they recognized each other by smell, they lived and died by smells. Alek's nose wasn't good enough to follow their secret ways. He had to find his own paths.

With four of the bigger, stronger boys, he set out to learn his new maze.

Alek crawled carefully on three limbs, moving slowly. His desperate dash from the new war had left his hands scraped and bloody, and the new scabs hadn't hardened yet. His back and thighs ached from the unfamiliar exertion, and his neck burned from holding his head up to catch the few, rare flickers of distant light leaking down. His hands would grow calloused and strong. So would his knee. But for now he moved slowly, absorbing the tunnels' turns and textures in the cool darkness.

Beneath the tiny holes of a storm drain, where thin sticks of sunlight pierced the darkness and made nine tiny dots in the dirt, Alek heard human voices and froze. The four Family froze with him, ears upraised.

Humans were dangerous. They left food, yes. But certain deaths, like the tasty pellets and those boxes of enticing smells, always stank of human.

But sometimes Alek could understand humans. He could learn things. Learn where food was. Learn where traps were. Learn where to go and where to flee. Alek felt a need to help, to prove himself to the new group of Family.

People were babbling and crying. One spoke loudly, others in quick scurry-and-stop rushes.

Alek struggled to find words again.

Television. The loud voice was a television, or maybe a radio. One of the cafes on the street? An open doorway?

The television voice. A human woman. "…have planted explosive devices throughout the city."

Alek froze. He knew explosive devices. Explosives hurt the Family. Explosives hurt everyone. Were any in the tunnels?

"Oh my God," a man said above. A metal chair leg scraped across the lid. "Oh my God."

A sidewalk café, then.

The television woman said "—urge everyone to remain in their homes and calm." Her tone shifted. "We're getting reports now of an explosion in the Holland Tunnel." The background noise changed, screams and sirens made tinny by the tiny speakers.

A real car horn blared, drowning out the television.

Alek perked his ears and listened, catching slices of the story through the quietly desperate bystanders and the occasional rumble of a truck's tires or the subway below.

"…demanding ten billion dollars, or they will detonate one Semtex device every four hours…"

Alek slumped back on his heels in surprise, knocking his head against the tunnel's stone ceiling. Bright red and blue circles flooded his eyes, coloring the darkness.

Money?

Someone started a war, for *money?*

Outrage bubbled up in Alek's chest. These people had so much. They gave everything so freely—yes, you had to pay the apple lady, but that was okay. They'd give you a *face* if you didn't have one. They tossed money in your hat if you asked. And someone demanded *more?*

Alek did not belong with these people. He knew that. He never could really belong to them.

But they'd welcomed him.

These good people did not know war.

They did not know how to fight.

Alek shook. His heart hammered against his ribs and furious bile rose from his empty stomach. His battered hands curled into clumsy fists.

The four boys surrounding Alek raised onto their back paws, noses in the air, chittering angrily. Tails lashed the darkness.

These people did not know how to fight for their lives.

Alek did.

Tiny shrieks of fury echoed down the tunnel.

5

The fastest two boys dashed down the dark tunnel towards the nest, leaving Alek and the slower two boys to follow as quickly as Alek could crawl.

Alek wasn't used to this work anymore. His hands burned. He'd jammed fingers on rocks and broken concrete and walls. He had aches and bruises and he thought the knee of his one leg was bleeding even through the denim. His futile anger had stolen his breath and left him trembling.

But every time he slowed, the two Family boys gently nipped the inside of his wrists to urge him on. Alek knew they weren't angry. He felt their concern. They knew he had no time for weakness.

Alek had been a boy before, when he'd first taken to the tunnels and joined the Family.

But now he was a man. A man with teeth.

He had something to protect.

People who didn't know how to protect themselves.

A young lady who knew selling apples, but not enough to fall down or to hide her face from falling glass.

With the boys to prod him each time he slowed, he scurried back to the nest before collapsing to his side to heave air into desperate lungs.

The nest churned with Family. Gravid girls had already squeezed into the deepest cracks. Behind the tunnel walls, amidst chambers dug from broken cinderblocks of a forgotten foundation, mothers loomed over pups and elders moved to block the cracks where others might come in. Alek felt them all, the determination to protect the Family.

Not even a madman would plant explosives to kill Family. But when war came, Family died. Alek knew that truth in his bones, and the Family believed him. Family never lied.

Alek felt his fury seep through the pack, passed by whisker and paw. The girls too newly pregnant to be slowed and every single boy churned around him, ready to tear any invader to bloody strings of meat.

But there was no enemy here.

Alek had to calm himself. His fury was right, yes. It felt good. He needed it.

But the Family couldn't fight this.

And really, what could he do? Alek knew war. More than once he'd fought for his life, twisting and grabbing and biting and clawing with another human in the tunnels over a scrap of food or just the right to live. Alek had lost himself in a swirl of claws and gashes and, more than once, a rock clenched in a bloodless hand, raised high over a soldier who would have murdered Alek.

But how could one fight explosives? Explosives hidden all over town.

Alek lay in the mud, in the safely tight drain pipe, soaking in the darkness and trying to think. He'd been too young to really understand before, but he knew the shape of war. In the old city, they started with guns. Here, they started with explosives. Both times, they made demands. Once the killing started, though, it would never stop.

He had to stop it before it started, before it got worse.

Semtex.

The television had said Semtex.

Alek knew Semtex. He'd seen it many times. Soldiers had stored it with food, or used food to trick you into setting it off.

How far could the whisker line go?

The Family was everywhere. *Everywhere.* In every wall and ceiling, in every tunnel. They knew conduits and passageways humans never could.

The Family knew how to deal with threats. Lock a hungry, feral cat in the basement with a pack of Family, and you got a bunch of chubby rats.

You couldn't fight this threat with claws and teeth.

The Family was also master scavengers.

Maybe they could scavenge this threat away.

Alek lay still and thought about Semtex. Forget the packages, the grenades, the wires. The Family would know nothing of them, could not even see them as Alek would.

Semtex was burnt orange, or red like a brick. It felt gritty between the paws, like a child's clay choked with sand. The greasy feel, somewhat like plastic, somewhat like fat, something all its own.

Alek remembered the grease, that bitter almond stink that drove nails up his nose and stabbed fear into your brain, the square brick shapes so unlike anything found in nature. He bundled it into a tight knot of sensation, a smell he could taste and grit he could feel and that color that meant death.

He stripped the human words off, boiling it down to the purest truth he knew.

And sent it to the Family.

Smasher of nests! Eater of pups! Find it, break it, scatter it like pellets! Scatter all of it! Find it all!

The effort left Alek gasping again, shuddering on the cold wet mud, the concrete at his back leeching his heat away but new sweat over his closed eyes. The Family accepted him, but they didn't think like him.

They understood well enough though.

Tiny paws scattered, shooting down tunnels and through cracks, going down the secret paths known only to the Family. Alek felt furry bodies churning against him, tiny claws pricking his skin, the warm rich smell of rat. He shivered on the muddy tunnel floor, cool concrete leeching his heat away.

Rats climbed onto Alek's stomach, his side. One draped across his neck. Warmth began seeping back into him, one furry belly at a time. One girl on his chest got very cozy and peed. Alek didn't mind. He was one of them.

The Family was still alert, but they trusted Alek. The threat was grainy and greasy and no good at all to eat.

Alek lay in his blanket of rat and listened.

He felt the knowledge diffuse on the whisker line, passing from paw to paw. It spread on scuttling feet, tiny nails ticking on metal floors and grabbing upright lines, squeezing under doors that people had not used for fifty years. A great living web of Family, all through the city.

A sense came back to him. It was gritty, yes, but too thick. Too stiff. Too hard to break. Alek didn't know what it was, but it wasn't Semtex. *No, not that.*

The knowledge passed into the sky, within the walls and elevator shafts of the tall buildings. *Not that smell, no. Not that taste. Closer, but not quite.*

Maybe this wouldn't work. Maybe it was a stupid idea.

The Family knew doubt, though. Doubt was an old friend.

Then a brush of whiskers on Alek's hand brought a new scent. It was everything Alek had remembered, but the bundle of smell carried notes Alek had forgotten. A rat's sense of smell was a million, a billion times better than a human's. Even stripped down to its barest outlines by the passing from whisker to whisker, the scent awakened Alek's memories.

That one. That's it. Scatter it!

The message went out faster now. The Family was awake—not only this small piece of it, but all of it. The whole Family, throughout this city, alarmed and ready to fight. And the Semtex smell was so sharp, so piercing, that with those incredible noses the Family could sense it from floors away.

Tight little knots of truth came back to Alek from everywhere. A bundle found inside a wall, chewed into chunks and scattered for body lengths. A bundle in a tunnel, in a floor, in one of the loud tunnels that shook and sent everyone scurrying for cover.

But the Family couldn't get all of it. There was a big pile of it, the biggest pile of all. It was with humans.

Almost drowsing beneath his sleek-furred blanket, Alek didn't want to move. He felt safe and tired. His hands and knee and even the stump of his missing leg ached.

But these people needed him.

The Family flowed away at a thought, giving Alek space to roll to his stomach and then to his knee.

One Semtex left.

In a space that needed not a rat, but a man.

6

Alek crawled out the same hole he had dived into, out in the same plaza where he'd bought the caramel apple the size of a grenade. He'd had to go back to get his leg. The tunnels would take too long, and nobody could hop across town on one leg.

A great big gray boy perched on his shoulder, tail twisted around the back of Alek's neck, claws clenched through the shirt and into Alek's skin. Alek felt the boy's fear, but the boy still gripped no more tightly than necessary to hold on. Once Alek dragged the drain cover back into place, he crossed his arms over his chest. The boy climbed down and snuggled in, his bright black eyes wide with fear and his feet pulled tightly against his body. The long smooth tail looped over Alek's arm.

Safe, Alek sent. *I protect you.*

The plaza had changed. Fire trucks and police cars everywhere. Big black vans with blue lights flashing from the roofs. Things that looked like little tanks, but tanks did not have shiny paint. Soldiers again, but fake ones. Real soldiers were not so clean and did not stand so straight.

The building that exploded had not fallen, but several floors up near the sky lay open to the air. Sunlight glared off exposed metal overhead and countless tiny shards of glass scattered all across the plaza.

The apple cart stood alone where the young lady had been.

Alek hoped she had escaped. Probably not, though. If you didn't flee right away, if you stayed in the smoke, you died. He'd tried to help her, but he couldn't have taken her into the tunnels.

If he didn't move, though, more people would die.

"Hey!" someone shouted. "Kid! Yeah, you!"

Among these people, Alek was the size of a boy. He bolted.

The city had changed. What had been bustling joy now had knots of people afraid to move. The cars had stopped, and some people had left them in the middle of the road. Televisions and radios blared from cafés and bars and open doors. Blackmail. Terrorism. Threats of more death.

Each pronouncement lashed Alek on.

At every storm drain he stopped. He lowered his hands to the slits in the steel, slipping tiny fingers into the gaps. Whiskers brushed his knuckles, offering fresh guidance. *This way. That way. Down this alley. Follow this tunnel, that tunnel.* The boy in Alek's arms huddled tighter against Alek's chest as Alek ran, worried by the light and the sound but comforted by Alek's constant assurance and the warmth of their touch.

Alek hadn't wanted to bring the boy. He hadn't wanted to risk the youngster. The Family had demanded, though, and he couldn't say no.

The whisker line guided them both to an old brick building tottering near the glittering waterfront. A giant box, sixty feet on a side and three stories tall, with a single row of windows at head height and peeling white paint and the outlines of five-foot-high letters somehow still visible, spelling out the name of a long-vanished business.

The letters, the name, tugged at Alek's brain. The Family did not use words. When he thought with words, his bond to the boy faded. The boy dug his claws in and lashed his tail. No member of the Family would be so close to a human! Alek had to split his thoughts, somehow set part of his mind aside to be human while letting most soak into the Family.

Alek stopped at a drain just outside the crumbling brick building. When told to, he wrenched the drain cover aside, let the boy slip into the darkness, and gratefully followed into the cool dampness of the drain tunnels.

He'd just dragged the heavy steel cover back into place when the sirens arrived.

7

Most people could not have fit down this tunnel. If Alek had been any larger, or worn heavier clothing, this tight tube of very old concrete would have trapped him. As it was, crumbling cement brushed his shoulders as he dragged himself forward.

A few yards up the tunnel Alek found another drain. It was in the right spot to be in the floor of the big brick building. Above, people shouted. Other voices answered, distorted by brick walls and bullhorns.

All around Alek, the Family waited. Alek had never felt the whisker line so strongly before. Mostly boys, but a small number of girls, all angry and ready to fight. This wasn't just one clan. It wasn't even one city block of clans. *Millions?*

The Family did not know numbers, let alone words for numbers. His connection faded. Rats shifted nervously around him, suddenly no longer Family.

Alek shoved the words aside. No such thing as numbers. There was only the threat, a threat that needed to be driven away or destroyed.

Once the whisker line felt solid again and Alek felt submerged into the Family once more, he hoisted the drain cover aside and raised his head.

The brick building was one large room. Shining metal rails ran along the ceiling, dangling flaking white buckets from rusty chains. A heap of ancient abandoned furniture covered one wall, warped dressers and broken desks and waterlogged couches forming a pile taller than Alek and running from wall to wall. An almost usable table had been dragged off to the side, near the giant roll-up door in the center of the opposite wall. Dim sunlight seeped through narrow, dirty windows along the ceiling. The space stank of mildew and fetid rot.

Men, maybe—no, no numbers. No words. No human things. Just see them. Don't listen to their words, either. Don't break the whisker line. Gleaming metal slung over shoulders and clipped at the waist, the familiar, mingled stinks of gun oil and sweat. They peered out the windows, angry and fearful at the flashing blue lights.

One man, the alpha, stood near the sole table. He had broken out a pane in the roll-up door, and shouted human words out at the world.

And in the middle of the room, a pallet half-filled with reddish-orange, greasy bricks that stank of bitter almonds. The eater of pups.

These men had already searched their nest. They knew that nobody could get in. And the ones outside had so much metal and made so much noise, they missed the sound of Alek setting the drain aside.

Alek let a boy—a different one this time, with a shorter tail and chubbier flanks—climb into his hand. He quietly rose from the drain, letting blood flow back into his hips and leg. He had to move carefully to ease the metal leg around the bend and out of the tunnel.

The Family had no tactics. But they knew stealth.

A black and gray flood poured silently from the tunnel. More rats scuttled out of the abandoned furniture, so many that they looked like a carpet, like grass, like the evening tide from the ocean.

Deep in the whisker line Alek walked towards the alpha's back, holding the boy in his hands. A boy alpha? Why would anyone let a boy be alpha? Boys quit halfway through anything. They couldn't even stash properly—once their tummies were full, they were done.

You only needed a boy when you had to make more rats.

Or when you had to defend the nest.

Alek made sure his metal foot made no sound on the concrete floor.

He stopped five feet behind the alpha, who still shouted out through the broken window. Alek ignored the words, instead focusing on the alpha's attitude, his belligerence. This so-called alpha needed someone to throw him on his back and bite his scrotes.

Nobody let you bite their scrotes. You had to surprise them.

The whisker line had almost swallowed Alek, but he managed to peel off a thin slice of his mind and form a single human word.

"Boo."

The alpha jumped and spun to see Alek.

And rats. Rats filled the floor. Rats crowded up behind the men staring out the windows. Rats dangling from chains and prancing across rafters.

At the alpha's shriek, the Family attacked.

Yes, the Family knew heartbreak.

But that was because the Family knew love. They knew what it meant to fight for those you loved. And Alek was one of them.

Rats raced up pant legs and dropped from above. Quick sharp fangs sank into exposed skin at ankles and wrists, slipped into clothes and nipped at biceps and thighs and more tender parts.

Guns fired, a hail of bullets spattering the ceiling.

Men screamed from everywhere.

The tide buffeted Alek, as Family ran up his legs. Rats flew from Alek's shoulders and from the top of his head, launching into space to clamp onto the alpha's face, his neck, even into the mouth hanging stupidly open.

A loud bang sent Alek staggering back, each step eliciting squeaks of protest as he struggled to maintain his balance. One edge of the great rolling door rippled and shuddered, then the metallic panels slid to the ground in a chorus of clatters.

Men outside. Men dressed like soldiers, but too clean. Men with guns.

Alek reversed his stumble, rats clutching his shirt and hair to keep their own balance. He waved his arms frantically. "Don't shoot! Don't shoot!"

The whisker line dissolved under the onslaught of words.

For a breath, every rat froze.

Outside the building, behind the men dressed up as soldiers, police officers and camera crews stood just as still.

Rats and humans stared at each other.

Then the rats whirled as one giant, squeaking mass. The tide receded back into the drain, into the abandoned furniture, into tiny gaps in the walls. Rats leapt from Alek's shoulders and plunged off his legs to dash for holes only they knew of.

Every man in the room lay on the floor, screaming and crying and begging for help, a ring of pain surrounding half a pallet of Semtex.

Aleksander stood on the concrete before the open door and stared out at the city, the police, the cameras, all the kindest people in the world.

Mister Counselor Henders had told him to avoid attention. He would be unhappy with Aleksander.

No war. Not here. Not ever.

8

The man from the television, wearing his expensive suit and waving a microphone under Aleksander's jaw, asked Aleksander what he wanted after all this. Aleksander said he'd never gotten to eat his caramel apple.

The next day, the young lady in the tight black T-shirt brought him one.

You'll Figure It Out

A charming pattern of daisies and roses and other flowers danced at the top of the treatment room's soothing pale yellow walls. Dozens of real framed photos, not smart paint, covered one wall, and a low planter bristled with grassy flowers just short of blooming, or maybe just past blooming. Giselle appreciated plants but her medical practice left no time for her own. They added a lovely scent to patient rooms, strong enough to hang around despite the air handlers constantly sifting away all the scents of really old, really sick people. The gray carpet felt soft enough to walk on without shoes, though she wouldn't dare go barefoot. Patients got ill, and she mistrusted antiseptics after all the drug-resistant bugs of the 2030s. A grandfather clock filled the corner by the window, its chrome faceplate intricately swirled with brass and black steel hands pointing right at the nine and the twelve. A wooden shelf held three rows of antique paper books, colorful thick spines faded with age. An old-fashioned screen hung from a ceiling bracket, poised to be comfortably viewed from the low bed sticking out from the middle of the opposite wall.

Three comfortable-looking armless chairs sat up against the wall beneath the window, enough to make it feel nearly crowded, but the chairs wouldn't be there if they weren't needed.

Multiple people visited this patient, often enough that they'd furnished their own chairs, rather than pirating them from the lounge as needed.

The thought warmed Giselle's soul, despite the chain of aches in her spine and the headache like a nail behind her left eye.

The tiny patient making all the noise didn't help.

They had a face like a map of medieval Britain's cow paths, bobbing over a shapeless gown or nightshirt that had seen better decades but was old enough to be familiar. Their hands ineffectually swatted at the sleek medical android standing by the bed. Each shout felt like a tap on the nail of Giselle's headache. She blinked, steeling herself, and the patient's shouts came into focus. "Get away! I need to go march!"

Giselle glanced up at the wall behind the bed. Out of the patient's view, smart paint flashed up the New Dawn Memory Care Center logo and the words MISS ALICE – AGE RELATED DEMENTIA – BEDBOUND – ADVISE COCKY CHEER.

Giselle put one hand on her hip, cradling her tablet against her side in the other. "Miss Alice! What is all the ruckus here?"

Alice swatted at the android's outstretched hands. "This mechanical beast won't let me get up. I've got to get to the march! It's vital!"

Giselle focused on keeping her voice light. "And which march is this?"

Alice must have had close to a century of practice packing scorn into her gaze, and Giselle felt every drop of it. "The Avalon march! We've got to get rid of him!"

Giselle didn't let herself grimace. The poor woman's mind had gone back to the 2030s. Trying to reorient her to 2054 would only confuse and anger her. At Alice's almost absurd age, what good would it do?

"You haven't heard?" Giselle said.

Alice peered at her. "Heard what?"

188

"Here, let me turn on the TV." Giselle raised her tablet. The words *Avalon Execution* were on the first screen, near the bottom. One tap, and the big hanging screen lit up with a news announcer mid-sentence: *—arrest of President—*

A huge grin stretched Alice's face, straightening some of her wrinkles. "They got him?"

"They did," Giselle said. "Why don't you watch the trial for a while? See what happens?"

Alice fidgeted. "These things take forever."

"It might go more quickly than you think." The compressed tale might hold Alice all day. Perhaps not. But if Alice was fixated on that sordid bit of history, the carefully selected news snippets might bring her joy.

The head of the bed was already shifting up to support Alice into the closest thing she'd ever get to sitting upright. The service android silently retreated into its cubbyhole, where it wouldn't loom and worry her.

Alice laughed and clapped.

Giselle couldn't help a little smile of her own.

Human ingenuity had driven down global warming and delayed the infirmities of aging. They'd fed the multitudes and cured rheumatism with a pill. Nobody could heal the brain without destroying the person within, though.

Giving people a taste of hope at the end of their days, despite their worn-out minds, was worthy work.

Eyes rapt on Avalon's perp walk, Alice had already forgotten Giselle.

Giselle followed the android's example and retreated from the room as quietly as possible.

She'd barely gotten out into the hallway and eased the door almost shut when someone said, "Doctor Giselle?"

A young kid, maybe twenty or so, stood right in front of the smart paint's copy of an idyllic landscape by some centuries-gone master, the name CHRYS in big letters on their pale blue scrub top, right over their heart. They had their hair trimmed to weirdly drape over the ears and frame their face. They had to be decades and decades younger than anyone here, but Giselle didn't have any way to tell if they were male or female either. When had the kids started all looking so androgynous?

"My name's Charybdis?" they said. "The school said I'm supposed to help you today?"

Another student. Hadn't she had one just, well, not long ago? Giselle's head throbbed deeper. How long would they keep throwing these kids at her? "Stand up straight, young... young person. And if you're asking, I have no idea if the school sent you so you should immediately find that out."

They took a deep breath and spoke almost properly. "The school sent me to assist you. My name's Charybdis, but everyone calls me Chrys."

"What kind of name is Charybdis?" Giselle waved her hand. "No, never mind. Not my business, my headache's making me crabby. What class?"

"Concrete Reminiscence Therapy."

"Third year?" Giselle said.

"Yes, Doctor."

Giselle squinted at Chrys' open face. "You ever done reminiscence therapy before?"

"Only verbal?" Chrys said. "I talked with some older 'uns about their growing up."

"This is my unit, young ma—person. This is my unit. What we're doing here, caring for people lost in their past, is sacred work, and I will not have you disturbing a one of them." She dropped her voice. "You try to reorient someone without my approval or tell them it's the 2050s, and student protection laws or no, I will throw you out the front door of my clinic so hard you *bounce*. Do you understand?"

Chrys had lost a little of the color from their face. "Yes, Doctor."

"If they sent you here, I imagine you've read my book? Or the one by what's-his-name's, that slacker?"

"I've studied both of yours."

Both of hers? They must mean both her book and that hack piece. She had the student just the right sort of nervous. Giselle nodded. Administration wouldn't dare assign her another lackluster lump that couldn't be bothered to do the basic reading. "You stay with me on rounds, do as I tell you, and save any questions for the hallway, away from patients."

Chrys nodded, trying to hide their intimidation.

Giselle turned away and permitted herself a tiny smile. Training the young was also sacred. People would probably call her atavistic for the little thrill she got from asserting dominance, but the truth was, she'd earned it. Nobody else had spent so much time researching into caring for the extremely aged. Or advancing their contentment.

And she had so many more ideas. Once technology advanced enough to support them.

Until then, she'd keep doing the work that made her life worthwhile.

The next patient, a man who looked almost old enough to remember Reagan, had allowed his android to bathe him and guide him through getting dressed but sat unresponsive in his chair. Despite his clean hair and scrubbed skin, the man somehow still smelled insanely old. The wall spelled out JACOB – AGE RELATED DEMENTIA – MOBILE WITH ASSIST – DISCUSS COMIC MOVIES. The letters were a little watery—maintenance must need to smack the server again.

Jacob caught Giselle peering and turned to look over his shoulder, but the smart paint swallowed the words before he could even glimpse them.

Giselle turned to the student—what was their name? CHRYS, right on their scrub top. How was she supposed to remember all these students, anyway? Part of the price of success. "Do they still show kids the Marvel series?"

"Marvel?" Chrys looked puzzled. "That's one of those old epics, right? Ninety-some flat films and a bunch of serials?"

"That's right," Giselle said. "They came out when I was a kid."

"Yeah, I saw a few. The one where the guy who could shrink fought the green growing guy was fun."

"*Ant-Man and the Hulk?*" Giselle laughed. "That one upset so many people."

Jacobs' face was already turning towards Giselle. His jaw was starting to work, lips opening and closing a fraction of an inch as if his mental motor was trying to turn over.

"It's not fair, fighting someone that small," Chrys said.

"Fair?" Giselle said. "The world doesn't care about fair. Besides, Ant-Man won."

"He shrunk down small enough to rewire the green guy's brain. And how would he find the right brain cells anyway?"

Jacob's voice sounded thin as the wind through a cracked window. "Stark's neural mapper. They explained way back in *Stan Lee Citadel*."

Chrys opened their mouth to say something, but Giselle made a one-handed cutting motion and said, "I never really understood that."

Jacob didn't need any more than that to launch into a ramble about movies from Giselle's childhood. She had vague memories of her youthful self being impressed by all the flash and spectacle, but what she'd really loved had been the talking raccoon and the raccoonlets with tiny laser guns.

Jacob had spent so much of his life with that fantasy. They left him happily watching *The Wasp and The Widow*.

"Excuse me, Doctor," said the student.

They'd been so quiet, Giselle had forgotten they were there. CHRYS, right there on their shirt. How was she supposed to keep students straight? "Yes?"

"I'm wondering." Chrys licked their lips. "Is that really it?"

Giselle said, "What do you mean?"

"We walked in and talked with this guy about an old serial."

"Movies."

Chrys blinked. "Shouldn't we be trying, I don't know… giving them something new to do?"

Giselle drew herself up straight despite her aching spine. "Such as?"

Chrys shrugged. "I don't know."

"What would you have him do?" Anger tensed her back. "Take up jogging? Did you count the chairs?"

"Chairs? No, why—"

"His room had one chair. His." Giselle fought to keep her voice from a hiss. "No visitor chairs. Whoever that man was, whoever loved him? Whoever he loved? They're gone now. But there's some*thing* he loved. Something that won't go away. And that love brings him joy."

"But maybe a group—"

"He's not going to remember names," Giselle said. "He's so old he can't make new memories. You make him play cards or something, something where he meets people and has to remember them, he'll get all confused and upset. Or would you just plug him into virtual and forget him?" She leaned into the student's face, almost spitting the words. "He. Deserves. Better."

Giselle whirled, glancing up the hall. The smart paint had rearranged itself into a forest scene, branches weighted with deep green leaves covering the ceiling and seeming to block out a sun that wasn't really there. The white rectangles of patient room doors and the delicious aroma of coffee made the illusion merely impressive rather than perfect.

One of the doors had a blinking white attention light above it. "There!" Giselle said.

She remembered herself in time to slow down and take a deep breath before pushing the door open.

The smart paint had opted for a plain off-white finish, with a faint woven texture resembling cloth. The only decoration was a plain wooden rack displaying several lengths of worn ragged cloth, most black but two red, each a few inches wide and about two yards long. Faint incense hinted at unfamiliar cultures.

The patient was on his feet, between the bed and the door. He was taller than Giselle, with broad but knobby shoulders poking through the plain white pullover shirt.

Strangely, the medical android was right by him, its arms on each side of him. The man had grabbed one of the android's hands in an uncomfortable-looking grip.

He mumbled, "Thumb on thumb. Fingers around blade edge. Blade edge. Hand position. Back straight. Follow-through." Face just short of tears, he flexed bony hands on the android's implacable fingers.

The wall behind the man spelled out SIFU AARON – AGE RELATED DEMENTIA – MARTIAL ARTIST – ADVISE DISCUSS MEDITATION.

"Sifu Aaron!" Giselle said. "Unhand my android."

"That should work," Aaron said.

"It's a machine," Giselle said. "A machine that keeps you safe."

"Came up behind me," Aaron said.

This was *not* helping her headache. "It thought you might fall."

"I fall all the time," Aaron said. "Hundreds of falls."

"Do you fall in places like this?" Giselle said. "Don't you fall in a, a…"

"Dojo," came the whisper from behind her.

Giselle glared over her shoulder. She told students to be quiet, and young CHRYS had broken that rule. She'd chew them out later. "Dojo," she said to Aaron.

Aaron stopped struggling and looked around him. "Floodlight consciousness," he muttered.

"That's right." Giselle had no idea what it meant, but it sounded sort of relevant. "You're in your room. There, those are your belts on the wall."

Aaron turned. The smart paint message faded when he studied the belts. "Red. Never mastered hapkido."

"But there's a bunch of black, right? You've learned a lot."

As Aaron's gaze turned back to Giselle, finally settling on her face, the patient description faded back into view on the wall behind him. "You could learn too."

Giselle laughed. "I'm way too old to start something like that."

"One of my best students didn't start till she was 62."

"Why don't you sit down and tell me about it?"

He raised a hand perpendicular to his face and one leg off the ground, and somehow sank gracefully to his knees.

The room had no chairs. Giselle grimaced. Ignoring the surging ache in her spine, she eased herself to the ground with considerably less panache. The motion sent her headache's throb surging, then it settled back down.

"Martial arts isn't about fighting," he began. "It's about mastering yourself."

Giselle listened for a few minutes, asking an occasional question when he needed prompting to continue. When the wall prompted, and he went into a long, enthusiastic discussion of controlling one's own mind.

The whole time, she fought to block tears. This man had spent his life mastering himself, only to have his own brain betray him at the end.

She had no idea how he managed to sit so still on his knees like that. She was sitting with her legs out to the side and one arm propping her up, and she was already aching from the palm of her hand up to the top of her head. Despite that extra support and the soft carpeting, her butt was already tingling from poor circulation.

Eventually she coaxed him into demonstrating what he was talking about. After a few minutes with his hands palm-up in his lap, his breathing settled into an impossibly slow rhythm.

With a total lack of elegance, Giselle managed to silently winch herself to her feet. She couldn't help grimacing at how the student hopped up so much more easily. Her legs throbbed and tingled with returning blood, but she managed to keep herself upright and stagger out the door.

The student closed the door this time and softly said, "I think we helped him."

"You think?" Giselle said. "That man doesn't need someone to listen to him. He needs to be useful." She flapped a hand. "He's got a skill he aches to use. You saw it. He won't be happy unless he can do the thing that he does, until he's useful, and he doesn't have the mind left for it."

A shrug. "What could we do?"

"You get to be that age, your mind comes and goes." Giselle let out a sigh. "What we need is the technology to predict all that. We'll know when his mind is going to be clear enough, and have someone here that he *can* teach. Leave him hints to help him keep his dignity." How many times had she explained this? Maybe she needed to write another book, to push people in the right direction.

But a book was work. Right now, she felt nothing but fatigue. "It can be done. I'm certain of it." The headache just wouldn't quit, and her back ached like she'd done something foolish. "We need just a little more tech."

The weight of the student's gaze felt like another burden.

After a breath, the student said, "My class time is over, Doctor. But thank you so much. I've learned a lot."

Their class was over? Good. Really, how long did she have to put up with students?

"For what it's worth," they said, "I think you'll figure it out."

Presumptuous puppy, so convinced they knew everything! Giselle barely stopped herself from rolling her eyes. "Off with you, then. And remember, all those old folks? There are *people* in there."

"I will never forget that." They smiled. "Doctor."

For a breath, Giselle watched the student walk away, down a hall that seemed too familiar. How long had she been here? The peaceful murals of foliage echoed through her mind not in feet, but in years, decades filled with writing a second book and testifying to Congress and a child that grew—

Giselle shook her head. A bizarre déjà vu, nothing more. Gone as soon as it came.

After dealing with another student, she needed a break. Sit down a few.

A cup of coffee.

Maybe even a nap.

Then, back to it. The work was really all that kept her going.

Good thing she loved it.

Lavender

I flung myself into our pickup's bed half a second before the rebel ammo dump blew. Even at half a mile, the sound slapped me flat on my back. Jimmy's mouth flapped, his shout inaudible against the crescendo of detonating ammunition, rupturing poison gas canisters, and overlapping napalm pyres. If the pickup had still had windows, the blast would have shattered them. I clamped my hands over my ears, but the sound shook my brain in my skull. As the echoes faded, the pickup's neglected engine roaring to life rattled my joints.

"Hold it, Kyle!" I shouted. "Don't run!"

If we sat still, they might not realize we had set the charges. Either Kyle didn't hear me, or his twitchy nerves made him shove the pickup into gear. With a series of bumps and lurches, our truck pulled from the bombed-out police station and onto Vernier Avenue.

A pillar of stinking smoke thick enough to support the sky billowed down Lakeshore Boulevard, completely obscuring the rebel camp half a mile south. A handful of colored dots on our side of the smoke were vehicles and staggering rebels. The blast had devastated the few remaining mansions along the lake. Fresh-shorn wood and shattered brick still rained onto broken asphalt and into the lake, a few chunks splashing out in Lake Saint Clair near the Canadian picket boat line. Distant screams and starting motors spoke in a tinny voice through the sudden quiet.

Kyle gunned our truck down Vernier. We crossed a hundred yards before shelled-out houses cut off sight of the rebels stumbling towards their own trucks.

I sank down in the truck bed, tasting blood. My tongue found a freshly broken incisor.

Jimmy put his head next to mine. "Maybe they didn't see us run."

Before the war, Jimmy said four years at college reading leather-bound books at crumbling New England colleges would get him a career. Now he said the rebels hadn't seen us. For the only man who knew how to raise the dead, Jimmy is an optimist.

Up in the cab, Karen screeched at Kyle. Karen can put a bullet between a man's eyebrows at a mile. I wouldn't want her mad at me.

We hurtled across Mack Avenue before I heard the first rebel truck skid onto Vernier behind us. It rose into sight over the hill: another battered pickup, this one with a machine gun mounted above the cab. I wished desperately for a tailgate to cower behind, even knowing that a small-caliber round would punch straight through one. "Kyle!" I shouted, my voice inaudible to my stunned ears. "Behind us!"

Our truck lurched faster.

Two motorcycles appeared beside the rebel truck.

Half the I-94 overpass still stood. Just not the half we were headed for. Kyle jerked the truck to the left, jolted us across the median, bounced into the opposite lanes, and rocketed us across the overpass. I clenched the side with both hands and anchored my feet against the floor bar as Kyle slewed around dead cars, scraped paint with a burned-out panel truck, and swooped into a parking lot.

How many rebel vehicles had I seen? Four? Five? We'd blown the biggest rebel stockpile on the east side, right where their Canadian backers dragged everything ashore. Even if we'd killed everyone inside the encampment, how many were on picket? A dozen, or dozens?

Jimmy could get us out of this. After a rebel terror attack killed our families, he'd shown just how thoroughly he could get us out of this. A few words from Jimmy, and we'd be safe.

I hoped he wouldn't. Raising the dead to avenge our families had taken his strength and ruined his sleep forever, and I didn't even know the full cost.

Kyle swung the truck into a shattered mall, raced through the food court, down the broad hall between pillaged shops, and beneath ambush-friendly mezzanines.

I closed my eyes. My hand clutched for the sachet of lavender around my neck, as if I could feel it through my body armor. My wife Lillian had grown lavender, made her own oils and perfumes with it. I had often found her by following the scent of lavender through our home.

Lillian had died with my parents.

I didn't care what the rebels stood for. Their demands meant nothing. Anyone who would bomb a family restaurant needed killing. That's war, the last one living wins.

Jimmy had taken his vengeance. I still needed mine. No matter how many rebels I killed, I still needed mine.

I forced my eyes open.

The truck bounced out the far side of the mall, veered around the bus shelter, and skidded into a left turn on the wrong side of Kelly Boulevard.

A tire popped.

My guts plunged.

The truck wallowed and slalomed sideways.

My hands wrenched from the side of the truck, driving my feet into the cargo bar. My mouth went dry. A panel of shredded rubber flew away behind us. A rim screeched on concrete.

I couldn't see the rebels among the burned-out wrecks behind us, but they wouldn't quit looking. If we kept running, they'd see us faster. Our best hope was to force them into a building-to-building search and hope they gave up. "On the left!" I shouted at Kyle. "That bank on the corner!"

Kyle might have been jumpy, but he could drive. The truck wrenched to the side, the screech of metal growing unbearable as he pulled us onto the side street. I hopped out while the truck juddered to a stop, assault rifle in hand. The building had brick walls, one entrance, and no windows on the side or back. The churchyard across the road wouldn't give the rebels any cover. If they tried to come up from the south they'd have to cross the Eight Mile Crater. I hoped that anyone behind us didn't carry an antirad suit. If we were lucky, they wouldn't recognize our stopped truck. If not, we'd have a few minutes to dig in.

Kyle and Karen piled out of the cab, gathering their weapons, while Jimmy watched behind us. I had well-fitting body armor and my light rifle, Kyle had ammunition satchels draped over his arms, Karen had her rifle and her appalling skills. We had a decent chance against anything rebel patrols might have carried on picket.

Inside, diffuse sunlight exposed a bunch of clumsy wooden spars that had once been furniture, scattered across shattered glass and stained carpet. The bulletproof glass over the counter had been knocked down, the counter itself tilted on its busted-up pedestal. The door protecting the two teller stations had been blown towards the customers. Nothing remained but ruin. The rebels had already devalued the dollar before the war got this far, but people with nothing grab anything. Protective brick walls still stood, however.

Braced in the corner where the counter met wall, I pulled my gas mask into place and raised my automatic rifle, aimed squarely at the doorway. Thirty-eight rounds left, then the four big slugs in my old revolver. I tried to slow my breathing, make my heart stop ratcheting, and glanced at those around me. Kyle, an ex-surgeon, leaning over the tellers' counter. My little brother, bookworm Jimmy, crouched beside the door. Karen, the regiment's most deadly ex-housewife, crouched beside Kyle, rifle already braced on the counter's broken granite. My family now. Losing one family had driven Jimmy and I into the war. I couldn't stand to lose another.

If the rebels found us, we didn't have anywhere to run.

My hand touched my breastplate, pressing the lavender to my chest in a whisper of comfort. Somebody, somewhere, still had peace. Love. A wife. Children.

I'd have peace, too. You kill and kill and eventually, you get peace. One way or another.

Nobody came down the road. Motors growled in the distance, then faded. Jimmy licked his lips and gave me a quick smile.

Something clattered outside.

Then noise swallowed me. The ground convulsed. What remained of the decorative ceiling shredded down. Concrete dust scoured my sight.

I instinctively jerked my hands to cover my ears, but almost hit myself in the face with my rifle instead. The breeze quickly ripped the dust to veils, but even though I saw debris hit the floor I heard nothing but a squeal. Kyle was curled beside me, clutching his chest in silent convulsive coughing. I didn't have earplugs, but he didn't have a mask.

Karen's chest moved slowly as she held her relaxation and focused on her rifle. Her hand squeezed once, twice, in eerie silence. I had no doubt that she'd glimpsed two different rebels through the dust, and that both had fallen. Jimmy dragged himself up the front wall, then wrenched his rifle around to fire off to one side.

A new crater marked the middle of the street, surrounded by pulverized concrete and shattered sewer pipes. The soldiers chasing us hadn't dragged artillery. How had they dropped a shell right there?

Something touched my back. I jumped. Kyle knelt behind me, his mouth moving urgently. I shook my head and put a hand to an ear. He grimaced and pointed south.

I peered around the doorway in time to see something arcing through the air. I shouted "Down!" and fell backwards, pressing my hands over my abused ears.

The rebels hadn't needed to cut through the Eight Mile Crater. They'd already had people here. We were the meat in the sandwich.

The impact felt louder this time, raining chunks of concrete and metal down on my armored back.

Quivering with shock, I made myself get to my knees. The road in front of our building had become a crater, taking the top half of the front wall with it.

Blood covered Karen's face but she held, squeezing off silent death.

Kyle wore his shirt over his mouth and nose, and wobbled on his knees to hold his rifle in position.

Jimmy's mouth hung loose. His eyes bulged. His breath came quick and hard.

Through the gap in the wall, I glimpsed rebels adjusting old pipes mounted on a trailer chassis. A home-brew mortar. It wouldn't aim well, but a few more near misses would kill us just as surely as a vaporizing hit.

We'd lost one family already. I couldn't face that again.

What made it worse was that Jimmy could save himself. He could save all of us.

Bullets pattered into the building. The rebels didn't have to close the distance, they could just let the mortar finish us, but fury and adrenaline controlled them. Any one of them who thought he had a target took a shot.

Jimmy wouldn't save all of us. I even understood that it would hurt. Like before, a handful of dead would end these rebels. All he needed was motivation.

No matter what I chose, the last one standing wasn't going to be me. I'd be damned if I'd let Jimmy and Kyle and Karen go down, too. I wished I had time to raise the faded sprig of lavender and breathe in any lingering whisper of scent.

Instead, I stood and stepped into the doorway.

I hardly cleared the brick before a river of bullets shattered against my body armor. They didn't penetrate, but hydrostatic shock cascaded through my bones.

It hurt less than I thought it would.

I tried to breathe, but a weight inside my chest choked my air off. I took in even less air the next breath, then the pressure inside me flattened my lungs.

And somehow, through the ringing silence, I heard Jimmy scream.

✳

For a precious brief flash of eternity, you treasure the smell of dying.

Then Something wrenches your eyelids up.

The scent rips away from you like duct tape, taking your identity and not only everything you love but the idea of love. The summoner stands nearby, screaming corrupt phrases in an ancient language, rifle dangling in limp hands. You can't hear the words, but you can feel their effect. The summoner beseeches Something, offering *everything*. Something responds, through you. Mangled Coptic phrases burn into your bones.

You remember that the summoner could save everyone. Whoever *everyone* is. You didn't expect to be one of those who got back up to help.

The silence is complete. Sound is motion. Your heart lies still. Your lungs don't heave air. You feel a trickle as Something yanks you to your feet. Blood drains from your brain, starts pooling in your feet. Your lungs hang limp.

Your body doesn't recognize that all-over tingle. Maybe your flesh decomposes already.

The summoner's anguish, his despair at losing his brother, his gutted heart, resonates inside you. The bottomless ache means nothing. Neither does Something's lust for the summoner's *everything*. Emotions possess only the living. You have an impulse to move, as a falling rock plummets. You lurch through the doorway, into the street.

A church across the boulevard. Dirt cascades from ancient graves, as Something drags others upright. Embalming preserved some of them for decades, but even those reduced to rags of skin over bone stagger forward.

An enemy stands in the street, hugging a weapon, staring at the churchyard. His mouth moves, head shakes, all silently. He doesn't see you staggering closer, doesn't see your hands until they close around his neck.

Gunshots impact your body armor as you twist his head off.

The slaughter lasts an endless static moment. Other puppets wear funeral vestments, or ashen remnants of what they wore when the bombs fell. Many are naked; troops whose comrades stripped their body armor. Bullets spatter decayed flesh all around you, bludgeon your breastplate and greaves even as you tear enemy limbs free.

Your eyes move in your head.

The eyes of the other puppets do not.

You didn't finish dying before Something took you.

The world is silent, except for the summoner's chant resonating in your flesh. You don't need hearing. You alone feel the millions of strings, through rebel camps and shattered buildings and broken homes all across their country.

More blood.

An enemy smashes an iron bar into your helmet. You bite through his wrist.

No enemies in sight. You stand still.

Someone grabs your shoulders. This intruder's face means as much to you as a brick wall or a broken bone. Not an enemy.

There—behind the burned-out limo. An enemy. Kill him.

You twist to free yourself.

The not-enemy releases you, his mouth moving in a shout.

Another man seizes you, face twisting as he stares into you. The summoner. His corrupt chant stumbles and ceases.

Something drops your strings, and you collapse.

You can't breathe. You haven't breathed for, for minutes? Days? Now you want to, need to, and your chest won't move.

Kyle fumbles for your pulse, then wrenches your breastplate off. Karen's scrabbling in the medical kit. In the corner of your eye you glimpse Jimmy's mouth stretched in a silent scream. He presses the barrel of a handgun under his chin.

Fresh hot light stabs your eyes. A knife stabs between your ribs, ex-surgeon Kyle sucking air from around your lungs.

Karen's hand is already coming down, the fierce adrenaline needle a burning knife straight into your heart.

***

My stagnant heart crashed into a gallop.

The ache of life shuddered through me. An eye was a pit of pain and tastes that shouldn't have left my guts filled my mouth, but that first breath forced my lungs open.

Everything in me clutched for the smell of dying, but it was gone.

I convulsed, knocking Karen away—how *dare* she drag me back! Death had given me everything, and she'd stolen it.

No. That wasn't right. My skull felt full of rags, my thoughts moving like... like something slow. Something about air and my brain. Thinking hurt. Easier to thrash my way to my hands and feet, then to my knees. I couldn't stand. Too much hurt. The armor softened bullet holes into bright bruises and broken bones. The shattered asphalt beneath my knees wobbled with the world.

Our lopsided pickup truck, by the bank. Sun beating down.

The burned-out limo. I'd sensed an enemy—a rebel—a *person* behind it.

I'd gone so far. I hadn't gone anywhere.

Karen stood back, staring at me, revolted. She'd watched my body tear apart enemies—*people*. Kyle leaned over me. "Can you hear me?"

I had to reach a long way for my voice. "Yeah." Even the joint of my jaw burned.

"What—" Kyle's mouth flapped. "What happened?"

No human had words for what I remembered feeling. But I knew the war was over. War happens, and you kill to avenge your loves, then the war ends and you somehow have to stop because the world's rules have changed.

Jimmy had traded himself for peace. If we could keep it.

I fumbled for words. "Don't. Kill."

"They're all dead," Kyle chattered. "You—all of them. Rebels. They're all."

"What did you do?" Karen hissed. She was my family, and I'd lost her. I'd meant to urge my brother to save himself and our little family. Instead, I'd hurt him so bad he traded himself to Something, and Karen would flee as soon as she could.

I wanted to lie on the rubble and let my heart stop. It wouldn't stop after Lillian had died, and it wouldn't stop now. I'd seen an enemy—no, a rebel, a traitor—no, a human being, someone who'd lived when their side lost—cowering behind that burned-out limo right before Something dropped me. I raised a shambling arm and pointed. "Don't. Kill."

Karen whirled, swinging her rifle towards the limo. "Bastard!"

Kyle pivoted his head every which way. War was better than what he'd seen me do.

"You!" Karen screamed. "Hands up come out or I will by God gut you!"

God? I didn't know if God was real. What remained of my gut told me that Jimmy had known, and Something had wanted him for it. But It wasn't any kind of God.

A desperate shout from behind the limo. "I give up don't please I give up!"

"Hands!" Karen was quivering, finger inside the trigger guard.

My throat hurt as I squeezed a word out. "Don't."

"Why not!" Karen shouted.

I dredged through the muck of my mind, hunting for words. "War over. I—" No. I wouldn't take credit. I sold my brother. "Jimmy. Jimmy, the war, ended. Don't."

Kyle's face went slack.

Karen glanced at me.

Killing in war was different. I couldn't say why, I just knew it was. Karen's horror of me would rot into loathing, but I could do this thing for her. Save her. "Over. Don't."

Karen's finger quivered on the trigger.

My chest heaved. I might never catch my breath again.

I found one more word to groan. "Please."

Karen shuddered.

Her finger loosened on the trigger. "You want to get ripped apart?" Karen shouted. "Come out and lie face down on the ground!"

My whole body burned, but the hollow burn in my heart eased. What was left of me still hoped.

Dying smelled like lavender. Lavender, growing stronger and stronger.

Keeping Friends

"I'm trying to decide if I should kill myself now, or wait five minutes."

My precognition hadn't warned me about Tom's call, but I hadn't asked it. I pressed the cellphone into my ear hard enough to hurt, trying to compensate for the crackling connection and the passing traffic. "You don't really want to do that, dude. You still have options. There's other meds out there."

"They won't work. Nothing works. There's no hope."

I sat on a bench and forced my hands to stay still. My friends are important to me—I have to keep them. If I failed, Tom might kill himself while talking to me. The thought heated my blood until the air felt cool. "Can I come down there?"

"Don't bother. I tried a knife, but it wasn't sharp enough to cut through my neck."

Tom had fought clinical depression for two years. Medication had taken the edge off, but not enough that he could return to work. The electroconvulsive therapy his doctor had prescribed required Tom stop taking all his medications. The edge had returned, and he was using it on himself.

"Are you holding the knife now?" I said.

"Yes."

"Do me a favor. Put it down."

"I need to sharpen it. That'll take both hands."

The phone clicked and I heard only silence, then the dial tone.

I forced myself to take a deep breath, then another, and willed my heart to slow. "I'll do nothing," I said. "He's not really going to do it. He's just trying to get attention." With that decision, I twisted the deformation in my brain.

The world around me skipped, displaying shattered fragments amidst frozen moments. Tom's cat lapping at pooled blood. Sheryl finding Tom. Accusations and counter-accusations over a closed coffin. Tears, and years of recriminations.

My gut burned, and I shuddered back to the moment. I couldn't do nothing.

"I'll call the police," I said aloud, cementing the decision in my brain. "Give them his address. Tell them what he told me. I'm going to do that next."

The decision changed my future, but weakened my precognition. The new future wasn't strong yet and hadn't yet solidified. Colors streaked the new images, and sounds skewed from lips like a badly dubbed film. Blood on Tom's neck. A police officer tumbling down the apartment stairs, Tom's knife buried in his arm. The stench of urine and blood. Parallel metal bars and scored, battered Plexiglas between Tom and I, new gaps in Tom's bared teeth as he spit at me.

Prison would be better than a coffin, maybe. But Tom wouldn't be my friend anymore. Precognition had already stolen my family, my children, and too many friends. I couldn't stand losing another.

"I'll go down there myself," I said. "See him in person. It's only thirty minutes to his apartment. Talk to him where he can't hang up on me."

Yet another change to my future distorted the new visions to the jagged edge of uselessness. I saw shards of Tom bleeding and my fingers fumbling at a phone. Tom's voice was unintelligible, but the anger was unmistakable. A glimpse of him at a party, the years turning his hair white; he laughed, then he saw me, and he turned away. The sudden set of his jaw reminded me of my wife when we left the divorce hearing.

The bench wobbled beneath me, the stench of bus exhaust more bitter. Tom would never forgive anyone for finding him like that. I'd save his life, but I'd lose him.

"I'll call him back," I said. "I'll talk him out of this." I'd never viewed four futures in quick succession. My precognition showed only an unintelligible jumble that hurt my ears and eyes and left the taste of hot copper in the back of my mouth. I didn't think that calling Tom would delay him more than a few minutes, though.

I licked my lips and made a call.

"Jimmy? Listen, I just heard from Tom. He's really really upset. I'm worried about him. You live right by him, don't you? Could you go and check on him?"

Jimmy would find Tom, and call for help. Tom would be there for me. Tom would never forgive Jimmy for finding him, but I'd be there to console Jimmy.

My friends are important. I have to keep them.

Burned Out Souls

I

The thick, humid air of a summer in a Florida swamp smelled so strongly of plants and tropical flowers, seasoned with a hint of rotting mulch, that it reminded me of unhappier times. Times when I thought I had a future in the military, serving my country and all that patriotic crap. Times when I thought I'd find someone to care about, marry her and raise kids and maybe feel like a normal human being.

Being dead inside was better.

Being dead inside meant I could lurk in a tree and study a multi-million-dollar house in the middle of a mucky bug-mobbed Florida swamp and count how many people I needed to murder without getting all teary-eyed.

Yes, there's other ways to rob a house. But hiring a man called Stabbity Joe as part of your team pretty much eliminates the whole "plausible deniability" thing. I'm not called Tranquilizer Terrance. You get what it says on the label.

And the woman we were robbing, one Jackie Aspen, was a corporate jackass who'd robbed her own employer.

We're just highly paid repo men.

With knives. And guns.

Miss Aspen had all the outside lights on, those yellow things that supposedly didn't attract bugs. The average bug density out here was about fifty bajillion per cubic inch, so the whole property looked swarmed. Buggy buzzing filled my ears.

The good news was, I didn't need the night vision binoculars to study our target. The regular ones did fine. The plastic eye-pieces felt damned hot in my eye sockets, but at least regular bin-oculars are lighter. I was already uncomfortable enough with my legs wrapped around a cypress and didn't need heavy night-vision goggles hanging off my forehead and crushing my sinuses. The climbing belt supported most my weight, but if I didn't anchor myself I'd go sliding straight down into the water.

Even if I didn't discover that an alligator had been lurking beneath me, my temporary partner would never let me forget it.

The stilt house sat on a peninsula barely attached to the rest of the land, raised a few critical yards above the slurry they called "ground level" in central Florida. Every wall was tinted glass, every corner painted bright reflective white, the roof a giant solar panel.

Elegant. But the windows were thick enough to resist any-thing smaller than a mortar. That elegant white trim was blast-re-sistant steel. And the building's core had a couple of those great big Tesla batteries. Killing main power wouldn't do anything but stop the air conditioning and warn them we're coming.

The place shrieked money.

Nobody was close enough to hear. It was over a mile to the nearest neighbor. The driveway was half a mile long.

Cut the phone line? All cellular. Same for the Internet.

Blow the stilts? Military-grade steel. We'd need a half hour to wire up the charges.

And the four mercenaries toting their big manly guns around circling the shoreline would object.

Miss Aspen didn't know we were coming, but she'd be an idiot not to guess.

The auction *was* the next day, after all.

We'd been hired blind; the broker didn't tell us who we were working for, and again, I didn't care. Aspen's employer had invested billions of dollars in this antibiotic, and expected to reap trillions. I didn't understand why blocking folic acid production in bacteria was so revolutionary. All I cared about was, Miss Aspen had copied all the data to a briefcase full of hard drives.

Miss Aspen had a second briefcase full of chemical samples.

The client wanted them both.

Our instructions said the client wanted her to serve as an example of what happens when you rob the company.

A horrible, horrible example.

That was where yours truly comes in.

Her photo didn't look like someone who deserved that. But, really, who did?

Were we working for Miss Aspen's ex-employer? Maybe. Or maybe we were working for an org that didn't want any of their employees getting their own ideas.

Bugs buzzed around me, loud enough to make normal conversation impossible. My nasty-smelling bug repellant was half a step down from DDT and probably twice as cancerous, but the gnats still battered at my cheeks and tried to clog my nostrils.

Once we finished, I'd find the most luxurious hotel room I could. Clean myself. Enjoy the payoff. Indulge all my body's appetites.

My partner pro tem Scott Dawson said, "I count four mercs on the ground, two inside on the main floor. Can't count the upper floor through those curtains." He was only a few yards away, up a separate tree, but the bugs out here buzzed so loud I couldn't hear him without the earpiece.

"Agreed," I muttered back.

I'd kayak towards the property. Just before the mercs hit the alarm, Dawson would drop them and launch his little helicopter drones. I'd penetrate the house and handle the two guards inside and any extraneous civilians. The drones would deliver the grenades to the driveway. When the four men out at the road heard the chaos and raced up in their Jeep, too bad for them.

Anyone in the place except Miss Aspen? Drop them quick.

That'd give me a good fifteen minutes with Miss Aspen before law enforcement got too close. They'd pass quickly for me.

Not so much for her.

The thought triggered a flicker of feeling; not of caring, but a sensation that I *should* care. That I should feel bad for what I was going to do.

I ignored it.

It went away.

Being dead inside had its advantages.

If I didn't return, Dawson would blow the hell out of the building. It'd send a different message, yes. We'd lose a touch more than half our fee, but Dawson wouldn't have to split it with me, so he'd be okay.

The door leading to the upper floor's outdoor balcony slid open.

A dead woman stepped out.

Everything I'd murdered within myself shrieked back to agonizing life.

2

This business with the knives started by accident, in a third world hellhole with air too thick to breathe, too thin to drink, and too stink-ass to sell as skunk bait. I spent six straight months greasy with bug killer. The officers tried to keep us busy, but one night a couple of lunkheads started throwing knives at the wall.

I watched, silently smug, waiting for the inevitable moment when someone would slice off a finger and win a valuable medical discharge. It'd be good for a laugh, wouldn't it? And I'd already read all these Patterson novels. After a couple weeks of lunkheads hitting every part of the wall except their makeshift target, though, I rolled my eyes too hard. My bunkmate, waiting for his turn to miss the inside barracks wall, noticed.

It was either throw a knife or catch a punch.

So I threw.

I didn't even walk up to the line. Just relaxed, looked at the target, let out a breath, and gave this silly cross-body toss from the far side of the barracks.

I hit the target dead-center.

Absolute, pure luck.

More luck: the knife stuck.

I sometimes wonder how my life would have been different if I'd said *Holy shit, I hit it.* Instead, as the other soldiers stared at the knife, at each other, and at me, I'd coolly nodded. "Gentlemen."

And went back to my bunk and my book.

I didn't dare laugh until I went out to piss.

Nobody asked me to throw again. A couple days later, they quit trying to lose fingers.

But the story got around: Joe Stabinowicz was a menace with a knife.

I have no idea who came up with the nickname Stabbity Joe.

But hitting that target felt... good.

So on those infrequent occasions when I had a little time and a little more privacy, I practiced. I turned out to be pretty good with knives. Guns, APCs, all those toys the service wanted me to be good with, nothing quite gave me that sense of clarity and precision as figuring out exactly how to put *this* particular knife through that *specific* two-inch gap into someone's pupil.

Eventually, the service and I disagreed on who should be in charge of my life. We parted ways, with prejudice.

Without charges, but with changes.

They'd taken a dumb-ass suburban teenager and abraded off all the civilization. They'd taught me not to mind killing. I don't like it, sure—it's messy. Especially with a knife.

It's not like I had any other job skills.

And isn't that the definition of a job? Getting paid for something you'd just as soon not do, but happen to be good at? A skilled man who gets in good with odd-job corporate mercenary brokers can make a good living. Knives are a specialty skill, yes. But when you need a knife fighter, nothing else suffices.

Life isn't all blood and guts, though. Freelancing had introduced me to Kit.

We'd shared half of a MRE in a burned-out building between Buraan and Bargaal. That's in Somalia. I'd bitten my hand to keep myself from belly-laughing at her desperation-driven jokes while those kids with knock-off AK-47s were trying to find us, and failed to hide my tears at her bravery. Certain we were going to die before dawn, we'd made love under smoke-veiled stars.

Somehow, we'd escaped that ruined city alive.

That one night hadn't changed my life.

It had changed my soul.

I hadn't minded killing people. But Kit's voice, her way of looking at things, even the way she smelled after a day of crawling for our lives through a city blitzed into a burned-out wreck, made me feel more alive than I ever had. Through her, I had the weird feeling that other people... mattered.

She carried empathy.

I'd caught it.

She made me want to be a better person.

And Kit, somehow, wanted me to stay with her.

Between beats of my heart, I discarded my career.

The world had other jobs for someone who didn't truly care about people. Used car sales. Real estate. Politics. I had lots of options. And Kit gave me this queasy feeling that maybe I could *learn* to care again. Maybe the service hadn't scraped off all my humanity.

I was horrified to learn how desperately I wanted that.

I'd escorted her safely back to her charity relief camp and hauled myself back to the coast to deliver the bag of flash drives that caused this whole mess. One last task before I returned to her.

An hour after I left, an explosion wiped out the whole relief team.

Letting someone taste that connection, that empathy, that completion of soul, and then ripping it away is one of the cruelest things you can do. It's even crueler than what happened to the three monsters who set that bomb.

Keeping them alive for a week didn't satisfy me. Nothing could.

But you can't stay in pain forever. Over the last five years, it's burned away.

Any compassion I had left burned away with it.

I kept freelancing because, why not? When I die, the Alfred Dow Somali Relief Fund gets a big chunk of change. Until that terminal date, I got to live a life a whole bunch of men envied. Fancy hotels where they called me sir. Well-dressed women who wanted stumpy, scarred-up me to undress them. Fast cars, international travel, intrigue and death and a black glory known only to those who order deniable blood on secret web sites.

I clawed enough pleasure from every day to bother to keep myself alive.

Kit never even told me her last name, but she showed me the man I could be. And left me the man I am.

Seeing Kit on that Florida rooftop deck hit my burned-out soul like a monsoon on the Sahara.

3

My heart thumped up my throat until it wedged there.

I couldn't breathe.

My legs, already locked around the coarse tree trunk supporting me, clamped tightly enough that the rough bark clawed into my thighs. My upper body went limp. If the climbing belt hadn't been supporting me, I would have flopped backwards and plunged headfirst into the swamp muck. I should have dropped the binoculars. They felt fused to my face, though.

The night, the countless bugs, my partner, the mission, all went away.

It couldn't be her.

But I hadn't seen her body.

I'd seen pieces of bodies, yes. Badly scorched and seared pieces.

I'd called out for her. I'd joined the locals searching the ruined camp. By the time I returned the locals had switched from searching to salvaging, but once they realized I didn't care about any of the loot, they let me get on with the search.

There was only one road in and out of that camp. I'd been on it.

She hadn't passed me the other way.

She was dead.

The woman on that rooftop deck couldn't be Kit.

My whole body shook, but my binoculars were utterly focused.

I knew that nose. The curve of that chin. One eye a little higher than the other.

Not possible.

If you live long enough, you'll meet the man who could be the twin of your father, or your best friend from high school. Or that weird moment when you come around a corner and see your reflection escaped from the mirror.

That's all this was.

This woman surrounded by a phalanx of bug zappers was Kit's impossible twin. That's all.

I fought to shake the feelings off. Tried to shift them towards rage. How dare Aspen do this to me? How *dare* she make me feel? The thoughts couldn't penetrate my shock, though.

My gaze couldn't leave the woman.

Suddenly, I hated her. Whoever she was. Kit already haunted my dreams. My nightmares. She shadowed any night I spent with another woman. I'd plant a knife in this woman's throat and one in her heart just for reminding me of what I'd lost.

The woman let out her breath and started to inhale.

Her right hand rose.

I went rigid.

She eased her index finger into that little divot above her lips and her middle finger to her nose as if dividing her breath, and inhaled.

My anger shattered into an impossible blend of certainty and confusion.

That gesture was burned into my shriveled heart. Every time Kit had needed to still herself, she'd done exactly that.

She couldn't be alive... but.

But.

Confusion paralyzed me. The bugs buzzing in my ears seemed a mile away. The tree trunk between my legs? Impossibly distant. My legs weren't part of me anymore. Dawson's shout could have come from the far side of the country or maybe the Moon.

Something clawed at the inside of my throat.

My body took over. I jackknifed in the climbing belt, coughing and choking, and something awful crunched between my teeth. A bug? I'd been so stunned I'd left my mouth hanging open, and one of those flying cockroaches wanted a taste of my extra minty Pepsodent. My ribs ached from not breathing and my mouth tasted of squashed crunchy insect and my heart was somehow still exploding inside my chest.

A bug between the teeth did what I couldn't do for myself, though. It forced my mind to reset.

Maybe the woman was Kit's twin sister.

Out of nine billion people, someone will look and act like Kit.

Perhaps the resemblance would dissolve up close.

The only way I could know which... was to get up close.

And I *had* to know.

I had to know this wasn't Kit.

My cough barely died when Dawson said in my earpiece, "Must have been one hell of a bug."

"Yeah," I wheezed.

"Have you ever even *been* to Florida before?"

"Har de har har." Sarcasm doesn't carry well over a throat mike. "Is it time?"

"I'm just waiting for you to finish your snack," Dawson said.

Our contract was clear: no survivors. I spat out shards of insect shell like fragments of my heart.

She couldn't be Kit.

But whoever she was, I'd make it quick.

For Kit.

4

My shallow-bottomed kayak slipped smoothly through the mucky water of the swamp channel. I dipped the paddle slowly and drew it lightly. The constant hum of the millions of insects would swallow slight noises, and the closer I could get to the house before the fun began, the better my chances.

All other things being equal, I'd rather not get shot.

My profession depended on speed. I'd left the clunky night vision headset back with Dawson. Wearing it weighed me down and limited my field of vision. Clunking around my neck, it complicated fighting. And I'd known more than one freelancer killed by strangulation on his own gear. I had a radio, a handgun most pros would dismiss as a toy, and a whole mess of knives.

Bugs battered my face and ears despite my greasy repellent. Heavy branches blocked out the night sky. If it wasn't for the illuminated house on its stilts and the massive trees around me, I might have been paddling through a black void.

The mercenaries guarding the house kept the teammate in front of them in sight as they circled the shore. They were young, though. The sort of kids who do two years in Infantry and think it makes them men to be reckoned with. All kinds of agencies will rent out a six-pack of Macho Idiots with a side of illegally modified AR-15s. You have to know the wrong people to hire bodyguards tough enough to stand against my type. Their camouflage long pants and shirts had to be sweltering in this heat.

As I approached I cut my paddle strokes down to two or three a minute. Move slow and silent, until you move fast and deadly. The kid coming up on this side of the house had the build of a dedicated bodybuilder. His skin gleamed through his open collar.

"Confirm no body armor," I muttered into my throat mike.

"Acknowledged," Dawson said in my ear.

Between paddle strokes, I tried to relax and breathe. This was the quiet before the avalanche. Once the action began it wouldn't stop.

I fought the urge to double-check my gear. I could feel the bandolier of throwing knives over my shoulder, and the other knives buckled at my waist. More knives at my ankles, and one in my collar. Soft-soled shoes. Plus the handgun at the small of my back.

Yes, I carry a gun, a little .32 automatic. I'm not an idiot. I keep my rep by stabbing anyone who can ruin it.

The deck is empty.

Whoever Kit's twin is, she's gone back inside. Even that army of bug zappers on the house's rooftop deck can't keep this infestation away.

Finding out who she was shouldn't slow me down more than a minute.

If everything went really badly, all I really needed was for her to speak. If she didn't have a British accent, it wasn't her.

I'd put her down quick. Nobody should suffer for picking the wrong friend, even if they died for it.

It'd be over, for both of us.

Another stroke of the paddle.

The kid playing mercenary moved with that slow, careful pace that said he had a whole bunch of walking to do tonight and that he didn't see any need to wear himself out before he was done. He'd done some sort of guard duty, then. And he had his rifle properly slung.

I coasted for a moment, then nudged the kayak forward.

The kid's face turned towards me.

He didn't see me. I was too deep in the darkness.

He looked like an alert animal. Not a predator. Maybe a meerkat. Something small and tasty.

I wanted to get closer before the shooting started. I tried to breathe more quietly and let the kayak glide to a halt in the nearly stagnant water.

He studied the darkness before shaking his head and taking another step.

Good.

He got most of the way around the house, letting another kid rotate into view behind him, before the sound of my paddle stirring water stopped him again. The kid's ears almost perked.

I rested the paddle across my knees.

This second alert in a minute had him spooked. I watched him juggle embarrassment against survival.

Don't worry, kid. Live another two minutes.

Instead, he reached for his shoulder mic.

Dawson was pretty good with a rifle. Not Marine sniper good, but with a stable tree to nest in, a good scope, and a flash suppressor, you'd never see him.

The kid dropped.

Two gunshots echoed through the night.

I paddled maniacally.

The other kid in view just stood there, his bug-catcher hanging open.

Two more gunshots, and he wasn't standing anymore.

Around a couple more trees and I'd have a clear run at the house.

Another kid came running up between the stilts, shouting, "Joe! Joe!"

Don't worry kid. Stabbity Joe is on his way.

That kid whirled with a bullet in the shoulder as two more gunshots split the night. Dawson followed up with two more, though. Another tombstone seed, planted.

That left one guard on the ground.

I rounded the last tree and dug deep with the paddle. The kayak shot forward.

Light flashed between the stilts. Something screeched past my ear.

I drew the paddle more fiercely and tried to pull my ears down between my buttocks.

Dawson's rifle barked twice, then twice again.

The last guard's rifle flashed in the darkness, but not at me.

Just short of the steep shore I skidded the kayak to the side, bringing the side up against the ragged chunks of torn-up concrete roadbed that reinforced the peninsula, and half-launched half-rolled up onto the land. One hand looped the kayak's line around a protruding lump of cement.

Dawson's gunfire split the buggy buzz. Twice.

The last guard screamed.

Dawson planted two more. The screaming stopped.

"Changing," Dawson said in my ear.

I clamped my hands over my ears, closed my eyes, turned away from the house, and crouched.

I didn't know who the Kit look-alike was. Or why she was there.

But I really hoped she didn't die before she answered my questions.

Before I could kill her.

5

People think of rocket launchers as monsters designed to take out tanks. They exist, yes. But rockets come in a whole bunch of different sizes.

Including some just right for blowing a door off its hinges.

Even with my ears covered, the sound rattled my skull. I could see the flash of light with my head turned away and eyes squeezed shut, as if it had traveled through my thick skull to reach my retinas. Before the echo died I rose, uncovered my head, and grabbed two knives from the bandolier.

You won't find these knives at Wal-Mart. This old lady in Tucson makes them for me out of recycled aeronautical steel. They're cut to fit my hands, perfectly balanced for the way I throw, and sharper than scalpels.

Holding them felt like coming home.

Dawson had put the rocket at the top of the door, shredding the upper half of it and knocking the bottom half wide open. Even at this distance, the smoke burned my sinuses.

I scrabbled forward, trampling the grass and charging up the clattering steel stairs to the door. The haze dissipated slowly in the still air, so I sucked a deep breath before launching myself into the cloud and through the door.

The rocket had inflicted a quarter million in furniture damage alone. I glimpsed cracked stone tabletops and shredded sybaritic leather couches, a busted-up television by IMAX and bar by Dionysus—

Past the sunken couch, a man in camo staggering to his feet, fumbling at his rifle.

I rotated my hips and twisted my right wrist, all in one synchronized motion.

I knew the blade would miss before it left my hand.

Even in the haze and heat I realized my body wasn't right. My heart should have pounded, but instead it jackhammered against my ribs. My throat felt too tight, my head pressurized, and despite holding my breath the stink of vaporized door seemed to burn in my lungs.

The mere sight of Kit's doppelganger had totally jacked me up.

No time for yelling at myself, though.

No time to cool myself down, either.

Recovering from the first throw let me launch my second knife.

The first blade sailed past the mercenary.

A heartbeat later, six inches of black steel buzzsawed across the man's neck.

If I was on my game, the blade would have planted in his voicebox—but no matter, he geysered blood and went down.

I'd already drawn two more knives.

I bolted forward before the man's body hit the ground, escaping the eye-burning noxious cloud so I could suck in something other than vaporized door, trying to loosen my shoulders so I could hit a target on the first throw.

Something moved to my right.

I jerked myself sideways.

The triple burst of gunfire stunned my ears, but the rounds punched the air behind me.

I spun on one foot, bringing the knife to bear, building momentum before I even saw—there, in the doorway, throw, throw!

But I didn't release.

My eyes needed a split second to register a young guy, teeth in the classic Rambo clench.

It wasn't Kit.

Kit's look-alike, that is.

Not her, so it made me angry.

My body was spinning so I finished the pivot, whirling in place and letting fly, recovering to rock back and launch the second blade, my empty hand already tugging another from the bandolier.

I didn't need it.

Rambo Junior had one of my blades in his chest and another through the side of his mouth. Nasty.

I've done worse.

But for some reason, I was shaking.

No, I knew the reason why my muscles quivered like a frightened bunny rabbit. My mind wasn't where it needed to be.

I'd quarter-second delayed throwing until I knew it wasn't Kit.

That familiar-looking woman was going to get me killed.

I'd get her to speak. Ask her name.

My brain would clear.

I could kill this foolish, illogical *hope* burning in my bones.

I would rather be dead inside than feel anything as horrible as hope.

"Main floor clear," I muttered into my throat mic.

"Good work," Dawson answered.

I felt a flash of gratitude that the guy hadn't seen my hesitation.

Shattered glass from the busted-up table crunched underfoot as I raced around to the bottom of the broad stairway leading to the upper floor. Stairways are a choke point, but at least this one rose to the end of a hallway rather than into open space. The smoke from the door was thinning and spreading, burning my throat with every breath. I tried to loosen my shoulders, ready to throw both knives.

Yes, I'd rather throw knives up a flight of stairs than use a handgun. I have a better chance of hitting.

The only real solution to charging a staircase? Speed.

Bolting around the corner, I saw her at the top of the stairs.

With a heavy handgun in both hands.

Aimed straight down at me.

I could have thrown right then.

I could have killed her dead.

But that face. It haunted my dreams. Dreams I loathed and welcomed.

I knew those shoulders.

The way she stood.

She didn't shoot, either.

Instead she said, "It *is* you."

Not just her body. Her mannerisms.

But her *voice*. Her inflection.

That British accent.

I froze. Knife in my hand.

She pulled the trigger.

6

I stood there like a carnival target, ready for any ten-year-old with a BB gun to pop me off.

Fortunately, she was already turning to run when she pulled the trigger.

Bullets sprayed, but all hit off to my left.

I'd only thought my brain was broken before. Kit had to be dead. All those hollow days since strobed through my shattered mind. The locals told me nobody survived—

Revelation cleared my brain like lightning.

Kit had been lying since the beginning.

She'd known about the bomb that destroyed her camp.

Those freedom fighters that had planted the device? They'd been guilty, sure... but they hadn't known where their orders came from.

She'd used me.

Used me to get to the camp, so she could blow it up.

My confused heartbreak came back together into a wholly different emotion: rage.

The one person I'd cared about since childhood had been a lie.

All that loss?

I'd mourned over something that had never existed.

With a few words—not even pretty words, just talking about how to survive and where to hide and wondering if the water pouring from that busted-off pipe was drinkable—with a few words, she'd convinced me to abandon my life.

I was just as much a sucker as any other guy.

Kit had betrayed my despair. And yes, it had been despair. I'd wallowed in despair until my soul had drowned.

Any secret hope I might have nurtured of feeling that way again?

Her appearance had scoured it out of me.

Once she died, once I recovered? Once I drank and screwed and ate and drank and screamed for a week, a month, a year?

I'd be peacefully dead inside again.

The way I had to be.

Part of me shrieked that Kit had been honest. That if I gave her a chance she'd explain, and it would all make sense. But I've been a freelancer for too long to believe that.

I needed an explanation, though.

I needed to know how she could destroy me that way. How many other people she'd destroyed the same way.

That meant I had to talk to her, just for a minute.

With a knife to her throat.

But my throat mike would pick up every word I said, and carry it to Dawson.

I trusted Dawson to carry out his part of the mission. I trusted him to carry me out on his back if I got hurt. But there's no way I would trust Dawson, or anyone, with anything so intimate as the short sharp conversation Kit and I were going to have.

I whispered, "Going up, going silent."

"Acknowledge," Dawson said in my earpiece.

My fingers found the wire connecting the transmitter taped to my chest to my throat mike. I deftly tugged it out of its socket.

I'm a professional. The opposition on one gig might be your ally on the next. You can't take losing personally. You can't do the victory dance in front of the other guy.

What Kit had done to me, though?

How much more personal can you get than slicing out someone's heart?

Time to return the favor.

7

When I was halfway up the wide mahogany stairs, the lights went out.

Perfect blackness swallowed everything.

I froze, knife in each hand.

Had Kit killed the power? She knew the house better than I did. Architect's blueprints don't compare to spending time in a place.

Or, I reminded myself, maybe Miss Aspen. The person who started all this, remember?

No way to tell, yet. I forced myself to stay in place while my eyes adjusted. Late at night, miles away from anyone out in this desolate swamp, light didn't even come in through the glass exterior walls. I couldn't even see the handrail an arm's reach away. The only way I knew which way the stairs ran was because I was facing up.

I'd gambled on leaving the night vision headset.

And I'd lost.

The loudest sound was my heart thudding in my ears.

The coppery stink of blood seeped through the explosive haze into my nose.

If Kit had night vision goggles, I was dead.

"You still with us, Stabbity Joe?" Dawson whispered in my earpiece.

He'd heard the gunfire. If I didn't answer soon, the clock would start ticking. Dawson was a professional. If he thought I'd gone down, well, there's no killing like overkill.

At the top of the stairs, dim lights faded on. Not enough to read by, but enough to show me the outline of the stairs. I forced myself to release an imprisoned breath. From the angle, the lights had to be close to the floor. Probably emergency lights. If I lived out in these boonies, I wouldn't want pitch blackness around the stairs.

Kit knew I was coming.

Feet to the far left of the treads, I bolted up the stairs.

The stairs opened onto a door-lined hallway. A pale white LED detachable emergency light hung from each power outlet. According to our intelligence, Miss Aspen used the room at the end of the hall, opposite the stairs, as an office.

Ears struggling to strain sound from the silence, I padded quickly down the hall. The soft soles of my shoes absorbed my steps.

The master bedroom door was pushed to, but not latched.

Kit might be behind this door.

The thought flooded me in a horrid toxic stew of hope and pain and despair and longing, so thick and strong that I had to stop for a breath to regain my poise. I couldn't throw a knife or even pull a trigger with trembling fingers.

Never again.

If anyone ever made me feel again, I'd cut their throat.

All I had to do was survive the next ten minutes. Or less, if Dawson started to worry.

But if I opened her office door, I'd almost certainly catch a gut full of lead.

Kit. The other side of that door. Ready to shoot me.

Think. I'd studied the blueprints.

I drew a deep breath and crept to the first door on the right. It was closed. I tucked the knife in my left hand back into my bandolier. Very, very quietly, I tested the knob.

It turned.

Hardly daring breathe, ignoring the sweat running down my forehead and the knot in my gut, I twisted the knob until it stopped.

I made myself take a deep breath.

When I saw anyone, I would throw a knife. No hesitation. None.

I flung the door open and hurtled myself through. Light spilled into the dark bedroom, silhouetting the low boxy shape of an orgy-sized bed and a looming dresser.

But I'd remembered the blueprints right. This bedroom had a second door, connected to the office.

A heavyset dark shape lurked in that doorway.

I want to say that I threw right away.

But my treacherous mind took in the crouching shape. The way light glinted off the long metal-and-plastic shape at its shoulder. He was poised to mow down anyone who came in the office door.

Something in me whispered that Kit had a handgun, not an AR-15.

The crouching man snarled an obscenity and tried to whirl his rifle towards me.

I launched a knife at his gut.

The rifle went off.

Three rapid bangs shattered the quiet.

I launched the second knife just as something slashed through my shoulder.

I couldn't die then. Not without answers.

The pain hit.

8

When people are still trying to kill you, you can't stop to inspect your wounds.

My right shoulder burned. So did the bicep.

But my fingers could still clench. Good enough for now.

Put any other shooters down. Drop Miss Aspen.

Thirty vital seconds with Kit.

Then tie off the wound.

The ranking surprised me. Was I willing to risk exsanguination to grill Kit?

Apparently I was. And I didn't have time to argue with me.

My right arm wasn't going to be throwing any knives, though. I gritted my teeth to tug my handgun out of its holster. Hugging my forearm against my ribs gave me enough support to hold the weapon steady. My other hand tugged a knife from my bandolier, then I was stepping around the mercenary's body.

No time to waste bracing myself.

I almost leaped through the doorway.

The office was sybaritic even by my standards, even illuminated by those weak LED emergency lights near the floor. A U-shaped desk supported gigantic but sleek monitors, partially hidden by two cheap briefcases. The couch and chairs looked like they'd suck you down and never let you leave.

More magnificent than that imagined view, though?

Kit.

She stood before the desk, legs spread, automatic in a text-book two-handed grip. She'd never appear on the cover of *Sports Illustrated*, but seeing her alive almost stopped my hammering heart.

Those eyes glaring at me?

She was too far away, the lighting all wrong, but somehow I could see their rich brown.

I was still moving, my feet propelling me sideways as I turned, bringing the gun to bear, turning so I could throw but too slow, way too slow, the pain in my shoulder deepening and blending with that in my bicep, growing hotter with each beat of my heart but not cold, not yet, wrenching my gun hand around but I can't make myself turn quickly enough to get a line on Kit and tell her to freeze—

"Hold it!" Kit shouted.

For a second, she didn't shoot.

It was long enough.

My knife was ready to throw.

My handgun, lined up for the shot.

At that distance, I couldn't miss. A knife in Kit's gut, and she'd still be able to talk. For long enough, at least.

You want to talk about treachery?

My knife arm refused to let fly.

9

Illuminated only by lights shining up from below, separated by fifteen feet of plush carpeting, Kit and I stared at each other.

She was beautiful. Smudged and smoke-stained, hair disar-rayed, blood trickling from a nostril, seeing her made my blood sizzle in my veins. Her every curve was perfect for me—you might not think so, but you're free to be wrong. She was proud and defiant, even in a bomb-tattered green pantsuit.

With my knife ready to throw, I had a sudden mental flash of ripping that ruined suit off of her. Seizing her in my arms. Being seized back. Kissing her so fiercely that my head whirls.

I cursed myself for ten types of screaming idiot.

Why didn't she shoot me?

I needed to know how she could use me like that. How she could give me that soul-destroying dose of compassion, and rip it away right when I realized I wanted it.

But somehow, I couldn't get my mouth to form the words.

Kit spoke first. "Why did you do it?"

Her accent was sexy as hell. I needed to ignore it. "Because I'm paid to." Why else would I kill those men?

"I thought we had something."

"I didn't even know you were here." The gun quivered in my hand.

"I'm certain you did not." Kit raised her voice. "Because you thought you killed me!"

Wait—what?

I opened my mouth but she shouted "Don't even try that with me. Don't you even try, Mister Stabbity Joe. That's what they call you, isn't it? You didn't find me in that bombed-out doctor's office. You picked me up there. You *used* me. You used me to get back into my camp. You left that bomb and walked away. If I hadn't been down by the well, you would have killed me too."

The heat in my injured arm and shoulder couldn't stand against the cold that flashed through me. I couldn't breathe. My gun was in my hand. My finger inside the trigger guard. Even in the weird upside-down lighting, the bore of her gun looked big enough to swallow my head, and I still couldn't fire.

Kit might not have been a killer. Not like me.

But anyone with that much rage coloring their face, that much fury in their voice? They're ready to kill.

My brain; knows she's lying.

She's playing me.

Again.

Looking at her? Face-to-face?

My brain doesn't let me do the right thing.

Staring at Kit's tortured face I said, "I don't want any misunderstandings." I drew a shaky breath. "I'm dropping my weapons."

Kit didn't flinch.

I opened my hands.

A dull thud as my gun hit the carpet.

The knife dropped silently.

Her face was as open as a brick wall.

I fought for words. "I didn't plant that bomb. When I came back, the camp was gone. That blast didn't just take you away from me. It took away…" My brain grasped for what to say next—then it was there, spilling out of me, coming from somewhere deep inside. "When I lost you, I lost everything worth living for. My heart died with you. Seeing you now? Truth is, if I had to choose between living without you and you shooting me?" The words hurt as they burst out but I couldn't stop, I couldn't stop anything. "Put a bullet in my chest, because I'm already dead and I can't stand pretending I'm not any more."

My mouth hung open.

I think I'd always known that. But hearing myself say it made it real.

Kit's gun shook.

Words aren't much good.

She was psyching herself up to pull the trigger.

Kit said, "Jackie. You can come out now."

10

My heart exploded. Again.

She'd played me. Again.

I'd been suckered in.

Again.

And I'd known it.

I was going to kill her.

Jackie Aspen stepped out of the attached bath, perfectly un-mussed but with the expression of a piglet who's wandered into the Big Bad Wolf convention. Even if she lived through the night, her career in corporate espionage was finished.

I'd seen flung bricks that looked kinder than Kit. She had her finger resting right on the trigger of her gun. "Joe," she said. "Back up. Further. Keep your hands still and open. Right up against the wall. Now move left. Right in the corner."

I glared hot death at the woman who'd destroyed me.

But obeyed.

"Jackie," Kit said. "Grab his gun. From the floor."

Aspen glanced between the two of us.

I tried to will her to death, too.

"Quickly, now!" Kit barked.

Aspen scuttled forward, crouching to grab my discarded hand-gun by the barrel.

Kit smoothly shifted her gun to a single hand and held out the other. "Here."

Aspen scurried back, offering Kit the gun with a worried smile.

"Good." Kit took the gun in her left hand. "Get back a bit."

Aspen stepped back from the treacherous, deceitful, two-pistoled woman who'd destroyed me.

Giving Kit just enough room to raise my gun and put a bullet into Aspen's forehead.

||

I should have moved, but the sight of my target's body crumbling like a sack of bricks left me stunned. In that half-second of paralysis, Kit had the gun—my gun—aimed back at me.

That'll teach me to carry a gun.

"I was empty," Kit said.

I'd been suckered with an empty gun?

I swallowed. Stuck in the corner, with my wounded shoulder oozing weakness into me, there's no way I could close the distance between Kit and I before she'd shoot me.

A quick move would have confused the issue. I could have grabbed a knife from my bandolier. Plant it in her throat.

My hands wouldn't move.

I'd spoken the truth. I'd rather swallow a bullet than kill Kit.

The thought… relieved me.

"I found the people who planted the bomb," I said.

Her chin tightened. "What happened?"

"They died." My lips were dry. I tried to lick them, with my parched tongue. "Bad. And slow."

Her shoulders loosened, just a touch.

We looked at each other.

"What now?" I said.

The gun wobbled in her hand.

With a hiss, she lowered it.

I didn't move.

"You hurt me." Kit shook her head. "You hurt me. And you being gone kept hurting."

"You haunted me," I said. "Every day without you was forever."

"It really wasn't you?" she said.

"If I'm lying, I'm dying." My nod made my brain wobble in my skull. "No, I've been shot. I might be dying anyway."

She stepped towards me.

The motion casts light into my heart, but I held up my good hand. "No—don't!"

She stopped, puzzled.

"I have a partner outside," I said. "The mission is, nobody walks away."

Kit grimaced. "My job was to get the auction winner, then put Aspen and the buyer down." She glanced at Aspen's cooling body. "Two months of infiltration, shot to hell. By *you*."

My laughter felt wonderful, despite the pain in my shoulder. "When did you start doing this?"

She rolled her eyes. "Just after some charming rogue told me what he really did for a living, and promptly tried to kill me."

Her words sobered me. "It wasn't… I didn't…"

"I believe you." Kit bared her teeth. "But it's been years. It's not that easy."

Her words shuttered the light in my heart.

Five years was a long time.

And five years of hate is a lot of hate.

I closed my eyes. "I get it." My mouth was impossibly dry now. I hadn't been hit anywhere vital or I'd be long dead, but a slow bleed is just as deadly.

But there was one last thing I could do.

"My partner's outside," I said. "If I don't come out, he's going to put an antitank rocket right into this place."

"Then let's go."

"No." The words tasted bitter. "The job is, I take those briefcases and everyone dies. You lay low. Give me... an hour. Dawson'll get me out as fast as he can. Oh, and don't take the road. He put grenade drones on it."

She nodded. "Can you make it?"

"I get to the kayak, I'll be fine." The rage still filled Kit's face... but it wasn't complete. There was something else there.

I took a final chance.

"Listen," I said. "Next month... I'm going to be up in, uh, let's say Chicago. I have a standing reservation at the Five Seasons. I'll be there a couple weeks. Take in some shows. Eat some really good food." I swallowed. "I won't be wearing a bulletproof vest."

"And what am I supposed to make of that?" she demanded.

I gave a one-shoulder shrug. "Whatever you want. But if I don't get out, we're gonna get blown up."

Kit licked her lips. She's still livid.

I couldn't blame her. First I destroyed her relief camp. Then I wrecked her job.

She lunged for me.

I didn't have time to brace.

She pressed up tight against me, hitting my hurt arm too hard but her lips on mine wash all that away. The sweet taste of her breath mingles with the dried blood from her nosebleed, and I don't care, it's Kit and gunshot or not I'm more alive than I've been in years.

She broke the kiss too soon. "You need to go," she breathed into my mouth.

"Stop by if you like." The words stabbed my heart.

Before I could think, I ripped my heart in half and stagger for the door.

Maybe she'd hire Dawson to put a bullet in me from a hundred yards away.

If she was truly angry, though? If she wanted to hurt me?

She'd let me sit in Chicago and wait.

I'd wait there forever.

I'd checked the briefcases and reached the door when Kit said, "Hey, Joe?"

If I look back? If I see her again?

I'll never leave. Dawson will blow us to cinders.

My heat is too full for me to form words.

I can't turn.

But I stop walking.

The love of my life says, "I'd rather see Chicago with you than walk around dead anywhere else."

Shattered Canvas

Yesterday, my best friend asked me to kill her.

Claire didn't put it that way, of course. I mean, if she needed someone to kill her I'd be on the shortlist of people she asked. She knows that if terminal cancer came for her I'd sadly but willingly help her to the garage, start the engine, crank some Legendary Pink Dots on the stereo, and close the door behind me as I left. I would've married her ten years ago, but even while we were kids I understood that she just didn't like boys that way. But together we'd repelled the neighborhood bully using the only language he understood, and that forms a bond you can't break even over decades. She understands people without them saying a word. It's part of what makes her a fantastic therapist.

And eventually I'd found my brilliant, beautiful Olivia — not that that had worked out well, but that wreck wasn't Claire's fault.

My other friends from those days have all faded, but even when life goes insane Claire and I still meet for breakfast every Thursday morning before work.

I look forward to those breakfasts in a way I've never explained to anyone. Claire can't fill that foolish, senseless, *stupid* gap that opened in my soul three years ago, but her company eases the silent ache.

Motor City Brew is a tiny place, wedged into an irregular gap between three 19th-century buildings in downtown Detroit. One wall is ancient red brick, recently sandblasted and scrubbed to expose bright red clay. Another is dark wood planks, exactly like the building next door. I'm pretty sure that the walls belong to the surrounding buildings, and that someone just put a roof over the space and called it done. But the thickly padded blue vinyl chairs invite you to sink into them, and the delicious smell of roasting coffee saturates the air, and the morning business-suit-drone crowd is too busy doing the grab-and-dash to intrude.

I can't stand coffee, but their tea is also excellent. And not only does MCB bake their own scones from scratch, they get real British-style clotted cream from I don't know where.

My first clue that something had happened came when I strolled in the door at 7 AM to find Claire had actually beat me there. She seemed to seethe in her seat, a nervous excitement that made her even more animated than usual. She'd already bought my tea and scone, so I hurried over and sank into my usual seat opposite her.

"I've got to tell you." Claire's words escaped as if pressurized.

I opened my mouth to say something. Without my morning tea, my brain felt too sludgy to even speculate.

She erupted with "I'm getting married!"

A hint of loss twinged in my heart, followed by a flash of embarrassment at my own selfishness and a flood of sincere happiness, mixed with just a little jealousy. "That's great! Did Temp ask you, or did you ask her?"

"We sorta asked each other." Her hands bounced around with every word. "It was a couple days ago, but I wanted to tell you in person. Hell, we've waited to post it on Facebook until I told you."

Friendship is an asymmetric thing. Just because Claire is my best friend doesn't mean that I'm necessarily hers. That she held silent until she could tell me face-to-face gave me this unexpected soppy feeling. I had to blink away a couple of tears before anyone noticed. "Oh, you didn't have to do that!"

She shrugged. "After all we've been through?"

My feelings were all tangled. I was happy for her, but part of me wondered if this friendship was going to fade too. That's what happens. People get married and move on. I managed to say "So when's the big day? Do you need any help paying for things? And congratulations. Temp has quite a catch."

Claire laughed. "I'm going to have to come up with a new name for her. Temperance is a mouthful, but she's sure not 'temp' anymore."

I couldn't help noticing that the chubby guy behind the counter was paying too much attention to us and not enough to his increasingly annoyed line of customers. I couldn't really blame him — it's not every day you hear a woman tell a male friend she's getting married. He probably thinks we both bat for the other team. "You'll work it out."

Claire's smile was radiant. "We will. And no, we're doing a small ceremony out at the farm next month, so it'll be cheap. We want to save our money for a house, and Temp's car is going to collapse into rust and plastic any day now. But there are a couple things you could do for me, if you would."

I gathered myself enough to pluck my mug of tea from the table. Yes, Motor City Brew uses real stoneware cups, ancient things, probably salvaged from some derelict building. The aroma of fresh-brewed black tea, with just a hint of real black currant, filled my nose. "Name it."

"First, I need you to be my maid of honor."

I grinned. "We're gonna have a helluva time finding a dress."

Claire pointed two fingers at me. "I know just the place. I'm thinking lace ballroom gown." She leaned in. "With a cummerbund, to make it manly."

I knew she was joking, but even if she wasn't I'd probably do it for her. "Then I'm in. What else?"

Her face grew intent. "I want you to paint our portrait."

She had no idea that she'd asked me to murder her.

✻

If my brain had been running more quickly, if I'd had my morning caffeine, I might have had a better answer. I might have found a way to tell Claire *no* without hurting her feelings. I could have deflected her, or changed the subject, or — or anything.

Instead, I'd hidden my shock and horror.

I'd forged a smile.

I know it looked fake, but there's nothing as distractible as a person happily announcing their wedding. Claire might have an uncanny sense of what people felt, but her pre-marital bliss worked in my favor.

And, damn me all to hell, my mouth had said, "I'll see what I can do."

Because that's what I always tell Claire.

Then I make it happen.

It would mean so much to us, she'd said. *To me.*

She's always been there for me.

I can do nothing less for her.

My studio's a converted loft in one of those early 20th century buildings that made people call Detroit the Paris of the Midwest. The north wall is all windows, and I pay extra rent to have them cleaned every week. The sunlight is almost luscious. My industrial graphic design consulting business has grown so much that

I've been forced to control my working hours by raising my rates to a truly ridiculous level. Yes, people might say that I've sold out, but industrial art is harmless. It's for everyone, so it's not for anyone. I can design billboards and make cars look alluring one after the other, and nobody will get hurt.

And it lets me pay for this fantastic space. I have the most luxurious desk you can imagine, built custom just for me, and a chair comfortable enough to serve as an acceleration couch on the Space Shuttle. If I have to do paperwork, I at least want to be comfortable. There's half a dozen free-standing cork boards, each as tall as I am and wider than my spread arms, mounted on wheels so I can arrange them as needed. Each has bits and pieces of a client's project thumbtacked to them, but I've rolled them all against the back wall where they hide the massive, framed prints of my most successful commercial work.

I know perfectly well I'm not doing any client work today. My creative brain has been in a complete logjam since Claire asked me for a portrait as her wedding present. Yesterday, rather than work, I compared seven months of credit card statements to the scanned receipts, filled out the corporate meeting book, and talked to the cable company about adding a landline to this place.

Heck, I even called my mother — *that's* how desperate I was to avoid being creative.

I want you to paint our portrait.

The whole problem is ridiculous.

My entire brain knows it makes no sense.

But my soul vehemently disagrees. And it's my soul that paints.

Anyone who walks into my loft knows I paint. My original oils cover the back wall, carefully arranged in a spectrum: red tones on the left, blue on the right, darker near the ceiling and pale near the floor. The canvases are all different sizes, ranging from a meticulous study of the Ambassador Bridge no larger than a postcard up to the three-feet-by-five study of the Fourth of July picnickers out on Belle Isle.

The whole loft smells of oil paint and turpentine, with an underlying hint of the ancient machines that this space had been built for. My easel stands under the windows, at precisely the spot with the best lighting, right next to an incredibly sturdy wooden table my younger self rescued from the scrap heap to use for brushes and paint and scrapers and all the other paraphernalia. Every client that walked into here couldn't help noticing that I was a real artist, that I did real paintings, and that I'd honed my craft over my life. A few prospective clients made a point of not mentioning my canvases, visibly dismissing my skill in an effort to drag my prices down. The others universally declared that my work should be hanging in galleries or museums, or that they'd better hire me to design their ad or mural or whatever while they still could.

A few years ago, I'd worried about running out of space to hang my canvases. I could only fit a dozen more without a degree of cramming that would harm the presentation.

That wasn't an issue anymore.

Maybe if I hadn't been so tight with my work, none of this would have happened. But I'd had the idea early on that I would be a Big Artist, that my work would be valuable, and I didn't want a bunch of juvenilia cluttering up my reputation.

Really, the only way I would create a painting for someone, the only way I'd offer a person a canvas, was if I loved them.

Part of me insisted I would have been better off giving them the cheapest, cheesiest Van Gogh I could find.

Oh, I still painted — if you cut off my arms, I'd learn to hold the brush in my toes. Once I finished a work, once it had dried and cured, I'd take a moment to study it. What had I learned? What could I have done better? The technique that I'd set out to practice, how had I done?

Once I'd learned everything I could, however...

One of the first skills an artist learns is cleaning canvas. I started with the scraper, transforming shade and color into innumerable meaningless, harmless flakes. They stuck to my arms, my hands, even my face. I keep my hair short, but somehow powdered paint still fills it. Once I removed everything that will come off without damaging the canvas, paint thinner and sandpaper strips off the rest.

Yes, I could afford a new canvas every time. But throwing them away after only one painting feels wasteful.

And someone might find a discarded painting. I can't chance that.

No, wait — those flakes aren't harmless. They're kind of slippery on the tile floor. I keep an industrial shopvac at hand to make sure I get every dot off of the cool gray floor.

Destroying my paintings hurts less than the alternatives. My heart knows that if I stopped painting, pretty soon I'd be chilling behind the wheel of a running car in a closed garage. Again.

And my soul insists that my art is too dangerous to exist.

One day I'd be tempted to give it away.

When my wife Olivia and I'd rented this place, the realtor had taken pride in pointing out the small but immaculate private bathroom, complete with shower stall. I'd laughed and said I would never need it. Olivia had smacked my arm and told me that I better not come home stinking of paint thinner, but she'd been smiling.

Not many people can handle being married to an artist. We're moody. Most people understand what drives us, but they don't understand how *hard* we're driven.

Olivia not only accepted that, she loved me for it.

It's been years that she's been gone, but I still have to close my eyes for a moment and breathe deeply through my nose to still myself.

When I open my eyes, that infernal blank canvas is still staring at me.

I haven't opened any paint. I haven't chosen any brushes.

The rack beneath the window has a canvas this size that's only had two paintings on it. I remember them both: a still life of corroded transmission parts that I'd successfully imbued with nearly organic life, and a view of the uninhabited Huron Metropark Beach last fall that I'd tried less successfully to saturate with subtle, non-Euclidean menace.

Photorealistic surrealism is a lot harder than you'd think.

But Claire deserved a virgin canvas.

I'd thought that perhaps I could fool myself. But my soul knew damned well that if I was breaking out a new canvas, this was a special painting. My creativity refused to stir.

I stared hollowly at the white void for long minutes, mind vacant, until I finally had to turn away and scream obscenities at the top of my voice.

This whole problem was nothing but chance.

I couldn't think of anything to do but walk through it again.

Maybe this time, my soul would understand.

✳

The first Painting of Death is one foot square, mostly in reds and oranges and yellows. It shows a young man with his back against a cinderblock wall, intent on a book, one sneakered foot raised to rest a sole against the concrete, against a city backdrop.

Dion Jarvis and I had been students together at the Center for Creative Studies, right here in Detroit. We'd both had an interest in Surrealism strong enough to tonk off some of our professors. I've always had a sense that the world is not what it appears and that if we look closely enough, with enough concentration, it will dissolve around us. Dion thought that people never looked that closely, but that great art could break people's self-imposed limitations and open their minds. We both had a point, sure—but which of us was *more* right? We'd taken our debate with full-on teenage intensity, both certain that we'd unlocked the Secret of Great Art.

Arguing art over drinks is fun.

But the best artistic argument is art itself.

That picture was of Dion. I'd painted it for Dion, to try to prove my point in one of our interminable but friendly philosophical wrestling matches.

It hung near the ceiling, over to the right, amidst the other pieces in similar tones. Looking at it now, I remembered that I'd wanted to make it bigger, but Dion lived in a rented room about the size of a shoebox. I'd told myself that a larger painting would be the same as shouting an argument — it might not make your point wrong, but it would make you more annoying. I'd spent days cramming everything I wanted into that tiny square.

The painting looked normal enough at first, even uninspired. Back then, I'd felt a burning rush of originality every time I picked up a brush, whether I deserved it or not. There's no drug as powerful or as exhilarating as youthful confidence. Looking back on it with another fifteen years of experience, I could see countless mistakes. The strangeness I'd tried so hard to evoke was way too diffuse. A younger version of me had painted this, and even I had to study the work closely to see what he'd been trying to achieve.

The painted Dion doesn't lean against the wall. He's part of the wall, an extrusion, a living being born of brick. That raised foot sitting almost flat against the cinderblock? It's part of the wall too, still connected by a tiny twig — human fruit not quite ripe enough to fall free. If you look close enough, the book is cased in rind, supported by tiny tendrils growing from Dion's hands.

The cityscape beyond Dion has a separate dysfunction. A more experienced artist would have continued the organic, vegetative theme. Instead, Younger Me had given the buildings an animal nature. Those great skyscrapers aren't concrete, but covered in fine fur. I'd needed a magnifying glass to fill in people on the distant street, behind Dion, and if you brought your own you could see that those people had too many or too few limbs to be human.

I peered closely at the red-stained clouds and made out the minuscule words, composed of characters I'd pillaged from the dead alphabets of forgotten languages. Younger Me had known what each of those characters was, and had this idea of adopting them throughout all his artwork. Some people might call that pretentious, but a working artist would recognize it as one of the many ideas we pick up, play with, and drop back into the slurry of our subconscious.

I had worked on that painting for three days while I was home over Thanksgiving break, the only time I felt confident I'd be able to conceal the work in progress. Mom had been annoyed, but I'd passed the project off as homework.

Dion had looked touched when I presented him with his portrait, but then he looked more closely and puffed up with friendly belligerence. "This is how you want to settle this?" he'd laughed. "Dude, just you wait until this weekend, I'm going to show you what *real* art is like."

Two days later, Dion slashed his wrists.

I'd known he was bipolar. Dion's temper was mercurial, constantly weaving between creative mania and despondency. I'd thought that made him pretty much like any other artist, except at a higher volume.

The funeral changed my mind.

Claire had come to the funeral with me.

His father found my signature on the back of the painting, and asked if I wanted it back. Dion had told me many times that his dad supported him, but really didn't get art, so I said yes.

Claire had to drive me home, painting clutched in my arms.

Studying the painting now made my chest tighten as if my asthma had returned. I had to blink away a tear. It had been over ten years, but studying my early brushwork brought Dion's loss crashing back onto me. I suspected that fifty years from now, the sight of this scrap of canvas would rip a scab off my heart.

Maybe I should play with dead alphabets again.

No. That was my brain, trying to distract me.

I had painted this for a friend. Someone I loved like a brother, with the irrational sort of friendship that you form when you first head out into the world and you're responsible for yourself, alone except for all the other minnows swimming with you, knowing that the pike are going to snap a whole bunch of you up but not you, you and your posse are going to make it. I had created this painting with a glad heart — with a little bit of *I'm gonna show you*, sure, because nineteen-year-olds are little shits, but with a glad heart.

I hadn't painted it to get Dion killed.

When I carefully painted every tiny figure, every strand of hair, every twig, I had no idea I was cursed.

"This is not a curse," I growled.

My voice faded into the vastness of the loft, the hollow space swallowing my words.

✳

The second Painting of Death is in the middle of my wall of canvases, at a comfortable eye height, right where I can clasp my hands behind my back as I study it. It's modestly large canvas, two feet by three, in bright, sunny colors. It's one of my few pieces without even a hint of surrealism.

And it's the only Painting of Death without a human figure.

I'd met Bryce when I was interning with a big advertising firm, and we'd hit it off almost immediately. We both loved the Detroit Tigers and loathed the Lions — although it's easy to detest a team with such an impressive multi-season string of losses. But we had the same sense of humor, and we both loved action movies so long as they had some kind of brain behind the explosions. Working late one night, I'd caught him listening to the Birthday Massacre album that had just been released that day. That sealed our friendship.

Bryce was twenty years older than me, and had been an ad man since he graduated from college back in the dark days before the Internet. I couldn't figure out why he wasn't married, or at least seeing someone, but one night we'd gone out to the bar to watch the Red Wings smash the Leafs' hopes of a championship. After a couple beers he'd admitted that he just wasn't interested in people that way, men or women.

That revelation changed our friendship. A twenty-two-year-old man looking for a woman to care about is absolute crap at the dating scene. Bryce had dated. He dated a lot, thinking that if he found the right person he'd actually be attracted to them. That's what happens, right? He'd been in his thirties before he found out that there were other people like him, and that it would be okay for him to end his pointless quest for The One and instead enjoy life.

But he was thrilled to share his experience with me. *No, don't talk to that girl, she's out to have a good time on her own. Nothing good comes out of spilling a drink on someone. Talk with her for five minutes, and if you have to work to keep the conversation going, she's not for you.* Once he realized that I wasn't going to belittle him for not jumping in himself, he'd even join in with a little bit of *yes, that is certainly a fine-looking lady. You should say hello.*

He had a fine aesthetic sense, just not the same sort of hormones.

Bryce had taught me how to talk to Olivia. And I had agonized for weeks on how to thank him. You don't buy a Tigers jersey for the guy who helps you meet the woman you want to marry.

But Bryce had a Golden Retriever that he loved more than anything, a daft animal that he'd named Einstein. I'd thought he'd meant it as a joke, but I guess he'd named the dog after a retriever in some old book. When the company sent Bryce to Chicago for a week to romance a client, he hired me to look after Einstein. I'm sure he expected "looking after" to include walks and feeding and a bit of toss-the-ball.

Maybe "paint a hyper-realistic portrait of my dog" wasn't on Bryce's list, but it was on mine.

Olivia had not only understood, she'd encouraged me. She'd spent the evenings with me, alternating between knitting a sweater for her mom and encouraging Einstein to sit still so I could capture his every detail.

Silly dog jumped in surprise every time he farted.

Most misnamed critter in history.

For five days I searched clip art sites all day long, gathering seeds for the overpaid, unimaginative "graphic artists" I interned for, then I spent long hours of the evening trying to reincarnate Einstein in two dimensions.

That last night, Olivia looked over my shoulder and said, "That's him."

I captured Einstein sitting at the end of the forbidden couch, his chin resting on the armrest. His ears have a little perk—not as if he's alarmed, but just enough to hint that he's on watch for his family. His fur is countless tiny brush strokes, each a slightly different hue of gold, fading to almost white around the muzzle and deepening to brown along his hips and belly. Einstein's tail lays with the tip of the tail raised, not actively wagging but showing his innate perkiness, the dangling fur fading to near translucency as it fluffs out.

Somehow, I managed to capture the placid joy in his eyes.

When Bryce dragged himself home Saturday morning, Olivia and I had met him in his driveway. I could tell the week had worn through his spirits. The struggle between "rudely telling us to go away" and "being gracious to the damn kids" flickered across his face.

Grace won out.

Barely.

Olivia grabbed the door. "We laid in a couple supplies for you, so you don't have to go out."

I grabbed his suitcase and escorted him in.

"I hope it was you," Bryce said to Olivia. "This young man can't—"

He saw the painting and stopped so quick he wobbled on his feet.

His eyebrows went up.

His head tilted, just a little, and one side of his mouth quirked.

"You son of a bitch," Bryce whispered.

I couldn't breathe.

"You…" Bryce shook his head. "You've…"

Einstein ruined my moment by rocketing out of the kitchen and crashing full-tilt into Bryce's knees. Bryce went down like a tower of children's blocks, cursing and laughing and grabbing at Einstein's massive ruff.

I was cursing too, but inside. Olivia laughed so hard she had to grab the back of a chair for support.

"Okay!" Bryce gasped. "Let me up, you maniac."

I reached a hand down to help Bryce up.

He surprised me by seizing me in a massive bear hug, pounding on my back. "Perfect," he said in my ear, voice shaky. "God in Heaven, it's absolutely perfect. That's him, that's totally him."

The words lit a fire in my heart.

"Least I could do," I managed.

I'd brought joy to a friend who'd changed my life.

And maybe my art was getting good.

Twenty-five days later, as Bryce and Einstein were walking along Woodward Avenue, Einstein lunged after a squirrel. His leash snapped.

Dog and vermin bolted into the path of an oncoming truck.

Bryce lunged after them.

Einstein lived.

Another painting came home with me.

✳

The third Painting of Death no longer exists, except etched on my heart.

And there it's going to stay.

If I'd been more thoughtful, paid more attention, I would have known better than to paint it. I'd given away two paintings as heartfelt gifts. Two people had died.

But it's not enemy action until three.

And we were getting married.

Olivia and I had spent hours talking about our lives together. Where we wanted to go, how we wanted to live, where we wanted to end.

I painted our lives together.

At first glance it was two old folks sitting in a glider, on a cabin porch. The stark shadows show that it's summer afternoon. Her hair is white. He has no teeth. You can see the comfortable silence between them. They've said everything. Shared everything.

It's their cabin. You can tell because there's a photo hanging on the wall, them and their four grown children, with *their* spouses and another generation at their feet. It's a small photo so the faces don't show up well, but you can see the smiles.

And because I was the one who'd painted it, I hid details everywhere. Olivia's Nobel Prize in Mathematics was a coaster. The words for happiness and success in a dozen different languages, concealed in scattered leaves and the rings left on the top of the hand-carved table next to the glider and in the condensation trickling down the glass.

There's only one truly surreal detail in the whole painting.

The two people aren't holding hands. They've grown together. They're literally *one*.

It's a picture of two people that won at life and are content to ride out the last few years together.

I put the last paint on the canvas at four PM the day before we married, only an hour before our rehearsal dinner. We'd planned a civil ceremony, so dinner was just "a few close friends coming over to the condo for pad Thai, good beer, and Cards Against Humanity." I'd wanted to get it framed before tonight, but this didn't need a big box store frame; it needed something custom. So I loaded it in the car and raced home.

I opened the front door to find Olivia glaring, backed up by five of our close friends. "You're late? Tonight?"

"I'm sorry." I remained in the doorway. "Trouble at the studio."

She waved a hand. "I know you're artistic, but this is our wedding. You need to be on time."

"I was almost out of time," I said.

"I was about to come down and get you."

Right then is when a spouse should apologize. Instead I said, "This couldn't wait."

Olivia crossed her arms. "What was so important? And come in, you're letting the bugs in."

Behind her, Claire and her date were giving me a truly impressive Death Glare.

"Listen." I stayed in the doorway. "Once we're married, everything that's mine is yours. I know, a husband can give his wife a gift, sure, but it's not the same thing."

Her scowl softened, just a little.

"If I wanted to give you something, truly give it to you as something from me to you, not as a part of *us*, it had to be by today."

I reached around the doorframe and hauled the painting in.

Olivia caught the whole picture, and everything it meant, in a glance.

Her scowl shattered into tears.

I had to show it to everyone. Then Olivia had to show it to everyone. I knew she'd find the ancient Sanskrit for *lots of really good sex* along the bottom of one of the logs, disguised as wood worm tracks, but I hadn't expected her to find it so quickly. Or for her to tell everyone. Or to post it on Twitter.

The pad Thai sat neglected long enough that we had to nuke it.

When we returned from our honeymoon, I took the canvas to the best frame shop in Detroit. Three weeks later, she stopped on the way home from lecturing at the university to pick it up.

When that monster flipped his testosteronemobile on top of Olivia's little car, the painting burned just like she did.

❋

I'd needed three lessons to learn that my art kills.

I can't give it up. I can't stop painting.

But of all people: *Claire.*

Claire held me together when Dion killed himself. When Bryce died, she helped Olivia load Einstein's portrait in the car.

I want to say she's never asked me for anything, but that's not true. We've been friends since we could walk. She's asked me for a bunch of things, all the sorts of stuff a friend can give.

And when she'd heard about Olivia, she'd raced to the condo. She's the one who heard my car running behind a closed garage door.

Claire came to visit me in hospital psych lockup. I asked her why she'd come to the condo. She said *I knew what you would do.*

I needed weeks to forgive her for rescuing me.

And I never told her—or anyone—why.

Yes, Olivia was reason enough.

But I've spent my life with my art.

And if I give someone my art, if I show them my truest heart, I kill them.

I whirl from Einstein's painting and storm over to the virgin canvas, intending to rip it from the easel and fling it down the chute, plus the easel, the bottles, brushes, everything, incinerate it all—

—but the taut white canvas square paralyzes me.

I could sooner saw off my own leg.

I stand frozen, heart hammering in my ears.

Dion. Bryce.

Olivia.

I couldn't add Claire to that list.

How many lessons did a man need?

I'd have to tell Claire no. She'd ask why.

I'd have to refuse to tell her.

I don't hide anything from Claire. Not when she asks.

It might rupture our friendship.

And I don't know if I can stand that.

Claire and I survived everything. I'd been sort of worried about introducing her to Olivia. Too many new girlfriends aren't happy to hear about old female friends. I'd told Olivia that Claire was gay, and she'd accepted that, but I'd seen that narrow thread of lingering suspicion. Olivia had even opened the conversation with "So, you're the favorite ex-girlfriend?" and I'd wanted to die.

But Claire had given Olivia a slow, direct stare. Not in the eye, but walking her body from feet to hair. "He's not my type," Claire said, "but if you get tired of him, look me up."

That shattered the ice—you can't fake that type of appraisal. And before long they chattered away like they'd known each other for decades. Claire has a sharp sense about people, she always knows what to say...

My thoughts stop.

My heart thrums in my throat.

Fresh sweat erupts along my back, my armpits, even on my face.

Claire understands people.

She'd driven me home from Dion's funeral, as I clutched my dead friend's portrait.

She'd helped Olivia load Einstein's picture into our car.

And Claire had been there when I presented Olivia with her wedding gift.

She'd been to my studio. She knew about the wall of canvases.

She'd seen my incomplete paintings.

She knew I was still painting.

I have to grab the table for balance.

She knew.

I'd probably leaked a million tiny hints nobody else would catch.

My head keeps spinning.

I never hung another painting, even though there's room for a few more. Claire would notice that.

My stomach is a knot of acid. My eyes pulse in their sockets.

I pound the table with a closed fist, screaming obscenities until my throat burns and I have to stop and lean on both hands to catch my breath.

Sweat from my face pocks the abused table. I have to close my eyes and try to recover myself.

What does she think she's doing? Okay, "my art kills people" doesn't make any sense. It's ridiculous, except for the bit where it's utterly true.

I have an urge to pick up the phone and yell at her for boxing me in.

I need to say no. It'll cost our friendship, but so what? At least she'll *live.*

And she's getting married. Friends drift apart after marriage. We say they won't, but they do.

I feel a chill.

Claire knows that too.

She's telling me that my fears are stupid.

If I give her a portrait, if she and Temperance hang it in their living room, they won't be able to forget me.

Or I don't, and they'll drift away.

The chill sinks into my blood.

Claire has bet her life that she's right.

The worst bit?

I trust Claire. I always have.

Our friendship wouldn't break *after* I told her no.

It would shatter when I *decided* to tell her no.

I stand there, hands resting on the table, trying to pull my shattered soul together and cursing my best friend, until I can breathe without quivering.

Trust? Or death? Damnation or friendship?

Finally, I wipe my eyes.

Dry my palms on my pants.

And pick up a brush.

About the Author

https://mwl.io

Never miss another new release!
Sign up for MWL's mailing list at
https://mwl.io

Novels and Collections (as Michael Warren Lucas):

Immortal Clay
Kipuka Blues
Butterfly Stomp Waltz
Terrapin Sky Tango
Forever Falls
Hydrogen Sleets
Drinking Heavy Water
$ git commit murder
$ git sync murder
Prohibition Orcs
Frozen Talons
Vicious Redemption
Devotion and Corrosion

Nonfiction (as Michael W Lucas):

Cash Flow for Creators – Relayd and Httpd Mastery – PAM Mastery
FreeBSD Mastery: Advanced ZFS – FreeBSD Mastery: ZFS
FreeBSD Mastery: Specialty Filesystems – Tarsnap Mastery
Networking for Systems Administrators – Sudo Mastery
FreeBSD Mastery: Storage Essentials – DNSSEC Mastery
Absolute OpenBSD – SSH Mastery – Network Flow Analysis
Absolute FreeBSD – Cisco Routers for the Desperate – PGP & GPG
FreeBSD Mastery: Jails – Ed Mastery – SNMP Mastery – TLS Mastery
Letters to ed(1) – Domesticate Your Badgers

The Networknomicon
Only Footnotes

See your favorite bookstore for more!